OUR LOVE IS THE REALEST

SHVONNE LATRICE

FIRST CLASS

PUBLISHING GROUP

ABOUT THE AUTHOR

<u>Other Works by Me:</u>

Good Girls Love Thugs 1-5
Falling for a Hood King 1-4
Married to a Distinguished Thug 1-3
She's Gotta Have It 1-2
Me & My Dope Boy 1-3
Yazir & Nina 1-3
Forbidden Love with a Thug 1-3
You Needed Me 1-3
Shorty is in Love with a Real One 1-4
I Got Your Back 1-2
My Baby Is a West Coast King 1-4
Our Love Is the Realest 1-3
She Got It Bad for a Heartless Gangsta 1-4
She Got It Bad for a Heartless Gangsta: An AK Christmas
Hood Boyz Fall In Love Too 1-3
Nobody Can Love You Like Them Roughnecks Do 1-4
She Gave Her All to the Hood's Finest 1-5

$19.99
ISBN 978-1-966375-28-9
51999>

WAAYIL

"Bitch, I said I wanted blue icing! *Blue,* hoe! Why the fuck is this green!" my girlfriend, Alba, shouted at the bitch working the bakery area.

"Ma'am—"

"Aye, it's aight." I waved my hand.

"I paid for—"

"I said it's aight!" I cut Alba off and stared down into her eyes. I prayed she heard every word I hadn't said with my stare.

I was close as a muthafucka to dragging her ass out of Kroger by her fucking hair, and trust me, I wasn't that type of nigga. It took a lot to get me hot, but Alba was hella close right now.

"Bitch," Alba mumbled as she snatched the cake and started to switch her ass out.

"My apologies." I nodded to the woman working the bakery counter. She just scoffed and shook her head as I followed Alba out into the parking lot.

"Keep acting dumb with me in public, Alba," I stated calmly as I opened the passenger side door for her.

She slid in, pouting hard, and I just closed the door behind her. Once I made it around to my side and got in, for some reason, she felt the need to open back up her big ass mouth.

"I paid good money and told her to put *blue* icing! I know that's your favorite color, baby; that's all," she whined.

"It's fucking icing that muthafuckas are gonna gobble down and forget about tomorrow! Like I told you before, keep turning the fuck up on muthafuckas and watch you regret that shit. I'm tired of yo' bullshit, Alba, for real."

"So what does that mean?"

I heard her turn in her seat as much as she could while holding the cake, as I drove through the parking lot to pull out onto the street. I ignored her and turned my music up, getting comfortable in my seat.

Alba acting a monkey in public wasn't new shit at all. Anytime a muthafucka did something she didn't like, she had to take it there and cause a damn scene. I was a low-key type of nigga, so I didn't appreciate that ghetto shit and her using all the bass in her small ass body to get her point across.

I swear to God I would never hit a woman, but Alba's ass had been asking for it for the fucking longest. Shit, the only reason I think I dealt with her stupid ass was because I did have love for her, and the sex was cool. I wasn't that muthafucka that got sprung off pussy, because to me, shit wasn't all that deep. Good pussy was everywhere; it was just finding the right bitch that had it. By saying that, Alba's personality was something I usually fucked with, but certain times, like today, I hated her ass.

"Baby, talk to me." She turned my music down as I pulled into the driveway of my parents' home.

I didn't say anything, so she just smacked her lips and fell back into her seat with her arms folded. Getting out, I closed my door and hiked my jeans up as I started towards the front door of the house. I could hear Alba talking shit as she got out and slammed my door so hard I thought the window shattered.

My birthday was today, and I'd saved up a lot of money to cop this Chevy, so she had me twisted and fucked up by slamming my door.

"Come here." I turned to face her and she slowed down her steps up my parents' driveway.

"What?" her voice trembled.

"Come here. You're slamming doors and shit, so I got something to say to you. And I don't yell, so bring it in."

"I'm sorry!" She stomped her foot like a toddler.

"Come here, Alba." After a few moments of hesitation, she slowly made her way to me and I gripped her arm roughly as hell before gritting, "Get yo' attitude together before I go across yo' muthafuckin' face. It's my birthday and I wanna have a good ass day for once. I don't need the bullshit, aight?"

She simply nodded, so I let her arm go and then snatched the fucking cake out her hands. I swear she could bring the worst out of a nigga. My mama said because of that, I needed to let her ass go, and sometimes Alba was making me believe that shit too.

"About time, nigga!" my twin brother, Nusef, shouted, hopping over the back of the couch.

"Man, shut up," I mumbled, carrying the cake to the kitchen where my mom, dad, and uncle were.

Nusef and I were adopted by my mother, Freya, and her husband, Theo Samuels, ten years ago, when we were eight years old. Freya and Theo were all about having a colorful household and shit as they called it, so even though they were black, they adopted my little sister, Midori, who was Asian, and then my little brother, Emil, who was Mexican. Then there was Wednesday, who was black like me and Nusef, and she was my little dog. I didn't say this out loud, but I for real felt like she was my blood sister verses Midori. Loved them both though.

"Put the cake on the middle counter, honey." My mom smiled as she placed a couple dishes into the dishwasher. "And, Sef, do not touch it!" She scolded my brother who just smiled widely and threw his hands up in mock surrender.

The adoption shit was a trip though because unlike most foster kids, Nusef and I weren't some children in and out of the fucking system for those first eight years of our lives; we knew our parents.

Life was pretty normal and shit until they got arrested for what I now know was check washing. According to our caseworker, my parents made over one million dollars forging checks and shit. I know I shouldn't have admired that bullshit but low-key, I did. Like damn, how they pull that shit off? Check washing wasn't no easy task in this day and age.

When I was around twelve, my foster parents would take Nusef and I to visit our parents, but as we started to get older, that shit stopped. They claimed that visiting the jail would be a bad influence on us since we were older. But now that we were eighteen, I planned to check on them for sure. I wasn't gon' tell my foster parents though because I was sure it'd make them feel some type of way, and that was the last thing I wanted. They were good to me and Nusef, and I didn't want them to think I felt otherwise. After all, they went as far as allowing us to keep the last names we were born with, which I appreciated.

"How does this look?" My little sister, Wednesday, spun around in some little ass dress and then smiled.

"Change that shit," I replied, feeling my face frown the fuck up.

Wednesday sucked her teeth and left the kitchen promptly. People always said I was more like her and Midori's father than my pops. He was just too lax for me sometimes, so yeah, I took it upon my damn self to set shit straight on occasions.

"I think she looks good!" Alba shrieked.

"Didn't nobody ask you," I stated lowly as I moved past her so I could go to my bedroom and change. It was already 6 p.m., and the backyard party was gonna start in just fifteen minutes. Shit, we lost most of our fucking time because Alba wanted to box the bitch at the bakery.

As soon as Alba and I got into my bedroom, I started to remove the shirt I had on since I was just gonna change that. My jeans and my white on black classic Adidas were just fine. Most of the mutha-fuckas coming tonight were just some homies and a few hoes from around the way, and I wasn't about to try to impress not a one of them.

"Baby, are you ready for your gift? I think it will stop you from being mad at me." Alba pouted with her pretty ass.

I let my eyes scan her thick frame that must have come from all that damn Puerto Rican food. She had a toned ass stomach, a fat ass, thick thighs, and titties that I'm guessing were D cups. Shit, a nigga didn't know. All I knew was that her body was on point like a mutha-fucka, and her head game was too.

"Hurry up," I smirked.

"Oh my gosh, Waayil! Not that!"

"Then what?" I furrowed my brows, suddenly irritated that I wasn't about to get some head before going down to the party.

"Look!"

She unzipped her little ass jean shorts and pulled them down a little past her thigh, before peeling back a white bandage. My eyes landed on the tattoo of my name on her thigh, and for a moment, I didn't know what the fuck to say.

"Why you do that?" I finally quizzed.

"Excuse me, nigga? You should be happy I did this! You know how many niggas wanna fuck me and I'm over here tatting *your* name!"

Not saying a word, I sprayed some of my cologne on and then left the room. After getting herself together, I could hear her ass following behind me.

"Happy birthday, bro." Emil smiled.

"Thanks, man." We slapped hands as we both started to descend the stairs.

"Papi!" Alba called after me, but I just acted like she wasn't there, making Emil chuckle. "Waayil!"

I could hear voices and music from a distance in my parents' large backyard, and a smile graced my face upon seeing my little sisters, Wednesday and Midori, cheesing at me and holding gift bags for me and Nusef.

"Don't worry it was cheap!" Midori giggled as Wednesday nudged her to say shut up.

I just chuckled lightly and took the bag to look inside as Nusef did the same. I nodded with a smile upon seeing that they bought us each a drawing pad and some color pencils. My brother and I loved to draw and anytime I got something that would attribute to that, it excited me.

"Happy birthday, little brother." I gripped the back of Nusef's neck and he snatched from me, making me chuckle lightly. I was three minutes older, and I used that shit to fuck with him.

"Fuck you and happy birthday, bitch," he spat as we laughed in unison.

We made it out into the backyard and I couldn't believe all the muthafuckas that were here already. I only went upstairs to change, and shit seemed to be in full swing already. Of course, Nusef skated through, eyes locked on the pretty bitches who I knew were more than willing to give up the pussy. Shit was tempting sometimes, but I just couldn't stick my shit in any bitch that was willing to give it away so freely. Especially not when Alba had me perfectly satisfied. I loved pussy, but a nigga didn't need one hundred of them muthafuckas.

"Waayil!" Alba called after me again, but I just continued to ignore her as I greeted some of the homies and my homegirls, and got a cup of Hennessy.

Taking a seat on one of the benches, I bobbed my head to "No Hands" by Waka Flocka, while checking my phone to see if I had any texts. I did, but not the one I was looking for, so I just pocketed my phone.

"Baby," Alba whined and straddled my lap, tossing her long light brown hair back. "You never talk to me, and I don't know what to say or do anymore." Not saying a word, I put the red cup to my lips and drank some down. "I love you, papi, that's why I got the tattoo. And I'm sorry about what I said upstairs."

Not in the mood to see her pouting and begging me for forgiveness, when in actuality I wasn't even mad... I just didn't care, I said, "You good, ma."

She giggled and then leaned down to peck my lips with her soft ones. I pressed her pussy down against my dick as I gripped her ass, before kissing her again.

"Rock Yo' Hips" by Crime Mob came on, and everyone outside hollered out in excitement. Alba quickly jumped up and started to grind in my lap to the music. My eyes were glued to her ass, but out the corner of my eye, I could see a group of girls come into the back-yard. When I looked, I could feel myself grinning way too fucking hard. No nigga with a bitch should be as happy as I was to see another girl.

"Give me a second, baby." I moved Alba to the side, got up, and lightly jogged to the group of girls.

"Happy Birthday." My best friend, Yikayla, smiled as she took a red cup from the table nearby.

Yikayla was very... different, so she had this weird ass short dress on that I'm sure she'd made herself. She was into designing clothes, and always shopped at thrift stores for her attire. She would take it home and add her own shit to it. I couldn't do it, but I admired that about her pretty ass. Only bitches talked shit about it because the niggas were too focused on trying to get at her because of how beautiful she was.

"Thank you." I finally smirked after taking in how she looked.

"Hello to you too, nigga!" her older sister, Dree, snapped.

"*You're* supposed to say Happy Birthday, Dree," Yikayla's younger sister, Jonaya, said, swaying her nonexistent fourteen-year-old hips to the music as she scanned the party. "Happy Birthday, bro!" Jonaya tapped my arm. "Wednesday!" she yelled before running off.

After Dree and their other sister, Rori, finally said happy birthday to me, they dipped further into the party.

Yikayla, Dree, Rori, and Jonaya were the Goode sisters or the *fine ass* Goode sisters as niggas called them. All of them were chocolate except Jonaya, but they all looked alike and were beautiful as fuck. I guess I was the only nigga in Memphis who didn't want to fuck one of them... I did— never mind.

"What you got this dress on for? And makeup?" I ran my thumb down Yikayla's cheek and she moved my hand.

"I can't wear makeup?"

"Who the fuck you wearing it for, though?"

"Nobody," she almost whispered, and shrugged one shoulder as she looked up into my eyes.

Yikayla and I were thick as thieves and had been since I'd gotten adopted by the Samuels. I remembered when she was always ashy as fuck and her thick curly hair was always a mess. Now at sixteen, she was turning into a woman, and I didn't know how to feel; beautiful chocolate girl with a slim thick frame and long ass hair. Her eyelashes were like old school fans, and her pretty brown eyes always sparkled. Her lips were never chapped, and she always smelled like that natural brown sugar soap she loved. Not to mention, she wasn't some hoe trying to give her pussy up to any nigga that gave her a compliment.

"I saw your car." Yikayla smiled.

"Yeah, man, I told you I was gon' get that shit."

"You did. So hey, I got—"

"Yikayla!" Alba interrupted, coming up to us. "You look adorable in that dress. It is too cute. I remember when I was sixteen and looked *adorable*." Alba smiled and then stood in front of me, wrapping my arms around her body.

Alba was two years older than me at twenty, but I swear it didn't seem like it. Had I not seen her ID and shit, I wouldn't have believed it.

"Yeah, I umm... I guess looking adorable is a good thing." Yikayla nodded, smoothing down her dress.

"Aye, so what were you saying?" I squinted my eyes at Yikayla, still holding Alba who was pressing her nice round ass against my dick. And best believe my lil' big homie was responding.

"Nothing. I'm gonna go make a plate and say happy birthday to Sef. Talk to you later, best friend." Yikayla started off.

"Wait, Kay, look what I got!" Alba stopped her.

When Yikayla turned around, Alba quickly peeled her shorts up just a little to show off the tattoo of my name. Yikayla stared at it for a moment, and then nodded with an awkward smile before continuing on her initial route.

As soon as Yikayla was out of earshot, Alba turned to face me and looked up into my eyes, while hugging my torso.

"I think she wants to fuck you."

"Yikayla?" my brows furrowed.

"Yes, *Yikayla*! You better not fall asleep around her or you're gonna wake up with your dick in her mouth."

"You have no idea what the fuck you're talking about." I pulled her into me and squeezed her ass.

"I know she—"

I cut her off with a kiss because I was tired of her accusations. If she only knew that it was me who wanted to fuck Yikayla, and not the other way around.

Everyone continued to have a good time, and then after we cut the cake and shit, my parents decided that it was time for everyone to get the fuck out. I was happy about that because I wasn't the most social muthafucka.

"Aye man, you holding?" my foster mother's brother, Harry, tapped me. This nigga was suspect as fuck, and I wasn't sure why my parents had taken his ass in a couple months ago. You could tell he was a fuck up just from looking at him. Nigga was older than my

Pops but still asking my mama for money. And it's obvious what the fucking money was for.

"Nah, and don't touch me, mane." I pulled Alba with me by the hand.

As we walked inside of the house, I saw this nigga named Latrell smiling in Yikayla's face. That nigga was a teenager when I was a fucking kid, so he had to be a cool twenty something, which meant he had no business in Yikayla's sixteen-year-old face.

"What?" Alba frowned.

"Meet me in the bedroom. Hurry up before my mama sees you."

Alba hit the stairs and I made my way over to Yikayla and Latrell.

"Aye, my nigga, I don't know if you heard, but the party is over so you gotta go." I draped my arm around Yikayla and stared Latrell in the face. I was a little taller than him but not much.

"Oh yeah, my bad. Kay, let me walk you home—"

"Nah, I got her."

Licking his crusty ass lips, he chuckled and said, "Come on, mane, what you doing? I know this ya best friend and shit, but we was talking."

"Get up outta here, my nigga. I'm not gon' ask you again." I was calm, but this muthafucka was pushing me. It was nothing for me to fight, but if I could prevent it, I liked to. Niggas liked to joke and call me quiet crazy, and even though I disagreed, sometimes the name did fit.

I could see in Latrell's eyes he wanted to say something, but instead, he just scoffed and turned to leave my crib. I looked down at Yikayla as I moved my arm from being around her, and she just shook her head with a smile.

We both left out and started towards her house, which was across the street and two houses down. My thoughts were going wild for the first couple steps, so there was silence between us. It wasn't an awkward silence though.

"That's what you like?" I quizzed her as we stepped out into the street to cross it.

"What? Latrell?"

"Yeah, Latrell. Who the fuck else?"

"I don't know." She shrugged, tousling her hair and hitting me with a whiff of her sweet scent. "He's cute and he's nice to me."

"He's old as hell, Kay. And he sells drugs."

"You sell drugs." She looked to me as we got onto her side of the street and started making our way down.

"Yeah, but I... never mind."

"You what?" she grinned.

I glanced up at the streetlight that lit up the super dark street, and then back down to her. I contemplated being completely honest, but decided to give her only half of the truth. I loved her and Latrell didn't, that was the difference amongst other things.

"I sell drugs because I need to make money for a greater goal. He sells drugs because he's trying to be the next Pablo Escobar. You don't need a nigga like that."

"What kind of nigga do I need, Waayil?" She walked up her porch steps as I stayed put, watching her sexy brown legs.

Sighing, I said, "I don't know, just not him, aight?"

She smiled as she came back down the steps, and then threw her arms around my neck to hug me tightly. I wrapped my arms around her torso, and closed my eyes as I inhaled the scent of her thick, curly hair. Turning my face slightly, I kissed her cheek and let my lips rest there for a moment. It was taking everything in me not to touch her lips with mine, grope her, or tell her that for the past month, I'd been dreaming about stroking that pussy and making her cum.

I didn't even know what happened, but it seemed like six months ago, the way I saw her was different. She was still my best friend, but I found myself getting jealous as fuck when niggas looked at or talked to her, or when she expressed liking some bitch ass nigga at school. I found myself eyeing her body when she would walk in front of me, and most importantly, I'd lie in bed at night and wonder what it'd feel like to be inside of her.

"Goodnight." She pulled away and stared up into my eyes.

"Night," I replied softly as I let her body go.

I watched her as she rushed back up the stairs and let herself into her house. Even when the door closed, I stayed there. I waited until I saw her bedroom light come on, and she came to the window to smile widely down at me. I gave her a smile back, and then turned around to head back to my house.

I had completely forgotten Alba was waiting for me, but I just planned to shut her nagging ass up with some dick.

YIKAYLA

Initiation

The Next Day…

"Sure Thing" by Miguel played softly through Waayil's car speakers as we sat in the parking lot of Family Dollar in Orange Mound. He had his drawing pad with a little book light clipped to it so he could see since it was dark outside.

I watched as he colored in the picture he drew, while sexily bobbing his head to the music as he sang along here and there. His voice was so beautiful, and he should have wanted to become a singer. He didn't want to though, because he said it brought too much attention, and if you knew Waayil, you knew he hated attention. I noticed as he got older though, attention from these Memphis hoes was inevitable because he was turning into such a handsome man.

Waayil was nibbling on his full bottom lip, with his hat turned to the back so he could see his work, as he nodded to the song. The little facial hair that he'd started to grow made him look so mature, as he sat there dressed in an open black and white flannel shirt, dark jeans, and his favorite classic white on black Adidas. He had three pairs of the same shoe, and never changed to a different style.

"Alba doesn't say anything about you drawing me?" I broke the silence, admiring the drawing of me that he was filling in.

"Wouldn't matter if she did," he replied nonchalantly.

Waayil wasn't the type to talk too much. It was funny because his twin brother Nusef was the opposite. If you went to a party, Nusef would most likely be getting it in with some big booty girl in the middle of the dance floor, while Waayil sat on the side and chilled, observing. I think his calm observant nature was the reason for his intelligence, because he was way smarter than his brother. Waayil would notice something coming way before Nusef or any of us, and it was because while we were doing the most, he'd be sitting back taking in his surroundings.

Waayil and Nusef looked exactly alike with deep chocolate skin, tall six-feet-three frames, and pretty honey colored eyes with specks of green. The only difference was that Waayil had deep dimples in his cheeks that showed even when he made the slightest movement with his mouth.

"She's pretty obsessive, Waayil. She wants all of your attention. We used to hang out a lot more before you got with her. And that tattoo? Please tell me that's fake," I scoffed.

I couldn't stand Alba, and it wasn't just a recent thing. I'd hated her ever since she'd gotten with Waayil. She was beyond thirsty for him, and over time, he just caved. Granted, Alba was beautiful, and it seemed every man in Memphis wanted a piece of her, but she was just so different from Waayil that I didn't understand why he liked her. I guess what I really mean is that she was so different from me...

"You jealous?" He chuckled slightly, not bothering to look my way, and continuing to color in his drawing. It was rare that he laughed, but when he did, it was usually only around me and sometimes his twin or foster siblings.

"Not even! I don't see you like that!" I screeched a little louder than I wanted to, taking a sip of my milkshake from Checkers to calm my nerves. And I guess that was because I was lying.

I wasn't sure when it happened or how it happened, but for the past few months, I'd been seeing Waayil differently. I didn't look at him like a brother anymore; I was attracted to him. The way he walked, *didn't* talk, looked, and when he would give me that closed mouth smile while squinting his pretty eyes. It was something he'd done since I'd first met him, but now it was the sexiest thing ever. I often wondered how it would feel to be with him physically, and was jealous to know Alba got to experience that.

"Okay." He snickered lowly, adjusting his hat and then reaching for a different colored pencil. His drawings were really good, and even though I felt like since he didn't want to be a singer, he should be a painter or something, Waayil wanted to be a tattoo artist.

KNOCK! KNOCK!

Waayil looked up from his drawing pad and put his things into the back seat before rolling down his window.

"You got that? I told you all or nothing so it's one hundred dollars. I didn't sit out here in this parking lot for twenty minutes for nothing, my nigga," Waayil sternly told the guy in the big white t-shirt and jeans. He was light skinned with brownish hair that was cut into a fade.

"Yeah, and I got you." The dude held up five twenties, and Waayil took it from him and hit the car light to make sure they were real.

Once he confirmed the money was legit, he turned the light out and stuffed the cash into his pocket. He retrieved some sort of narcotic that was small and tightly wound in plastic, then handed it over to the boy who excitedly accepted it.

"How you doing, ma?" the boy nodded his head up to me, eyes roaming my frame as he licked his lips.

DANK!

Waayil opened his door with force, sending the dude to the ground groaning.

"Get the fuck from over here, mane. She's sixteen," he told him, closing the door back, rolling the window up, and pulling out of the parking lot as I chuckled.

I wouldn't say Waayil was bat shit crazy, but he had his moments. Just because he didn't say much and wasn't the most boisterous guy, didn't mean he wouldn't get down. I'd seen him fight plenty of times, but it was always because someone started with him. Waayil was a pretty peaceful guy until you fucked with him.

"You didn't have to hit him with the door," I chortled as we pulled into the drive-thru of Church's Chicken, wanting some food just before they closed.

He just adjusted his hat, sending his cologne permeating through the car before he rolled down the window. He always smelled so good, and it was never over the top.

Waayil ordered our food, and then we ate it right there in the parking lot. I hated doing this because we were surrounded by crazy mumbling bums and criminals out here. But of course Waayil didn't care. He wasn't scared of much; of anything really. Whatever he *was* afraid of, I had yet to encounter it.

"I'm not ready to go home," I said once Waayil got back into the car from trashing our food.

"Kay, it's almost midnight." He cranked the car and started to pull out onto the street. "I know, but it's Friday and it's summer, Waayil. Not like I have to be somewhere tomorrow."

"Well, you wanna come to the crib? I ain't doing shit but playing video games and smoking until I fall asleep."

"Okay." I nodded. Anything that involved him sounded good to me. For some reason, tonight I didn't want to leave him.

He gave me that closed mouth smile, making his dimples appear and his eyes light up as he sped down the street headed to our neighborhood, Midtown. I admired him as he dipped through the streets, maneuvering the car so smoothly like some gangsta. Like always, my mind started to wander to what it was like to sleep with him. Alba was so fucking lucky. Bitch.

We finally made it to his parents' home, and once we got into his room, I removed my sandals and sat on the edge of his bed while he cut the TV on and the lights off. He removed his precious Adidas, stuffed them with tennis balls, and then took off his watch and chain. Waayil wasn't flashy, but he looked better than the niggas who were.

He took a seat next to me, and started to roll up. Once he lit the tip, I watched him take a pull with his sexy lips.

"Can I try?"

He looked to his right at me, eyes naturally low like always. He was smirking, showing off his dimples, before he finally handed it to me.

"Tuck ya lips in so you don't burn 'em. You too pretty to have some burnt ass lips and shit." He removed his shirt, exposing his body, which was starting to get more defined since he and his brother stayed in the gym all summer.

"Fuck!" I dropped it on my thigh and burned myself because I was too busy lusting over his chest.

"Damn, ma." He laughed, picking it up and inhaling on it like nothing happened.

"Oww." I caressed my wound. He laughed and then leaned down to kiss the burn on my thigh, gently, which brought on a tingle between my legs.

"Better?" He smiled up at me and I nodded.

I was *done* with smoking, so once he was finished, he went to brush his teeth and then came back. He grabbed his controller, and then powered up his game system so it illuminated the bedroom. He showed me how to play for a little bit, and then he turned it off and laid back on his bed. I cuddled up next to him, and he draped his arm around my shoulders. This was something we always did, so it wasn't anything special.

Taking a deep breath, I sat up a little and looked down into his honey colored eyes. He stared back up at me in the dark bedroom, looking so handsome, and I could tell he was wondering what I was doing. Leaning down, I crushed my lips against his, not even believing what I was doing. To my surprise, he kissed me back and then slipped me some tongue. I'd never kissed anyone, let alone tongue kissed, so I wasn't even sure if I was doing it right. I must have been though because he didn't stop me, and our breathing became heavy.

"Yikayla, nah." He finally pulled his lips from mine.

"Waayil, I love you," I replied frantically, anxious to get him to change his mind about us stopping.

Running his hand down his face, he sat up and shook his head.

"Kay, I got a girl."

"You love her?"

"It don't matter if I do or not. Fuck."

"Do you love me?"

He stared at me for a little bit, and then started to pull on my dress in an upward motion. I lifted my arms in the air, allowing him to pull it over my head and toss it to the side. He unhooked my bra, threw it as well, and just stared at my half naked body for a moment. It made me nervous because I was hoping he wasn't disappointed, since I wasn't as developed as Alba.

He kissed me hungrily, positioning himself on top of me as he tugged on my panties. I was turned on by how badly he wanted me, and how passionate his kisses were. Everything felt so right that I was praying like hell that I didn't suddenly wake up.

Waayil eventually ripped my underwear, and then dropped his head down to suck my nipples. It felt so good, and the moistness between my legs signaled that. He trailed his lips downward, sucking different areas of my body as if it were covered in some sweet topping, and then placed my legs on his shoulders.

"Waayil, what are you doing? No."

I'd seen women get head in movies, but I didn't want it. It just seemed strange.

Typical Waayil didn't reply, he just began to flick his tongue over my clit. At first I wanted him to stop, but once he started doing whatever the hell he was doing, I was happy as fuck he hadn't listened to me.

Pressing my thighs into my stomach, he snaked his tongue around my clit before sucking on it softly. I tried to stay quiet, but soft moans began to escape my lips uncontrollably as my chest heaved.

"Oh my gosh," I mumbled, as he buried his face further.

I could feel liquid dripping down and I was so embarrassed. I'd heard boys at school comment on a vagina being wet as hell, and I always thought that was disgusting. But with the way Waayil was moaning as he ate my pussy like it had the cure to cancer, I could tell he didn't think it was nasty at all. He was sucking, slurping, and licking me something fucking serious, while holding my thighs in place with his strong hands. If Alba got this, no wonder she was so possessive.

"Fuck," he commented, just before the feeling he was giving me intensified to the point where my body froze and trembled as I gushed.

"What happened?" I quizzed breathily as he trailed his lips back up my body.

"I made that pussy cum." He grinned sexily, standing up to push down his boxers and jeans.

I stared hard at his long, thick, chocolate dick, as he grabbed a condom from his drawer. He placed it on the nightstand next to his bed, and then climbed between my legs. Before I could say anything, his tongue was down my throat and I could taste the minty mouthwash he'd just used prior, letting me know that my vagina didn't really taste like much.

"Waayil, I asked if you loved me," I reminded him in between kisses.

Stopping, he stared down into my eyes and caressed my hair with his hand before saying, "You know I do, Kay. You shouldn't have even asked that shit. I ain't got to say shit for you to know I love you."

I nodded before he pressed his lips against mine again.

I gasped when I felt the head of his dick at my opening, and once he saw it wouldn't go in, he placed my thighs over his forearms. Sucking my lips passionately, he forced a little bit inside of me, causing me to whimper. It was *so* painful, and he had me in a position where the only thing I could do was grip his biceps.

"Shit," he grumbled against my lips, pushing more of himself into me and making me whine. I felt like I was being ripped.

I didn't know how much dick he had left, but when I saw it earlier, it looked like a lot. I wanted to tell him to give me a second, but the pleasure in his face motivated me to stay strong and just deal with it. I'm sure Alba didn't complain, and I wasn't going to either.

"Mmm," I cried softly, tucking my lips in and closing my eyes to hopefully think about something else.

"Look at me," Waayil demanded, moving in and out of me slowly.

I opened my eyes to look at him like he'd asked, and he slipped his tongue into my mouth. A few seconds later, I started to feel some pleasure, which prompted me to moan a little bit louder. I was whimpering into Waayil's mouth as he sped up some, slamming into me and causing my juices to spill over. That same feeling from when he gave me head came over my body, just before I *came* again. By this point, it was feeling so good that I could barely talk. He had me speechless, yet the way he sexed me, appeared to be completely effortless on his part.

Waayil pressed my hands into the bed and hammered me harder and faster, while covering my mouth with his to muffle my moans. My vagina was sopping wet to the point where I could hear him plunging inside of me.

"Fuck," he growled, and it felt good to know that I was pleasing him as well. "When I pull out, Kay, I want you to put it in your mouth," he instructed.

Oh, fuck! I don't know how to suck dick, nigga!

Instead of spilling my thoughts, I nodded as much as I could, just before I came yet again. He pulled out of me, and I sat up to take him into my mouth. He palmed my head and guided me up and down, and I just sucked on it like I did a Popsicle. I prayed that I was doing it right because if not, I was gonna be embarrassed as hell. When I saw him toss his head back and moan subtly, I jumped for joy on the inside.

"Swallow for me." He looked down at me with his beautiful eyes, before tucking his lips in to expose his dimples. My God this was the most handsome man I'd ever seen.

Suddenly, I felt a warm liquid seep into my mouth and out of reflex, I just swallowed it because that's what I assumed he was referring to moments prior.

"Damn," he panted, chiseled abs rising and falling right in my face as I wiped my mouth.

I felt like a porno star at the moment. I always thought girls exaggerated when they said losing your virginity made you feel different, but it was true. I kind of felt like a hoe, but at least it was with a man I loved, and at least it felt good to me. All the girls I knew, including my sister, Dree, said they had yet to cum with sex, but I had done so on my first time, and multiple times.

Waayil fell back, head at the foot of his bed, and then he tapped my thigh to come lie on top of him. He still smelled so good.

"My legs are shaking, Waayil." I breathed heavily as he chuckled softly, declining to respond. "Why didn't you use the condom?" He just looked down at me and pecked my lips a few times before letting his head fall back. One thing I loved and hated about him was his refusal to talk when he didn't feel it was necessary. "Did I do a good job?"

"I busted... so yeah."

"Waayil!"

"I'm serious, Kay. If a nigga don't nut or if it takes too long to nut, that means ya pussy is whack. Yo' shit is far from that though." After some moments of silence, he said, "I don't want you doing that with anybody else, aight?"

"I won't." I shook my head. I hadn't even thought about sex with anyone but him.

"Waayil, I had a—" His little sister Wednesday burst into the bedroom, prompting us to cover ourselves quickly. She stared for a second and then said, "I-I'm sorry." She closed his door soon after.

"Are you gonna go check on her? I'm so embarrassed," I giggled.

"Nah, she's good."

I just laid my head back down on his chest, inhaling his scent and enjoying the sound of his soft breathing. His presence was like a drug to me.

~

The Next Morning...

"Yikayla! Yikayla! Get up!" I heard my little sister Jonaya's voice as she rocked me roughly.

After Waayil fucked me a second time, we rested until about 3 a.m. and then I snuck home so that when my mom and stepdad woke up, I would be in my room. When I got home, I brushed my teeth and took a quick hot bath, because I knew that would make me doze off. I was on a high from my time with Waayil because I was excited about what was to come between us, so I knew I would have been up all night without that bath.

"What, Jo?" I frowned up at her.

"The police are at Waayil's house, and he's getting arrested! Come on!" She rushed out the room and I quickly followed her, not caring that I was barefoot and in my pajama shorts. The throbbing pain between my legs and on the bone that connected my thighs to my pelvis didn't even slow me down.

Running out of my house, I saw everyone who lived on our street was outside being nosey. I rushed over to where my sisters were, and watched as the police brought Waayil out in handcuffs. His mother was crying, his father was holding her, and I was just so confused. What the hell could Waayil have done between the time I left him and now to get arrested?

Waayil and I made eye contact but he quickly looked away, obviously disappointed in himself for doing whatever the hell he'd done. My stomach was in knots and I felt like crying because it seemed like we'd both finally gotten what we wanted out of our relationship, and now it was possibly over. I wanted to scream his name, but my voice was nowhere to be found.

"What did he do?" my older sister Dree quizzed, folding her arms as my little sisters Rori and Jonaya watched with wide eyes. My mother hugged me into her when she saw tears stream down my cheeks.

"Come on back inside of the house." My stepfather Jasper came and attempted to block our view. We turned to walk back to our house, but I kept my teary eyes glued to the scene because I was simply baffled.

When I saw the EMT's wheel a body bag out of Waayil's home, my jaw dropped in horror.

1

YIKAYLA "KAY" GOODE

"**S**hut the fuck up! I can't even hear!" I barked at my sisters as we sat around the table in the dining room. My boyfriend, Roscoe, was doing a radio interview and I wanted to make sure I didn't miss a word.

"Girl, please. What station is this anyway because I've never heard of it?" Dree spat, rolling her eyes. Some days I couldn't stand the bitch my older sister had become. If bougie were in the dictionary, her picture would be right next to it.

Silence was among us as we listened to the radio guy ask Roscoe question after question. I couldn't help the smile that was plastered on my face from hearing my man's voice. I hadn't seen him in almost a week because he had a few shows out of town, so at the moment, I was craving anything I could get. Part of my excitement was also because I knew he'd be back home this evening, and I was beyond ready for his homecoming.

"Last question, my man, what's the dating life like for you right now? Are you single? In a relationship? Let the ladies know," the radio host inquired.

My little sister Jonaya looked at me with a smile, as Dree rolled her eyes and Rori stared at her phone, texting away like always.

"Nah, man, I'm doing me right now. Music is my girlfriend."

"What?" Dree, Jonaya, and I exclaimed in unison.

"What happened?" Rori looked at all of us, waiting to see who would answer her annoying ass first.

"I told you he wasn't shit. That nigga ain't even a real rapper. Ain't nobody heard of his shit but you and his bum ass friends." Dree shot up from her seat and rounded the counter to go to the fridge.

"Dree, shut up." Jonaya shook her head and looked at me.

I was still floored by Roscoe's answer. We'd been together for five years now, and just eight months ago, he'd decided he wanted to become a rapper. I guess the drug thing hadn't worked out for him, so he wanted a new venture. Even though he was twenty-eight and should have been decided what he wanted to do with his life, I supported his change of plans. And this is how he repays me? He denies me on fucking radio? At least it was some underground, Internet radio and nothing big, because that would have been even worse for me.

"Is someone gonna tell me what happened?" Rori quizzed with a frown, smoothing down her already slick edges.

"Nigga said he was single." Dree came back to the dining room and bit down on a piece of toast covered in avocado.

"Wow, so—"

"Excuse me." I got up from the table, ignoring Rori's attempt to get caught up. She irritated me with that bullshit, never paying attention because the only thing she cared about was her nothing ass nigga, Gavin.

My sisters and I led completely different lives; some shit I didn't agree with, but at the end of the day, I loved them all the same.

Dree was the oldest, then me, then Rori, and last was Jonaya. We all had different fathers and yes, we were close as hell in age. My mother had four children and four baby daddies by the time she cele-brated her twentieth birthday. She didn't marry any of them, so she chose to give all her daughters her last name.

On the upside, she wasn't dumb about it. She got a lot from each of our fathers before they dipped, and she really struck gold when she married my stepfather, Jasper. Jasper was like a father to us all and had been in our lives since I was five years old. He was much older than my mother, and he was rich as hell considering the fact that he was a renowned plastic surgeon.

Despite my mom's fast and flighty ways as a young girl, I'd never been without. I really wouldn't call her a good mom because she was always in her own world and never really disciplined us, but she wasn't as bad as she could have been. I loved her and she loved us, and that was all that mattered. And on the bright side, her self-centered ways caused us all to be strong since we were pretty self-sufficient.

As soon as I got into my bedroom, I closed the door before dialing Roscoe. He had me fucked up if he thought he was gonna get away with that bullshit. No wonder he didn't tell me about the interview. I just happened to go on his Facebook fan page and saw he was promoting it.

"Hey, ma, I was just thinking about you." Roscoe smiled into the phone.

"Oh really? Because you told that radio host you were single, so excuse me if I'm surprised that you were *thinking* about me."

Sighing dejectedly, he replied, "Yikayla, I only did that shit because I told you how bitches like to come for rapper's girlfriends and shit."

Nigga had been a rapper for two seconds but was acting like he had so many wild and crazy fans. I had yet to see someone ask for his autograph, or hear his music at the parties across town.

"Roscoe—"

"Yikayla, baby, I'm gonna be home today and when I see you, I wanna take you out and enjoy some time together. I don't wanna argue over some bullshit. I love you; you know I do. And shit ain't been easy since you went away to school, but now that, that shit is done, we need to keep shit tight, right?"

"Yeah." I smirked as I plopped down onto my bed.

I'd just graduated from Tennessee State University with a business degree this past May, and being in a long-distance relationship was hard as hell. Yeah, I was in the same state, but it was pretty far from my home in Memphis.

Things between Roscoe and I got even harder when I had our one-year-old son, Lonan, because it frustrated me that he didn't see him like he should have. My stepfather agreed to pay for my apartment out in Nashville, along with any other amenities I needed so that I could graduate college while still taking care of Lonan. However, my stepdad wouldn't allow me to let Roscoe come live with me. The only way he could was if he paid for half of the bills, and since he couldn't, Roscoe only saw our baby and me once or twice every two months, unless I came home for a visit.

I was hoping to have my own place when I came home to Memphis after graduating, but having a degree didn't mean automatic employment, unfortunately. Plus, I was into fashion and there was no blueprint to achieving such a goal.

So for now, I was just working in my mother's Waffle House here in Midtown near Highway 70. My mother didn't complete high school and didn't have any expertise in really anything, so my stepfather bought her the Waffle House to give her something to do when she was bored. My little sisters and I were thankful for it because whenever we needed money, she would let us work. Sometimes I hated it, but it kept me with a little spending money until I could use my degree.

"Aight then. I should be by your crib around 7:30. Wear something nice for me, aight?" Roscoe pulled me from my thoughts.

"I will, baby."

"I love you, Kay."

"I love you too."

We hung up and I smiled widely until my bedroom door came flying open. I rolled my eyes when I saw Jonaya and Nusef walk in like they owned the place.

I rubbed my baby's back as he slept soundly on my bed with his pacifier in his mouth. He was so beautiful with deep caramel skin like his father, and soft curly hair. I loved him so much and I couldn't help but feel like Roscoe didn't care as much about him. He never asked about him when we would talk on the phone while I was away, and even now, when he didn't have him, it was like he didn't exist.

"Sorry, Kay, but this nigga wanted me to ask you if you're coming to the little party tonight?" Jonaya giggled as her best friend, Nusef, threw his arm around her.

Everyone thought they were fucking and it *did* seem like it, but Jonaya assured me that wasn't the case. She told me everything, even shit I didn't want to know, so I believed her. Plus, Nusef was always calling her a little sister, so I doubt he was sticking his dick in her. He may have been a hoe, but I think smashing Jonaya was even a bit much for him.

"What party?" I played dumb. I knew exactly what today was, but I had no plans on celebrating that bullshit.

Smacking his teeth, Nusef replied, "I know you know, but Waayil is coming home today. Well, actually, he's out already, but he'll be over this evening for the party."

"Oh."

"Oh?" Jonaya folded her arms and stared at me. "So you're not gonna see your best friend?"

"He's not my best friend anymore, Jo, and you know that."

After Waayil got the book thrown at him for murder, and sentenced to life in prison, we did keep in contact for a couple months. We wrote letters constantly, and I'd fallen more in love with him each time I ripped open an envelope. That was until he called and told me to stop communicating with him.

I ignored his request at first and still wrote, but he never responded and stopped calling. What made shit worse was that he let

Alba come see him and everything. I only knew because she bragged to everyone about her nigga in jail and all the correspondences. I cried every night for months over it, until I met and started getting closer with Roscoe. About a year later, Roscoe and I made things official.

Fast forward to now, when I got home from school, I found out Waayil's sentencing had been reduced because they changed the crime he was charged with to a crime of passion. So now, he was out after only six years, and tonight they'd be having a party for him. But fuck that. I was gonna be out to dinner with my man, and not celebrating the homecoming of the nigga that I thought loved me.

"My brother is gon' be hot if he don't see yo' ass there," Nusef interjected, leaning his tall frame against the door. Sometimes it was hard to look at him because he was identical to Waayil, minus the deep dimples and relaxed demeanor. Nusef bore the same deep mocha skin and pretty honey colored eyes with specks of green. His teeth were perfectly straight, and like his brother, he always smelled nice.

"I doubt he will notice. Now if you'll excuse me, I have to go to the nail shop." I climbed off my bed, picked up my baby, and grabbed my purse and phone, leaving Jonaya and Nusef in my room.

"Where are you going?" Dree asked once I got downstairs, lowering her law school book as she sat on the couch in the living room.

"Nail shop." I adjusted Lonan on my hip.

"Oh, I'll come too."

I rolled my eyes when she wasn't looking and once she had her shoes on, we left out. Just that quickly, Waayil had ruined my day. It didn't even matter that I was gonna see the love of my life tonight.

∾

That Night... Around 7:45 p.m....

I was sitting in the living room by myself, all dressed up and ready to go. My nails were freshly done, my brows were waxed, and I was smelling scrumptious. Lonan was sitting next to me in his carrier, passed out, since I'd played with him all day after coming home from the nail shop. He'd just had his dinner, and now he was knocked.

All of my sisters were across the street at Waayil's parents' home, celebrating his jail release. I could faintly hear music coming from the house, even though I tried to tune it out with a few YouTube videos.

"Oh, honey, I didn't know you'd still be here." My mother came down the stairs and smiled. Right on her heels was one of her little boyfriends, who hugged her from behind and kissed her neck.

Since my stepfather, Jasper, was an in-high-demand surgeon, he worked long hours, was always on call, and had to do some work out of town occasionally. By saying that, he sometimes left my mom with room to play the field, and that's exactly what her ass did. She would sleep around a little bit, and once my stepfather returned for a long period of time, she would end it... I guess.

I didn't like it, but I couldn't exactly tell my mother what to do. And snitching on her to my stepfather just didn't seem like the smartest move to me. Yeah, Jasper was like my father, considering the fact that I didn't know my real one, but I've seen too many times where stepfathers or stepmothers switch up once the marriage was over. I loved Jasper, and I appreciated all that he had done and still did for us, so sorry if I wasn't ready to let go of it all.

"Roscoe is just running a little late," I replied, toying with my purse strap.

"Why don't you go over to the party ya siblings were talking about?" Her boy toy smirked. He looked like he was about my older sister Dree's age, and had a few gold teeth in his mouth.

"I'd rather not."

"You haven't seen Waayil in months, honey, you should go."

"Ma, please."

My mother shrugged and then walked to the large kitchen with her boo in tow. She was so in her own world that she had no idea Waayil and I weren't close anymore. She must have still thought we wrote letters to one another. I rolled my eyes at the sound of she and her freak, laughing and flirting from afar.

Frustrated, I pulled out my phone prepared to text Roscoe, but he beat me to the punch.

Baby: *Hey can't make it tonight. My ride home flaked.*

Me: *Are you fucking serious?*

Baby: *Unfortunately. But my phone is about to die so I will hit you when I get it charged. Love you.*

Tossing my phone on the couch cushion next to me, I leaned forward and ran my hands through my long dark hair. I wanted to cry, but I refused to as I took my son upstairs, changed him out of his clothes, and put him in his crib.

"Mommy loves you, Lo." I smiled and pressed my lips against his soft bouncy cheek, before turning on his mobile and then the baby monitor.

After changing my shoes to my Nike slides, I grabbed the extra baby monitor and left my baby to sleep in peace. I went down to my stepfather's bar room and grabbed a bottle of Grey Goose, before heading back up and going outside to sit on the porch steps. I sucked my teeth at the sound of the party across and down the street at Waayil's, before taking a large gulp of the vodka.

"Ah!" I grunted, wiping my mouth and frowning at the strong taste. I usually had this with juice or something, but tonight I needed it straight.

As I sat there sipping and feeling miserable, I noticed a dark figure crossing the street and heading towards my house. It looked like Waayil, and as soon as the thought crossed my mind, my stomach started to knot up. How was it that after all these years, he still gave me butterflies and had me a bit scared to be around him?

Once the streetlight shone down on the tall dark figure, I realized it was in fact Waayil. He was wearing dark jeans, a black hoodie pulled over his head, and his same classic Adidas, which I guess he bought once he was released earlier. He gave me the prettiest, widest smile, making his dimples appear and his beautiful eyes sparkle. As he neared me, I watched him with my mouth slightly ajar, and almost moaned at the scent of his cologne. It wasn't his usual from back in the day, but it was a nice grown up touch.

"So you wasn't gon' come welcome me?" He stopped in front of me on the porch steps, and shoved his tattoo covered hands into his jean pockets. His beautiful chocolate skin was flawless, and so were his pearly white teeth. He was taller than he used to be, and way more built, but not in a WWF wrestler kind of way. He was perfect like he'd always been.

"I umm... I—" I'd lost my train of thought taking in this beautiful specimen. He looked so damn good with more facial hair. He was a man now and I loved it. "Why would I do that?" I finally gained some composure.

He chuckled softly and took a seat next to me on the porch, as I discreetly covered the baby monitor sitting in my lap. I'd made it clear to Nusef and his foster siblings to leave my life out of any conversation that they had with Waayil, so I was sure he had no idea I had a son. I wanted him to find out on his own. And honestly, I knew that if he didn't hear about me, he'd miss me more.

As we sat next to one another in silence, I was so damn stiff that I had to remind myself to inhale and exhale. If he so much as breathed on me, I would cum all in my panties.

"Yikayla." He said my name lowly in his much deeper voice. It had a sexy raspiness to it too. Everything about him had gotten sexier, and it was to the point where I kept my eyes on the house across the street instead of looking his way. Every time I inhaled, his cologne would invade my nostrils. Even though I wasn't looking at him, I couldn't escape his presence.

"Shouldn't you go back to your party?" I finally said, feeling his eyes on me but still refusing to look his way.

"I will, but I wanted to see you. I was looking forward to walking in the house and seeing your pretty ass face." He cleared his throat and leaned forward, letting his forearms hang off his knees. "Baby, I don't want you to be mad at me."

Don't call me baby in that sexy voice. You sound and look too good.

Laughing, I repeated, "You don't want me to be mad at you. Who said I was mad?" I shrugged and took down some more of the vodka. It burned like hell, but I held my breath so I wouldn't fold in front of him. I wanted him to see... or at least think I didn't give a fuck. And I shouldn't give a fuck because I loved Roscoe.

"You won't even look at me."

To try and prove him wrong, I turned to my left to face him and felt my heart rate speed up. Why was he so damn handsome? With the way I was reacting physically, you would think I hadn't seen his twin almost every day for the past two months. But I guess no matter how much Nusef looked like Waayil, he wasn't Waayil.

Staring him in his hazel eyes, my right leg began to subtly bounce, and my palms began to sweat, as I held onto that Grey Goose bottle for dear life. Waayil licked his lips, not seductively, but it still turned me on. He just gazed into my eyes, obviously high, without saying a word.

"There, I looked at you." I quickly turned my attention back to the house across the street so I wouldn't have a heart attack.

"I'm sorry, Yikayla."

"For what? For lying and saying you loved me just so you could take my virginity? Or for not even talking to me for the past five and a half years."

"I didn't lie and you know I didn't lie. I'm not even that type of nigga; well, I wasn't then. I would never be that way towards you."

I blinked repeatedly in order to hold back my tears. He was right; Waayil wasn't that guy who would lie to a girl to get in her pants. It was something I found sexy about him. He liked sex like most guys, but he didn't go out of his way to get it or act as if he needed it to breathe, like his twin brother. Nusef was a mess, but he was just like hot pussy Jonaya. I guess that's why they were so cool with one another; two hoes in a pod. I loved them though.

"Doesn't matter now."

I could see him nodding his head slowly out the corner of my eye. And since he was no longer staring a hole through the side of my face, I stole a glance. He had his lips tucked in, and his dimples had taken center stage as he stared out at the street.

"So this is how we gon' be? Like we never knew each other?" he quizzed, and turned to me with squinted eyes.

"I don't really care at this point." I stood up and when I did, he eyed my body lustfully for a few moments before he rose to his feet as well. He was so damn tall. "Goodnight, Waayil, and welcome home."

I turned to go inside of the house. The screen door closed behind me, and as I closed the wooden door, he stood there planted on my porch with his hands in his pockets, his beautiful eyes lowered, dimples on display, and his lips tucked in.

As soon as the door closed, I fell against it and breathed heavily for a few seconds.

"Lord help me," I prayed lowly as I shook my head.

2

WAAYIL CHRISTIAN

"Oooh shit, Waayil," Alba whimpered and cried as I fucked her hard from behind. I watched as her ass jiggled and moved every time I slammed into her with force.

Her pussy was just as good as I remembered, but I wasn't no dumb nigga. Never had been and definitely wasn't gon' act like one now. Someone had been in this pussy, but right now, I didn't care to complain. And frankly, I didn't care enough about the situation period. Long as that nigga stayed away long enough for me to bust, I was good.

"Fuck," I grumbled, going harder, slapping our sweaty skin together while groping her smooth ass cheeks.

I watched as she clenched her teeth while gripping the fuck out of her sheets, just before I yanked her head back by her hair. Drilling her hard, I sucked on her neck, making her spill in no time. As her body jerked, I pounded her pussy feverishly until I nutted hard in the condom. I'd only been home for two days, and Alba and I had been fucking like animals in heat around this bitch.

I carefully pulled the condom off as Alba laid on her stomach, panting heavily. Slipping out of her king-sized bed, I walked to the bathroom to flush it and turn the shower on. I may have only been out for a short amount of time, but I had shit to handle and didn't wanna be laid up in the house with Alba all muthafuckin' day.

The only reason I was still with her ass was because it really didn't matter to me if we stayed together or not when I got arrested. I was gon' be locked up for forever, at the time, so her still trying to be my bitch while I did that bid was on her ass. I admit I was grateful for the money she put on my books and shit, even though my brother and parents had me, and I appreciated her visiting me, taking my calls, and writing. However, if she thought I believed that she hadn't been throwing that pussy to other niggas while I was away, then she was dumber than she acted, and she acted dumb as fuck sometimes.

I ain't know if I was gonna end shit with Alba because honestly, being in a relationship and shit was the least of my priorities; being in one with her at least. As long as she was straight with just taking this dick for right now, then I had no complaints.

"Going somewhere?" Alba came and stood in the doorway of the bathroom, tying her robe around her body, and still breathing slightly heavily.

"Yeah, I got some errands to run and shit."

"And what about me?"

"What about you?"

I spread toothpaste onto my brush as I looked myself over in the mirror. I had a mark under my eye from the few fights I'd gotten in while being locked up. I was cool, low-key, so most of my time in there was pretty calm. But like always, you had muthafuckas who wanted to test ya gangsta or prove shit by fucking with the quiet nigga they assumed was a punk. I deaded that shit quickly as hell though. In no time, niggas knew I wasn't the one to fuck with, and I didn't need to talk nonstop to prove that shit.

"We haven't sat down and talked or anything, Waayil! I mean, I feel like we need to go away or something and just do us to make up for lost time."

"We can talk another time, Alba. I have shit I need to do and have set up. Fuck you expect, me to lay up in here with you all fucking day?" I frowned. I flossed my teeth and then rinsed my mouth with Listerine once I was done brushing.

"No, but I wanna talk about where we're going! We're not teenagers anymore, Waayil, and I held you down for the whole six years you were locked up!"

It's like I jinxed myself by thinking she'd be cool having the same setup we'd had six years ago. I should have known she would assume that 'holding me down' would result in her getting a ring as soon as I was released into the free world. Sadly though, that shit wasn't happening no time soon, and if I did settle down, I highly doubted it would be with her.

"Did you? Did you hold me down?"

She just stared at me, so I chuckled subtly before slipping into the shower. Once I was clean to my liking, and done thinking about all the shit I had to put together in my fucking life, I got out and dried off. After I slipped on some boxers, sweats, a t-shirt, socks, and some Adidas slides, I put my hat on and headed for the door.

"I'm making breakfast, Waayil." Alba stopped me.

"Wrap it up for me," was all I said as I left out of her crib.

The Chevy I purchased for my eighteenth birthday was still in pretty good condition. My family kept it up for me by letting it run here and there, driving it a few places, and keeping up with the oil changes. I was happy as hell to see my baby parked in the driveway of my parents' spot the night of the party. I just knew I wasn't gon' have shit to whip once I touched down, but damn was I glad that I was wrong.

Slipping into the driver's seat, I checked my texts then replied to a few as my mind drifted to Yikayla. I hadn't seen her since the night of my party, and I missed her ass like crazy. I thought about her nonstop while I was locked up, and at times that shit drove a nigga nuts.

Pulling out, I decided to try and get a conversation out of her ass again. The last time we spoke was awkward as hell because I didn't quite know what to say to her. It was foolish as fuck of me to expect her to welcome me home with open arms and forget about the last six years of us being apart, and me continuing to fuck with Alba. I had my reasons though, and if I could go back in time, I'd do that shit all over again.

I made it to Yikayla's parents' home, and smiled when I saw the car that Jonaya said belonged to Yikayla. I didn't know shit about her life, so I didn't know her schedule or anything. By saying that, it felt good to know that I came at a time that she was home.

Taking a deep breath, I got out of the car and frowned at the sun beaming down on me. It was hot and humid as fuck in Memphis right now. I should have been used to it, but I wasn't anymore.

As I made my way up the steps, Yikayla's older sister, Dree, came rushing out like she had to be somewhere an hour ago.

"Damn, nigga, you ain't been here but two seconds and you're already on Yikayla tough. Let me find out y'all fucked before you left."

I'd assumed Yikayla told people about what had happened between us, but I guess not. I wasn't gon' be the one to do it though.

"Nah, nothing like that. She inside?"

"In the back by the pool. I don't think she wants to see you though. I don't blame her. Y'all were best friends and then you cut her off."

I ignored Dree's comment and entered the house to see their mother, Natasha, on the couch in some little ass dress, exposing them chocolate legs. Natasha was fine as fuck, and she was known around Memphis as being the finest mama. Nothing about her showed that she had four kids, and she used that shit to her advantage. Muthafuckas knew she let loose when her husband was away. I didn't get how *he* didn't know.

"Waayil!" Natasha beamed, tossing her hair back and throwing her arms around my neck. Like three of her daughters, she had deep brown skin, long hair, long ass eyelashes, and big brown eyes.

"Hey, how you been?" I asked, peeping through the house to see if I could spot Yikayla in the backyard.

"Great, great. How are you though?"

"Much better than I was last week." I grinned as she laughed.

"I bet. Well you are even more good looking than I remember." There was a moment of silence before she said, "Oh, I'm sure you're looking for Kay so I won't hold you up."

I nodded as I slipped my hands into my pockets, before making my way through the large foyer, and out into the backyard.

I spotted Yikayla in the big backyard, sitting on one of the lawn chairs. She was wearing some weird ass shorts that looked like it used to be a dashiki, and a black bikini bra. Her hair was hanging down her back and all over the place like usual. For as long as I'd known her, she never did her hair, but it didn't take away from her beauty. I watched her for a moment as she bobbed her head to whatever was playing in her headphones, while probably sketching clothes.

I made my way over to her, and sat down in the lawn chair that was next to her. She paused for a moment, not looking my way, before taking one of her earphones out and glancing at me briefly. I didn't know why she couldn't look at me.

"You busy?" I smiled, peeping the dress she'd sketched.

"Yeah, I am actually, so if it's not an emergency, I'd like to be alone."

"Why you being so mean to me?" I touched her smooth thigh, that made me lick my lips unintentionally.

I remembered being in between them like it was yesterday. Eating her pussy invaded my mind, and I felt my mans down below bricking the fuck up with the quickness. I immediately wondered if she'd been with anybody else. Shit, of course she had, but I didn't wanna believe it.

"Please don't touch me." She brushed my hand off. I inhaled sharply, enjoying the sweet nutty scent she'd smelled like since way back. It was some natural shit that she'd made herself.

"I can't touch you now? You ain't have a problem with me touching you before."

"Because *before* I thought we were friends, but I realized we're not." She kept her eyes on her pad, but was only scribbling. "Waayil!" she shouted when I snatched it and placed it behind me.

She stood up and tried to reach around me, so I used my free hand to bring her down into my lap, making her straddle me.

"Don't tell me I can't touch you, Yikayla." I was serious as fuck. Whether she wanted to be or not, she was mine. She was mine well before I slid up in her and put my name on her pussy.

She tried to get up, but I held her tighter, keeping her sketchpad behind me with my other hand.

"Waayil."

"You missed me?" I whispered and kissed her neck. Fuck, I didn't think I'd be on her like this when I got out. Feelings were rushing over me like a muthafuckin' tidal wave and it was bugging me out.

Yikayla turned her head as I planted soft pecks on her smooth milk chocolate collarbone. On God, I wanted to eat her ass up right now.

"Waayil, I have a boyfriend and you need to let me up."

"You got a boyfriend?" I smiled, hiding the slight anger that lingered in me. She nodded as her eyes scanned mine. "He know I'm out?"

"No! I don't know!" I noticed she'd gotten more comfortable in my lap as I brushed my thumb up and down her smooth back.

"You ain't warn him that you was about to get stolen?"

"Waayil."

"I'm serious as a heart attack, Kay."

I didn't know who her nigga was, but his time with Yikayla was up. And if she didn't want to let his ass know, I had no problem doing so. If he wanted to get his ass whooped over Yikayla, then I wasn't gon' be the muthafucka to stop him.

"You think you can just come back and be my man? I've been with my nigga for five years and... and—"

"And what? Huh? You been with him five years and during that whole time, you thought about me. Tell me I'm wrong. Tell me there was a time where I couldn't have gotten out of jail and taken you, during that five years."

Shaking her head constantly as she looked off, she said, "It—"

"Look at me."

She turned to face me and replied, "It doesn't matter. I'm with him."

"Let me take you out."

3

———————

YIKAYLA

"Take me out? I can't, I have shit to do today, and you can't just waltz in here and make me change my plans."

As I ran off with as much attitude as I could muster up, Waayil kept that sexy ass grin on his face. His deep dimples were showing the fuck out, and his beautiful cocoa skin looked so smooth under the bright sun. I watched as he licked his lips slowly, preparing to speak. I wanted him to let me out of his lap because for one, I didn't want my sisters to see us; and two, I felt like I was gonna leave a wet spot on his sweats from how drenched he had me.

"I ain't say today. I can't today, but this Friday I wanna take you out. Aye, but if I was talking about today, yo' ass would have come."

"Why do you wanna take me out anyway?"

"Least I can do since you already gave me some," he replied lowly, squinting his honey colored eyes as he kept strong eye contact with me.

I wish you would stop looking at me like that with your fine ass.

Him bringing up the night we made love, and me feeling his big hands on my body, was way too much for me right now. I was sweating like a damn overworked slaved in this moment, and I was sure he could see it.

"Whatever."

"Nah, but I wanna talk to you. You've been asking me what happened since it happened and I wanna tell you, but over food."

"It won't be a date."

"It's a fucking date, Yikayla."

He finally let me up and I couldn't get into the other lawn chair fast enough. He reached behind himself to grab my pad and then extended it out to me. Taking it from him, I felt his eyes on me as I shoved my pencils into my pouch.

"When you get this?" He grabbed my ass when I stood up, catching me off guard.

"Waayil." I chuckled and turned to face him so he wouldn't do it again. "You have to go. I umm, I have some errands to run."

He cocked his head a bit, keeping his full sexy lips tucked in as his eyes shined brightly under the sun. He finally rose to his feet, towering over me, and I felt myself getting even hotter.

"Can I at least see yo' room? I just wanna know if it's the same."

"Is that all?"

"Yeah, that's all. This ain't some ploy to fuck. You know I wanna fuck you so it's no point in me trying to scheme my way into that."

"Well it won't happen anyway." I moved past him and I could see he was following me back into the house.

"It already did. It was good too."

His voice was low when he said it, sending chills down my back as we ascended the stairs.

"Hey, Waayil," my sister, Rori, waved to him, carrying a duffle bag. I was sure it was some shit her boyfriend, Gavin, had her ass doing. My sister could do so much better than a weak ass dope boy like Gavin.

"Sup, Rori. Fuck is in that bag?" Waayil frowned.

"Nothing, nigga." She smiled and kept moving down the hallway past us.

"My room, just as you remember it I'm sure." I led Waayil into my bedroom, holding the door open as he came inside.

I closed the door behind us.

"Yeah, but I see you got rid of a lot of shit. Not this sewing machine though. Still making yo' own shit." He snickered, picking up a new piece of fabric I'd acquired.

"Yeah, and the other new addition is..." I reached into the baby crib on the far-right side of my room to pick up my half sleep baby. Waayil was so enthralled by my sewing machine and fashion stuff, that he didn't notice the crib, changing table, and baby walker across the room. "...Lonan. Lonan, say hi to Mommy's friend." I moved his arm up and down, and fixed his navy-blue onesie.

When I made eye contact with Waayil, his lips were slightly parted. I couldn't really tell what he was feeling at the moment as he stared at my baby hard.

"You got a baby, Kay?" he quizzed, voice barely above a whisper.

"Yeah."

I moved closer to Waayil, and he kept his eyes on my son the whole time. He sat down on my bed, and surprisingly, reached out for him. Carefully, I placed Lonan into Waayil's strong arms, and they just stared at one another for a little bit as Lonan cooed and talked baby nonsense.

"How old is he?"

"He just turned one two months ago," I replied and rubbed my baby's back.

"Gemini like me, huh?" Waayil grinned, but then it soon faded as his hazel eyes continued to run amuck all over Lonan. "He's cute. I uh... I ain't gon' lie, I'm a little jealous of his father."

His confession made me smile a little for some reason. I was never one to get off on making someone jealous, but oddly, him being envious of Roscoe for being Lonan's dad was cute.

"What? Waayil, jealous?" I sat next to him on the bed.

"Don't get used to that shit. So his daddy is ya boyfriend, huh?"

He passed Lonan back to me, and I kissed him as he grabbed a handful of my hair in his little hands.

"Yep."

"He got you for five years and a baby," Waayil said more so to himself as he laughed lightly and shook his head.

He stared down at his tattoo covered hands and squinted his eyes like he was thinking about something. He then turned to make eye contact with me. I didn't know what to say, and it was obvious that he was disappointed.

"I wanted to wait for you, Waa—"

"Nah, it's cool. So Friday, just be ready to eat, aight? And bring him too... I mean, if you want to and shit." He stood up and scanned the rest of my room, lingering on the baby furniture for a moment, before rubbing Lonan's hair gently.

"Okay, don't be late."

He just gave me that closed mouth smile while squinting his eyes, before he left the bedroom. I played with Lonan for a minute, and about twenty minutes later, his father was calling me.

"Hey," I answered, keeping the phone in place between my shoulder and ear.

"What's up, you—"

Lonan cut Roscoe off by talking loudly to me in baby language. I chuckled and kissed his perfect nose.

"Shut him up so I can get my fucking sentence out."

"I'm not gonna shut him up, Roscoe. It's good that he's trying to talk!"

"Whatever. I'm outside, so come on."

"Okay." I sighed, not even in the mood to go anywhere after his comment. Not to mention, my mind was still on Waayil.

I slipped some baby sweats on Lonan since he was already in a onesie, and then I put his socks and Nikes on. After grabbing my baby's bag and his sweater, we left out of the house.

Roscoe still didn't have a fucking car seat for our son, so I had to place my things into his car before getting Lonan's car seat out of my vehicle. After buckling our son in, we were finally on our way to wherever.

As we drove off E. Parkway, I was just happy as hell that Waayil didn't run into Roscoe and vice versa. Roscoe was very jealous, and although Waayil wasn't really the envious type, he was a little possessive when it came to me. He'd been that way ever since we became best friends.

"Is that cologne I smell?" Roscoe frowned as he made a left, and then came to a red light. I felt him look at me as I tried to figure out what to say.

"I hope not because I am definitely wearing perfume."

"Humph." He pulled off. "I definitely smell cologne on you. You been around that homeboy who did you dirty?"

"Who?" I looked at his side profile, playing dumb.

Like our son, Roscoe had supple caramel skin and pretty curly hair. Any girl with eyes was attracted to him, and sometimes I wondered why he'd chosen me. But I guess it was just something about me because I had two of some of the finest men Memphis had to offer, interested in me. Don't get me wrong, I was the *furthest* thing from ugly, believe that, but both Waayil and Roscoe could have any woman they wanted.

Roscoe didn't have anything on Waayil though, and I wasn't the only one who thought that. Nusef was already Roscoe's competition, but now that Waayil was back, Roscoe just might fade into the darkness.

"Waayil, Kay. You know who the fuck I'm talking about." Roscoe pulled into his complex and found his designated parking space. When we first met, he told me his mother lived with him, but over time, I realized it was the other way around. Even the car he drove was his mother's; he just basically manhandled her out of it, so eventually she'd gotten a new one.

"I haven't been around Waayil like *that*, I was just around him and a lot of other people. He just got out and the block is still celebrating," I quickly lied.

Chuckling, Roscoe replied, "Shit, I know you ain't dumb enough to fuck around on me, especially not with some nigga like him."

I almost came to Waayil's defense, but I knew that wasn't a good idea.

We both got out of the car, and instead of helping me get Lonan from the car seat, Roscoe's attention was on his damn phone. I unbuckled my son, and as I did so, I saw a receipt sitting on the seat next to him. It was just a Hardee's receipt, but what caught my attention was the date on it. It was the day *before* he claimed his ride home to Memphis had flaked. I knew it because the next day was Waayil's release date, which was embedded in my mind.

Snatching the receipt up, I double-checked the date and the address to be sure it was the Hardee's out here. I had so many fucking questions as I clutched the receipt tightly and pulled my baby from his seat.

"You went to Hardee's three days ago?" I held up the receipt.

"I don't know, why?" he shrugged.

"This receipt says you went to Hardee's on Summer Ave. three days ago, Roscoe."

"And?"

"Weren't you still in Nashville this day?" I looked at the receipt again for the time stamp. "This was a little after noon, so what the fuck!" I hollered, not knowing what to think.

"Quit all that fucking yelling and shit out here, Yikayla! That shit ain't mine!"

"This is your fucking card number at the bottom, nigga!"

His facial expression changed, almost like he knew he'd been caught. Yeah, I knew the last four of his card number. Muthafucka *barely* used it because he *barely* had money, but I had a pretty good memory.

"Yikayla, I was in Nashville that day. I don't know, I didn't even take my car, which you know. My mom must have used it."

"Your mom chose to drive this bucket instead of her brand-new Toyota?" I adjusted Lonan on my hip.

"She does that sometimes because her car is a gas guzzler."

Moving past him quickly, going towards the apartment, I said, "I'm gonna ask her and see."

"Kay, she ain't home."

I glared at him hard, and then just turned around to keep walking towards the apartment. I didn't know what to believe. Roscoe had never done anything like this, and right now, I had no way to disprove his lie. I had a mind to call Hardee's and ask one of them cashier bitches if they'd seen his ass. Shouldn't be that hard since he was a famous rapper, right?

Once inside the apartment, I sat down on the couch and placed Lonan to his feet. He walked right over to his father's DVD collection and ran his little hand down them.

WHAM!

Roscoe smacked Lonan's arm hard as fuck, prompting my baby to open his mouth with no sound coming out because he was in that much pain. Tears immediately began streaming his plump cheeks, before finally, his vocal chords came through.

"What the fuck is wrong with you, Roscoe!" I barked, hopping up and grabbing my baby to console him. As Roscoe stared at us angrily, I pushed his head back extra hard. I wanted to claw that muthafucka until he was unrecognizable.

"He needs to learn to stop touching shit! Always running his hands over my shit and I'm tired of it!" Roscoe snatched his hoodie off over his head before darting to the back.

"It's okay, baby," I cooed to Lonan, kissing his small arm and then his cheeks as he wailed uncontrollably. "Fuck this."

I grabbed my purse and baby bag, then headed for the door.

"Where the fuck you going?" Roscoe rushed to the front.

"To get food and then we're gonna go home."

"We're supposed to spend the day together." Roscoe frowned deeply.

"No, you're in a bad mood and if you hit him again, I may stab you. We can try another day."

"Wait, wait, wait." Roscoe gripped my arm but not roughly. "I'm sorry. I'm sorry, I'm just stressing over this music shit, and... and... and money, and then I got y'all depending on me. We can go get some food, and then come back to chill or something. Okay?" His voice was calm, and his eyes were sincere as he kissed Lonan for the first time in months.

"Okay." I sighed just as his phone rang. I was only agreeing at this point because I was starving and he drove me here.

The name Sham popped up on his cell, and he quickly hit ignore before slipping it back into his pocket and opening the door for me.

I couldn't wait until Friday...

4

———————

WAAYIL

"*Waayil.*" *I heard someone sniffling as I laid in my bed. I'd just walked Yikayla home about an hour ago after making love to her, and that shit was still fresh on my mind.*

"Wednesday?" I turned to look over my shoulder to see my little sister crying. Her hair was down, and her light face was bloodshot red. "What's wrong, baby?" I sat up, immediately angry about her appearance.

"Can I sleep in here with you?"

"Umm..." I looked around my small bed. I ain't really want her lying in it because I just fucked in it, but how could I tell her no? "Yeah, but can you tell me what's wrong with you, ma?"

She sat next to me and leaned her head on my shoulder, so I draped my arm around her.

"I promised him I wouldn't tell."

"Who?" My brows dipped as my blood began to boil. I had no idea what she was talking about, but her mentioning that a nigga had something to do with it pissed me off.

"Un-uncle Harry."

I gripped both sides of her face and made her look at me.

"What the fuck he do to you, Wednesday?"

"You promise you won't get mad?" she whispered. It was late as hell at night, or early as fuck in the morning, depending on how you looked at it.

"Nah, I can't promise that. Tell me what the fuck he did, or I'm gonna go ask that nigga my damn self."

"He's been raping me, Waa— Waayil!" She screamed my name because before she could finish her sentence, I'd pulled my Glock from the shoebox under my bed, and was out the bedroom door.

BOOF!

I burst off into that muthafucka's room on one hundred, chest heaving up and down. I still had on my clothes from walking Yikayla home, and because of my anger mixed with all the clothing, I was burning up.

"Wake yo' ass up, mane!" I snatched the blanket off my bitch ass foster uncle.

"What? Huh?" He shot up off the bed, hands up in mock surrender since I had my gun pointed right in the middle of his face.

"You like to fuck young girls, my nigga?"

"What? Waayil, I don't have time for your thug games!" he hissed.

"Did you fuck my little sister!" I roared so loudly that I swear the walls shook and the floor moved under me. My face was so twisted up that I could feel it, and my heart was beating faster than it ever had. My trigger finger was itching at the moment, and if this muthafucka said the wrong thing, his brains would be decorating these fucking walls.

"Waayil?"

"Get out the room, Wednesday!" I barked to my little sister, not even bothering to look over my shoulder at her. I could hear the door close though. "Answer me!" I growled to my uncle.

"Is that what that slut told you?" He had the nerve to laugh, and unfortunately for him, that shit pushed me over the edge.

"Shit," I mumbled, letting the shower water cascade down my face as I remembered the night I'd somewhat ruined my life.

Did I regret killing that nigga? No, but I wish I hadn't have gotten caught. What he did to my baby sister was unforgivable, and he didn't deserve to live. I was never irrational with shit, I always thought it through, so me killing him wasn't an impulsive reaction. I wasn't that nigga that just blew up over every little thing. In fact, I tried to let most shit slide. But if you did some unthinkable shit like that muthafucka, then I would react right then and there.

Thankfully, my parents forgave me for what I did when they found out why I did it. They felt guilty as fuck for bringing his criminal ass into the house and giving him access to Wednesday. I couldn't imagine holding such a burden, but it was over, and Wednesday didn't hate them for it.

Once I was clean, I stepped out of the shower and brushed my teeth. At the moment, I was staying with my twin, Nusef, and I was already tired of it. Even before jail I liked my own space, but being locked up just intensified my need for solitude a lot more. Don't get me wrong, I still liked hanging with my brother and the homies, but just not for a long ass time. However, I could fuck with Yikayla until the cows came home.

I smiled at myself in the mirror, after I spit out my mouthwash, at the thought of her. Yikayla had always been beautiful, but seeing her as a woman was some other shit. Her body was crazy, perfect to me, and her sexy Hershey skin seemed to have this damn glow to it.

Her having a baby was fine, but I just wished she didn't have to fuck another nigga to get it. Just the thought of another muthafucka knowing what it was like to be in between her legs bothered the fuck out of me. Him being her boyfriend was the least of my worries because, like I'd told her, I was coming for her, and he'd just better bow out or get his ass handed to him.

"Nigga, you almost ready? You better not had been jacking off in my fucking shower." Nusef stared me down as he sat on his couch, phone placed in his hand.

I just laughed and went into the spare bedroom to put on some clothes. Once I was dressed, I sprayed on some cologne and grabbed my phone. I saw Alba had texted me five fucking times, along with a few others, and I already knew why. She was tripping over the fact that I didn't want to spend the night with her ass last night, and that I'd decided to stay with my brother instead. We were just on two completely different pages right now, and living together was only making shit worse. I was trying to hold out a little bit to somewhat spare her feelings, but I didn't know how much longer I could play fake with her while being around Yikayla.

"Aight, let's go," I told Nusef once I reached the living room, turning my phone on vibrate because Alba had me sick of hearing my phone ring.

Nusef and I left his crib and I just enjoyed the feeling of the sun beaming down on me. As we made it to his car, I yanked my sweatshirt over my head, forgetting that it was summer and hot as hell right now.

"You excited?" Nusef quizzed once he had his air blasting and the car running.

"Yeah, I am. I don't wanna work right away though. I feel like I need to build up to that shit, you know?" I glanced at him and he nodded as he pulled off Goodwyn Street.

Before I could even speak again, we were turning into the small shopping center on Highland Street, and I smiled widely as hell seeing the tattoo shop my brother opened.

Once Nusef and I turned eighteen, we got this big ass lump sum in our bank accounts. It was actually two; one from our real parents and one from our foster parents. The one from our birth parents was a surprise because I'd assumed that shit would have been voided due to their charges.

As y'all know, I got arrested shortly after my damn birthday, so I didn't have a chance to do shit with it. I bought my little Chevy using drug money. Anyhow, I agreed to let Nusef put our money together to open Monarch Tattoo. Hearing about the shit was one thing, but actually seeing it was another.

"Damn, you really did this shit."

"What, you thought I was fucking around?" Nusef chuckled as he swooped into a park.

"Nah, you know better. I would hate to fuck you up over playing me." I half joked as Nusef scoffed and shook his head.

"Aye, don't bring that jail shit to the shop, Waayil. Put all ya shanks and shit in the trash right over there. Can't have you plunging that shit into the employees and customers."

We both laughed at his comment as we made our way towards the entrance of the shop. When we stepped in, I took a moment to admire and take in my surroundings. The walls were covered with different drawings that my brother and I had created over the years, along with a few other things I didn't quite recognize. I nodded approvingly at the nice furniture for patrons to sit on, and how it didn't smell like a bunch of dirty broke muthafuckas and old pennies like most tattoo shops out here. I was so caught up in the view of this shit that I hadn't noticed my homeboy, Sax, and a few other people in the lobby area, waiting to greet me.

"My bad, bro." I chuckled as I slapped hands and hugged Sax.

"You had me worried for a second." He grinned widely and patted my back lightly before moving out of the way so I could see the other people.

"Hey, I'm Chiara, with a C-H," said some pretty ass girl with smooth caramel skin, a curvaceous ass body, and full lips that low-key had my dick doing its morning stretches. Her hair was a brownish red color, some shit I had never seen before. Usually these Memphis hoes went Kool-Aid red or nothing. Chiara's pretty brown eyes shot right through me as she slipped her small soft hand into mine.

"What's good, ma. I'm—"

"Waayil," she giggled lightly as my brother and Sax sucked their teeth. I just nodded to let her know she was right, and licked my lips at how stacked she was.

"Moses. I tattoo here." A male employee approached me and shook my hand.

"Venus. I tattoo as well." Venus was pale as hell, but pretty. Her features made it obvious she was black though.

"Nice to meet you," I replied, and glanced to my left to see another pretty girl hugging Nusef around the torso, while he had his arm draped around her.

"Oh, this is Rebecca." He smirked, and both Sax and I just smirked. "She's the assistant manager."

This muthafucka, Nusef, would never change. I honestly didn't know how he stuck his dick in so many bitches and was able to sleep at night. These days, women were just as frivolous with their pussies as streetwalkers, and I already knew if a bitch gave me some shit, I'd kill her ass. By saying that, it was best I stayed picky with who I gave this dick to.

"Well, Waayil, since I'm the receptionist here, I guess I should show you to your tattoo room." Chiara palmed her chest and flung her hair from one side to the other.

"Yeah, aight." I tilted my head back to get a look at the waiting area once more, before following Chiara to the back. Watching her fat ass sway from side to side was a nice ass view, and I almost bumped into her ass when she stopped.

She turned to look at me with a pretty, knowing smile, and I just gave her a closed mouth one, letting her know she was right about whatever the fuck she was thinking.

"You have dimples! Oh my gosh! I love dimples!"

I just tittered lightly. It was the only difference between Nusef and I. My mother had deep ass dimples, looking like an older version of Lauren London.

"You don't talk much I see." Chiara led me into the station and I smiled subtly, seeing my name on the door as I slipped my hands into my jean pockets. "So yeah, this room is yours. It's the biggest one besides Nusef's. Your brother was so excited that you were coming back and..."

Chiara ran off at the mouth as I surveyed the room. Although we had completely different personalities, Nusef knew me well and knew just how I would want this shit to look. Knowing that I would be doing some shit I always wanted to do, and at one point thought I would never be able to, had a nigga feeling all warm and shit inside. Then to know I co-owned this place? Shit. The only muthafuckin' thing that could make shit better right now would be having Yikayla, and feeling her soft thighs wrapped around me again.

"Hello, sexy!" Chiara snapped her fingers in my face with a grin.

"Don't snap at me," I stated calmly, not looking her way, and continuing to maneuver around the room.

"My bad," she responded lowly. "So you have a girlfriend or—"

"Excuse me."

I slipped out of the room and headed towards the back of the shop to look around. I didn't ignore Chiara because she was ugly or some shit, but she wasn't at the top of my list right now, and I didn't care about anything she had to say.

As I made my way back to the front, looking at shit on the walls in the hallway, I heard Yikayla's name and then my brother groan.

"What you say about Yikayla?" I interrupted the conversation going on between the employees in the lobby area. My eyes were hard on that Moses nigga because I recognized her name in his voice.

"Ummm." Moses scanned everybody in the room, and it was silent as I waited for his answer. "Nah, she's cute as hell. I was seeing if anybody knew what was up with her and her baby daddy."

"Oh, that's over with; well, will be come this Friday."

"Oh shit, well maybe I can get in that shit!" He laughed, but Sax and Nusef stayed quiet so his laughter ceased. Rebecca, Chiara, and Venus just watched with confused expressions.

"Moses, right?" I moved in his direction.

"Yeah." He nodded repeatedly like he was nervous.

"I'm gon' give you a pass because you're not really aware of what the fuck you're saying right now, mane. But Yikayla is off limits; that's mine."

Moses stared at me with parted lips for a little bit before saying,

"Oh word? Damn I ain't even know. On God, I didn't know. I just knew y'all were close or used to be homies according to ya brother."

"You good. Just don't let that shit happen again. I'll kill a nigga for mine." I looked around the room at the decor once more, and with a smile, I said, "This shit is nice!"

Everyone just stared at me like I was crazy, before nodding and responding lowly in agreement.

Waayil Christian was back and there were certain things I was staking claim on; Yikayla Goode being one of them.

5

———————

YIKAYLA

I stood in front of the mirror, holding up dresses in front of me to see which one looked better. I smiled when I spotted Lonan in the middle of my bed, staring at me with his cute self. Suddenly, the thought of what I was doing tonight made me feel bad because I'm sure my baby wouldn't approve of me going out with someone other than his father.

Letting out a heavy sigh, I shook the thought from my mind and continued to ponder on what I should wear tonight. My palms were sweating like crazy and my stomach was in knots. I kind of wished Waayil would cancel because I was *that* fucking nervous to go eat with him.

This man and I had been tight as hell growing up; like, I would tell him everything, even when my period started and how bad my cramps were. Yet, here I was, so nervous that I was about to go to Jonaya's room and ask her to give me some weed. I didn't smoke much, but I knew it'd calm my nerves.

"Red or black, Lo?" I turned to face my baby who was on his belly, watching me with his curly hair all over the place. He giggled but then turned away because someone knocking on my door caught his attention.

"Ooooh, a dress?" Jonaya leaned in the doorway and my other little sister Rori was right behind her smiling just as widely.

"Actually, no, I was hanging up some things that I just got from the cleaners. I'm wearing jeans and a top," I lied.

I'd told everyone who would listen in this house that me going out tonight with Waayil was just an old friends thing, so there was no way I could strut out of here in a damn dress. Plus, I had a man, and I shouldn't be wearing stuff like this for another nigga anyway.

"Sure." Rori laughed before pulling her phone from her pocket. "Gavin is here so I gotta go. But use a condom tonight," she added before turning on her heels and laughing with Jonaya.

Once Rori was down the hall and hitting the stairs, Jonaya looked to me and smiled gently. It made me smile back, because I knew what she was doing it for.

"I know you missed him," she finally spoke, walking over to pick Lonan up.

"I mean, yeah." I shrugged. "I missed him just like you all probably did."

Jonaya just nodded slowly, then kissed Lonan's cheek before taking him to her bedroom. Growing up, I hated having so many damn sisters, but nights like these, when I needed a babysitter, I loved it. I couldn't have asked Roscoe to watch him because he would have been wanting to know where the fuck I was going without him, and why so late. Not to mention, he never liked to be alone with Lonan.

Once Jonaya closed my bedroom door, I went to brush, floss, and rinse my mouth with Listerine, then I got into the shower. I used my regular soap, but then went over my body again with some scented shower gel from Victoria's Secret since I had a perfume and lotion to match.

I couldn't help but to grin as I rinsed my body. Jonaya was right; I did miss Waayil, but that did nothing to help the queasiness in my stomach. I hadn't felt this queasy even when I was pregnant with my son.

After drying off and spreading my matching lotion on, I spritzed my slightly damp body with the perfume, and then got dressed. I decided on a pair of skinny jeans, a white tube top that I'd decorated with pretty African patterns myself, and then some white sandal stilettos. My hair was never a concern of mine, so I let it hang freely and just put on my jewelry.

By the time I was dressed, something told me to look down out of my window, so I did. As soon as my eyes laid on Waayil, leaning up against that Chevy he'd gotten for his eighteenth birthday, a smile spread across my face uncontrollably. It was already dark outside, and the streetlights seemed to only illuminate his beautiful dark skin.

Relax, Yikayla.

I took a deep breath, went to kiss Lonan goodbye, and then let my mother, Jonaya, and Dree know I was leaving.

When I stepped outside onto the porch, I slowed down as I made my way towards him, trying to control my breathing and having a silent pep talk with my feet so I wouldn't ankle-break in front of him. He hadn't seen me since I was just a weird, naive teenager, and I wanted him to witness the woman I had become. So falling on my ass in these six-inch heels wasn't really a part of that plan.

Chewing his gum sexily as his pretty hazel eyes took me in, he leaned up off of his car and brought around some flowers he'd been hiding behind his back. His eyes scanned me from head to toe, and when he licked his lips, his dimples appeared like always.

"Damn, Kay," was all he said, serious expression embedded in his face once we made eye contact.

"Is that a compliment?" I tried to have a little bit of an attitude to make up for how vulnerable he'd had me by the pool earlier this week.

Typical Waayil didn't respond to my question, and I guess it was because I already knew the answer. He reached the flowers out to me as he moved closer. His cologne invaded my nostrils, and as his body kept coming towards me, the butterflies in my stomach turned to big ass bald eagles.

He was dressed in a black short-sleeved polo shirt, dark jeans, a black baseball cap, and his favorite white on black Adidas. A simple but nice chain laid nicely against his new muscular pecs, and the shiny watch around his wrist was a nice touch against his smooth yet strong chocolate arms. He stood over me and when he leaned down, I prepared myself for the greatest kiss in history; however, he pressed his lips against my cheek as he hugged me, then backed away with a grin.

I cleared my throat out of embarrassment, before following him to the passenger side of the car where he opened the door for me. I looked around the inside of the vehicle as he made his way to the driver's side, and I could tell it had been cleaned and fixed up. It smelled like lavender in here, which made me chuckle a little bit. Lavender was so feminine for a man like Waayil to have in his car.

"You didn't wanna bring ya baby?" he quizzed as he cranked the car.

"Uh, no, he needs to be asleep by a certain time," I replied, as he backed out of the driveway. Leaning back in the driver's seat, a closed mouth smile graced his sexy face just before he licked his lips. "Is something funny?"

Looking over at me with one eyebrow raised, he said, "Nah. But I'm happy to know you planned to be out with me for a minute."

Lord, when did his voice get so deep and sexy?

"Actually, no, I just wasn't sure if you were gonna be late or something."

He chuckled at my terrible lie, while nodding his head and turning on his blinker. Everything this nigga did was sexy. The way he whipped the car through the streets like he owned them, how he slowly bobbed his head to the soft music coming from his stereo, and even the way he sniffled occasionally.

My eyes cascaded down his large, but not too muscular frame. I wondered how good he looked under it all. I could still feel him between my legs that night, kissing all over me and groping me like he didn't have enough hands to touch all the places he wanted to. It was six years ago, yet, I remembered every detail about that night. I couldn't tell you anything really about the sex I had with Roscoe, and we'd just fucked two nights ago.

Don't get me wrong, Roscoe was pretty good in bed. But for some reason, sex with him could never compare to the night I lost my virginity to Waayil. According to Roscoe though, I'd slept with some old boyfriend and lost my virginity.

He was already jealous of Waayil, even though he'd never met him before. It was because a lot of nights, my family would bring up Waayil and how close we were, in the midst of telling stories about us all growing up on the same street. By saying that, Roscoe didn't need to know that not only was Waayil a big part of my life because we grew up together, but he was also a big part because he was my first... everything.

By the time I pulled myself from my thoughts, Waayil had stopped in front of The Bar-B-Q Shop on Madison. I loved this place, even though they took a while to bring you your food. It was worth it though.

"I'm glad I didn't wear my good clothes," I joked, hitting the release button on my seatbelt.

"I ain't know you had good clothes."

"Fuck you, nigga! Not everything I get is from thrift shops!"

We both laughed in unison as he reached for something in the back seat. I waited for him to get out, and once he did, he rounded the hood and stepped onto the sidewalk to open my door for me.

When we walked into the establishment, it was slightly packed due to it being a Friday night. We didn't wait too long though, because the manager knew Waayil and me, and didn't want to keep us waiting. He was a good friend of my stepfather.

Once seated by the window, Waayil and I both ordered the slab of ribs, half wet and half dry rub. My stomach was grumbling and still consumed with butterflies. Once the waiter left, Waayil and I just looked at one another for a few moments. Getting nervous, I glanced out of the window to give myself a break.

"Why you don't like looking at me?" He sipped his iced tea, then squinted his eyes like he was thinking. I loved when he did that.

"I don't know why you think that." I tried my hardest to keep eye contact with him. He was just so fucking handsome and I was just tense as fuck, making it difficult to keep my eyes on his.

When I felt my hands perspiring, I rubbed them up and down my jeans.

"I don't *think* anything; it's a fact. Every two fucking seconds, yo' ass is looking somewhere else. I'm ugly now or something?" He grinned because he knew damn well he wasn't ugly. Looking like a chocolate god with hazel eyes and the perfect amount of muscle and facial hair.

"No, Waayil, you look the same, I guess. But like I said, I have no problem looking at you."

"I don't have a problem looking at you either." Biting his lip as his lids lowered, he added, "Damn, you got so fucking pretty, Kay."

His voice was low and honest as he gazed at me, and I felt like I should have clipped some suspenders to the waistband of my panties to keep them from sliding down and taking my jeans with them.

"I wasn't pretty before?" I sipped my drink for the hundredth time out of nervousness. He laughed because he could tell; I knew he could. How was it that he still knew me so well?

"Yeah, you were pretty as hell before, mane, you know that. But being a beautiful teenager is different from being a beautiful ass woman."

His phone started to ring and before I could see the name on it, he hit ignore and shoved it into his jean pocket. I forgot he had a girl-friend for a minute.

"Alba?" I inquired like I didn't care.

He ignored me, giving me that sexy smirk that made his dimples show as he laced his fingers together.

"Waayil!" Some girl ran up to our table and bent down to hug him. Her perfume was louder than a fucking rock n' roll concert, and so was her blue hair.

"What's up, Alyssa?" Waayil replied. I watched his eyes move down her body as she stood up straight from hugging him, and it made me roll my eyes.

"I knew you were out, and I've been trying to catch you!"

"Word? For what?"

"To chill, but also because I need a tattoo. Nusef told me you were gonna be tattooing when you came home. I missed you though, so the tattoo can wait until after we—"

Completely cutting her off, Waayil gestured towards me and said, "This is my friend, Yikayla."

"Oh shit. Yes, I remember you! You're Dree's little sister!" she cheesed. She stared down at me, and it was like for the first time she realized that Waayil and I were here together.

"Nice to meet you, Allison," I gave a fake smile.

"It's Alyssa," she corrected me, but I pretended to be occupied with my phone.

She and Waayil talked for a few moments and then finally, she said her goodbyes to us both, which I didn't respond to.

"You mad?" Waayil's big hand reached across and caressed my thigh. I almost moaned at the feeling, but instead I dropped my phone like a loser.

"No." I moved my leg from his touch. "Mad over what?" I placed my phone in my purse after picking it up.

"Jealous, I mean."

"No, ain't nobody jealous, Waayil. Why would I be jealous of that hood rat? You think just because you fucked her I'm gonna be mad? I have a boyfriend, okay!" The whole time I ran off at the mouth, Waayil was dying laughing, fist to his mouth and everything, which kind of made me feel stupid. I tried not to chuckle as well.

"Kay, baby, I know you. You're mad as fuck right now. I never smashed shawty though." He turned his hat to the back so he could see me better, just as we got our food delivered to our table.

We held hands to pray over the food, and then dug in, letting the conversation between the other patrons play as our background music. I could barely focus on my food because I didn't understand why I was jealous of Waayil's interaction with Alyssa. I was perfectly fine with my relationship with Roscoe until Waayil came home, so what the fuck was my problem?

Waayil suddenly waved one of the employees over and said, "Can we get this to go?"

My heart started to thump thinking I'd done something to turn him off. We'd literally just gotten our food five minutes ago and he already wanted to leave.

"Sure." The girl smiled and nodded, switching off way too hard. I sucked my teeth on the low because I knew she did that for Waayil. I had forgotten how hot he had the girls back in the day, and honestly, unless they were blind or lesbian, then it was expected.

"Why are we leaving?" I quizzed Waayil once the girl left.

"Because it's too fucking loud in here and I wanna talk to you." He spoke without looking at me, as he dug in his pocket for his phone and wallet.

Just the thought of being alone in a quiet space with him, had me about to throw up for the tenth time tonight. I found comfort in the fact that we were in a somewhat crowded space with one another, now he wanted to be alone? Shit.

We got our food packed up and then got back into Waayil's car. As we drove to wherever, he turned on some low R&B music and started to sing along. I could feel myself smiling a little at the sound of his beautiful voice. It was just as silky and perfect as always. I glanced over at him, watching him smoothly turn the wheel to make a right, while effortlessly letting the notes of the song flow from his perfect lips. When he saw me watching, he gave me that same smirk like always, then went right back to singing.

I was so caught up in watching him, that I didn't realize the car had stopped at the Holiday Inn.

"Waayil, why are we—"

"Get out." He cut me off sternly, shutting the car off and sliding out of his car.

I just did as he asked, still wondering what the hell he assumed was gonna happen tonight.

6

———

WAAYIL

The look on Yikayla's face was funny as fuck. She'd been on edge all muthafuckin' night, and I admit that shit stroked ya boy's ego a bit. It was hella comical how she tried to pretend to be all tough and shit, like she was only out with me because I'd asked. She knew damn muthafuckin' well that she was out with me because she wanted to be, and that's all it was. But I'd let her continue to play the role if that shit made her feel better.

"Come on." I looked at her as I started towards the entrance of the hotel.

I knew tonight I'd be out with Yikayla, so I had this shit booked in advance. It wasn't like I planned to get some pussy; I just wanted to be alone with her. And since I didn't have my own shit popping off yet, a hotel was my only option right now. But shit, if her legs opened for me tonight, best believe I was getting in between them.

"I have a boyfriend, Waayil," she replied, following behind me to the hotel entrance.

I ignored her ass because she was just running her mouth at this point. Plus, she was telling that shit to herself more so than to me. She was trying to convince herself of some shit and I wasn't in the mood to be a part of that conversation. It was obvious because even though she'd said she had a nigga, she was still following behind me like I'd asked her to.

Since I already had my room key, we went straight to the elevator and up to the room. She didn't say one word the whole time, until we got inside the room and I cut the lights on.

"All this for me." She chuckled and set her purse down.

I admired her pretty ass smile. Damn did I miss that shit. It was like her smile, body, and pussy had been etched in my mind the whole six years I was away from her ass. I fucked Yikayla only twice and couldn't forget the shit.

"Yeah, I got this for you. Well us." I sat down on the bed and when she tried to walk past me, I pulled her down into my lap again so that she was straddling me.

"Waayil, stop." She wiggled her body a little to try and get away.

"Look at me for a second and I'll let you go."

Her chest rose and fell slightly as she stared off at the window. Finally, she turned to look down into my eyes, and I just gazed back up at her for a few. Moving her hair from her face, I adjusted my arm around her frame, bringing her into me some more.

The room was silent, but I could hear how heavily she was breathing.

"I make you nervous?" I inquired lowly. She just shrugged her shoulders and tried to look off, but I gripped her chin to prevent it. "You know I love you, Kay."

"No you don't."

"Yes I do, ma, fuck you mean? I ain't been out of jail a week and look where I'm at? I'm not at the crib with my bitch, I'm here with yo' ass."

"Then why did you cut me off and keep shit going with her!" She broke free from me and hopped up like my lap was on fire. "You told me to leave you alone, but you kept up with Alba! And you expect me to believe you love me?" Her voice was trembling slightly, and her eyes were glazed over.

"Kay, I told you to leave us be because I thought I was gonna be in jail for the rest of my fucking life, ma! You deserved better than being tied to some nigga in jail! I ain't want that shit for you, so I let it go! Alba don't mean as half as much to me as you do, so yeah, I kept up with her ass so I wouldn't be lonely. That's all the fuck it was!"

I stood up to move towards her and she stepped back. Tears were streaming her cheeks now, so I kept walking to her until her back was against the wall, then I thumbed them away.

"Why couldn't you just be honest and let me decide?" She stared up into my eyes as I held the sides of her pretty mocha face.

"Because I knew you wouldn't agree to that shit. I refused to hold you back from living yo' fucking life just because I loved you, Yikayla."

"I was depressed for a year!" she hissed.

"You ain't the only fucking one! I was locked up, thinking about how you was probably laid up with another nigga and forgetting about me!"

The thought of Yikayla fucking with some other nigga kept me up all night sometimes, even years after we hadn't spoken to one another. Sometimes when I got pussy during my bid, I'd have to imagine her.

"You knew that wouldn't happen," she whispered.

I couldn't take that shit no more, so I began sucking her soft ass lips while squeezing her nice round ass. I was taking it easy because I wasn't sure of what the fuck her reaction would be, but once I realized she wasn't gon' stop me, I slipped my tongue into her mouth and began tonguing her ass down hard as fuck.

We were moaning and everything, as we kissed like we'd clearly both been thinking about it since we'd split up.

I gripped the waistband of her jeans and started to unbutton them as quickly as possible. Like I said, I knew Yikayla like the back of my muthafuckin' hand, and if I didn't get her out of her clothes fast enough, she would stop me.

As soon as I had her zipper down, I slipped my hands down into her lace panties, but wanted to punch the fucking wall when I felt her small, soft hand grab my wrist to stop me. I knew it. I knew she was gon' halt this shit.

"Yikayla." I groaned out of frustration as I kissed on her sweet-smelling collarbone.

"Waayil." She nudged me off of her but when I didn't get back far enough, she slipped past me as she fastened her jeans.

For a moment, I just faced the wall, leaning up against it to get my thoughts together so my dick would hopefully go down. After taking a few deep breaths, I'd gained enough composure to turn the fuck around. When I did, I saw she was sitting on the edge of the hotel bed, fidgeting.

"Why you stop me?" I broke the silence.

"Should I pull out a scroll of reasons or do you just want the obvious?" She picked her head up to look up at me, and I got lost for a moment because of how beautiful she was. I didn't know how I'd gotten by six years without seeing her.

"Yikayla, I told you why I did what I did!"

I was frustrated by this time. She had to fucking understand. I had no idea my parents would get me a lawyer to have my case looked over again. Shit, I went in thinking I'd be there for life, and because of that, I made a lot of decisions that I probably shouldn't have. Shit, that I still needed to fix now that I was out.

"It's not just that! You have a girlfriend, Waayil! A girlfriend that has always been there! She was your girlfriend when you slept with me, she was your girlfriend while you were in jail, and at this moment... she is *still* your girlfriend."

"I don't give a fuck about her!"

"And that's fucked up! You guys have been together for years and you don't give a fuck about her?" Yikayla squinted her eyes in confusion.

Sighing heavily, I sat down next to her and adjusted my hat. I could feel her looking at the side of my face, but before I could give her eye contact, I had to get my thoughts together.

"Baby, when I say I don't care about Alba, what I mean is I would be willing to leave that situation alone to be with you. I had planned to do that shit before I got locked up, but as you know, shit got in the way of that. I got love for Alba because like you said, I've been with her for a while, but I shouldn't have to be with her forever because of that shit. I love you, and I wanna fuck with you, not her." I kissed her neck gently and felt goose bumps rise on her forearm.

"Even then, I'm in a relationship, Waayil."

"You don't wanna be with that nigga."

"Yes I do."

"No you don't, Yikayla. You're here with me, so you can't be that dedicated." I pecked her lips. "I know you." I whispered against them before delivering another one, more sensual. She tensed up once she realized what she was doing, and then stood up from the bed.

"Stop saying you know me, Waayil! You don't know me anymore! I'm not the same teenager that foolishly let you take her virginity while you had a girlfriend! I... I love my boyfriend, and he's the father of my child. The three of us are a family."

"You love him more than you love me?"

"I umm, I love you guys differently. You're my friend, and I love you like one. But I'm *in love* with him."

I nodded slowly while looking up at her. I didn't believe her ass, but then again, she was right about her not being the same girl she used to be. The Yikayla I knew, was the weird ass sixteen-year-old who used to make her clothes and not do her hair. Now, she was a grown woman with a sexy ass body, wearing heels and shit. I could still see that she added her own touches and designs, but she was different. I hadn't really taken the time to see that because I was so damn wrapped up in my fucking feelings for her.

It fucked with me a little bit to know that I couldn't just come home and have her ass like I'd wanted. That was all I fucking thought about after the judge banged his gavel and said I was a free man. But like I said, I loved Yikayla Goode with all my damn heart, and if she didn't love me then I was gonna work on making her ass love me. I was a determined ass muthafucka, and it was gon' take way more than a speech to make me give her fine, weird ass up.

"I'll take you home then," I finally replied.

She was silent for a moment and her eyes followed me as I rose to my feet.

"Thank you," she whispered almost, grabbing her purse up.

I hoped she didn't think this shit was the end, because it was just the muthafuckin' beginning.

7

YIKAYLA

I hadn't talked to Waayil in two days, basically ever since our date ended. However, what I'd said to him and how he reacted played in my mind repeatedly. I was in love with Roscoe, I really was, but I wasn't sure if I wasn't in love with Waayil too.

A part of me was angry with Waayil for basically choosing Alba over me, and I believe that was what was keeping me from completely falling again. He didn't deserve my love, yet, it was so hard not to give it to him. Not to mention that, that asshole just took me home and didn't try to change my mind. Deep down, I knew he didn't believe me, and it annoyed me that he knew me so well. He could just look at me sometimes and know what I was thinking. How was it that years later, he still possessed that power?

"Ugh!" I punched my pillow after slamming my phone down.

I was apartment hunting on this little app I'd found, but I could barely concentrate. I quickly checked to see if I'd woken Lonan and when I saw I hadn't, I breathed a sigh of relief.

I felt someone watching me, so when I looked over to my doorway, I saw my older sister, Dree. She was holding that same damn law book like always. Law school didn't start for another couple weeks, but she claimed she wanted to be prepared so she read anything on law she could find.

"Upset?" She smiled, slamming the hefty book closed before sauntering in my room and sitting down at my vanity. She fluffed her fresh press out before turning in my direction.

My sister was the exact definition of aloof. She was very pretty though, with her smooth, blemish free dark skin, silky, shoulder-length black hair, big brown eyes, and a body that we'd all inherited from our mother. I had yet to meet a guy who didn't fawn over Dree or talk about how sexy she was. Matter fact, the word fine had been associated with the Goode last name ever since I could remember. Dudes acted like my sisters and I were the crème de la crème; my mother too.

"No, I'm not upset." I sat up. "You're wearing that to the party tonight?" I quizzed, looking at her outfit.

"Do they have VIP?"

"It's an outside barbecue party, Dree."

"Then I won't be there. I don't do shit like that anymore. If I can't wear my nicest stilettos and dress, I can't go. You shouldn't be going either, Yikayla."

"Well I'm going."

"Why? To see Waayil?" she smirked.

"No, Roscoe is gonna be there so why would I—" I stopped talking once I realized what I was implying.

"Ooooh! I knew you wanted more from Waayil! You just admitted it too!" Dree laughed loudly, clapping her hands like she'd just discovered the craziest thing in the world.

"No, no, no. You were implying that I wanted Waayil, and I was just saying that Roscoe is gonna be there, so why would I..." I just stopped and shook my head because I realized there was no way out of what I'd already basically admitted. Plus, my speech only made Dree laugh harder.

"You ain't got to lie to kick it, Kay."

I ignored her as I pulled out my jean shorts that I'd decorated, making Dree groan at the sight. As she blabbed for the hundredth time about how excited she was for law school, I dug through my drawer for my sleeveless lace top that I'd sewn together myself.

Whenever Dree would talk about law school, it always made me think about my career. I didn't go to fashion school like I'd wanted because my stepfather Jasper told me he wouldn't pay for that. My mom didn't care if I went, but she didn't hold the purse strings; Jasper did. So Jasper and I came to an agreement that I would go to school for business and that down the line, my degree would be helpful in my fashion career.

The problem was that now I felt like not going to fashion school hindered me as far as opportunities. I had no idea how to break into the fashion industry, but I needed to do something. Especially since Dree was actually doing what she'd wanted to do since we were little girls.

"I'm too ready!" Jonaya walked into my room with Rori following behind her. Jonaya had on the littlest shorts I'd ever seen, but that was how she always dressed. She would walk the streets naked if she could, but since she couldn't, she wore as little clothes as possible.

"You coming?" Rori stared down at Dree with her arms folded.

"Now you know them little ratchet get-togethers are not my scene." Dree scoffed as she rose to her feet.

"'Cause you boring, bitch!" Jonaya half joked, making us all laugh, even Dree.

"Bitch, I ain't boring. I just don't believe in spending my time with these wannabe niggas around the hoods of Memphis. Show me to the parties with the doctors and lawyers, and then I'll be game."

"Gold digger," Rori chimed in, prompting us all to giggle.

"Have a good time, ladies." Dree pranced out, typing something on her phone.

I quickly changed, as Jonaya and Rori started to drink some of the Patrón that Jonaya had taken from my stepfather's bar downstairs.

He was gonna get a nice surprise when he came home to see all the bottles of liquor that were gone. But shit, my sisters and I were of drinking age, except Jonaya. She had one more year.

Once I was dressed, I took my baby to my mother's room. He was already fed, bathed, and asleep, so she just had to watch him.

I only had one shot of Patrón before my sisters and I left to go get into the car.

As soon as I cranked up, Jonaya turned to look at Rori in the back seat and said, "Please don't emasculate all the cute niggas by bragging on Gavin."

The three of us chuckled before Rori said, "I'm your older sister, boo. I do what I want. Plus, why would you want a weak nigga? Weak niggas are most likely dumb niggas too."

"Because dumb niggas have the best dick," Jonaya retorted. as I pulled down the street slowly, searching for my party playlist.

Rori just sighed in disappointment at our younger sister, after we all laughed.

Once I had my playlist popping, the three of us danced and sang along the whole way to the party.

I pulled onto Carver Avenue, the area that was pretty much a street with a lot of grass, trees, and open space. The homies always threw little ghetto ass parties over here, and they were fun as hell. I swooped into a park, or what was gonna be my park tonight, and then turned down my music.

"I dare you to take that to the face," I challenged Jonaya who raised her eyebrow like 'really?'.

She took the rest of the Patrón down. It wasn't even that much at all, yet, she felt the need to twerk in her seat when she finished like she'd accomplished something.

As soon as we got out of the car, we were getting greeted by some of the girls and guys we knew, as "Sit Down" by Kent Jones was playing loudly as hell. There weren't many people we didn't know, or who didn't know us Goodes. Being in the midst of all this, made me smile because I was so happy to be back in my city for good. Nashville wasn't home, and living there just wasn't the same as Memphis, despite them being within the same state.

We started to move through the party, right to where the barbecue was. The air was sticky and hot, even though the sun was setting already, and weed smoke filled the air even though there was a lot of open space. Cars of all kinds were parked any which a way, some with music coming from them and others abandoned for the night. The mosquitos were in full effect, but like always, we paid them no mind as we trucked it through the somewhat high, crunchy grass. The partygoers didn't care either because they were clearly enjoying themselves. I loved the smell of it all, and I think that was because I'd been away too long.

"Damn, ma." Some dude grabbed my hand, but I slick pulled it from him and kept it pushing.

My sisters and I danced lightly as we made our plates, and once we had everything, we made our way to one of the cheap white tables, joining Waayil's sister, Wednesday. Midori had gone off to college in Rhode Island, and his brother, Emil, didn't really hang with us like that.

"Hey, boo." Jonaya smiled and hugged Wednesday. Rori and I followed suit.

I prayed and as I was about to eat some of the potato salad, I spotted Waayil's car. Music was coming from it, but I couldn't tell what song because the sound system over the party drowned it out.

Fork full of food in hand, I kept my attention on his car, debating whether or not I should go over there and tell him I didn't really mean what I'd said. I wanted him to know that I *was* in love with him and that... shit, I don't know, maybe we could be together somehow. I just didn't know what I would do about Roscoe or even if I really wanted to break up the family I had.

"I'll be right back," I said to my sisters, finally deciding to just go talk to Waayil and see where the conversation went. I knew he was alone because Nusef was making a plate, and his other friend, Sax, was right behind him.

I made my way to the car, and bobbed my head a little when I realized Waayil was listening to "Ether" by Eric Bellinger. I smiled thinking I would hear him singing along, but when the smoke from his blunt cleared a little, I could see right into the car. Alba was right there bobbing her head on his dick, and he was laid back smoking, while caressing the back of her head with his free hand.

My feet seemed to be stuck, so even though I wanted to walk off, I stayed there paralyzed. Just as I found the strength to move, Waayil turned to see me. I quickly spun around, embarrassed that I'd just been standing there like some voyeur.

I didn't make it far before I felt Waayil's strong hand grip my arm, but I yanked away out of reflex. I had no right to be as mad as I was... but I was. I wasn't sure why I expected him to no longer be dealing with Alba just because he took me to eat, especially since I'd basically told him we would never be.

Waayil's face twisted slightly in confusion as he stared down at me. He looked so clean in the navy-blue Memphis Grizzlies jersey, dark jeans that weren't too baggy, and Nike Huaraches of the same color as the Jersey. He turned his hat to the back like always, allowing his honey colored eyes to pierce through me as both of us waited for the other to speak.

"Why you acting mad?" Waayil finally quizzed, folding his strong tattoo covered arms across his broad chest.

I'd never been so turned on by a man like I had been with Waayil. I finally understood why some bitches were straight up hoes. Shit, if they were around niggas as fine as Waayil all the time, how could I blame them?

His chain blinded me a little, as well as his matching watch, and his cologne screamed grown and sexy.

"I'm not mad, I just wanted to give you guys some privacy."

"Nah, you—"

"Waayil." Alba walked up, fixing her hair and staring straight at me. She still looked like a hoe just like she did six years ago. She gave me the same look she always did too, like she was suspicious of me.

"Aye, give me a minute. Go make me a plate," he told her as she slipped her hand into his. He quickly let hers go, and she just stared up at him for a moment. He spoke to her with his eyes, and then nodded towards the food, prompting her to do as she was told.

"Waayil, we don't have to talk. I swear I'm not mad." I chuckled awkwardly. I was so fucking mad I was surprised I hadn't burst into flames.

He didn't say anything in response, he simply took my hand into his and led me to one of the trees some ways away. Once over there, he pressed me up against it, and then towered over me, causing my breath to get caught in my chest as I took in his perfectly shaped lips.

Squinting his eyes for a moment, he said, "I thought you ain't love me."

"I-I do, I just said I'm not *in* love."

"Yet you stood there for way too long watching me get head, and then ran off like Snow White in the woods when I caught you."

Chuckling at his comparison, I shook my head and said, "No, I was just surprised."

"You know I'd rather have you on ya knees sucking my dick."

"Waayil!"

Why did I low-key want to though?

"So you ain't in love with me, ma?" He spoke so sexily and low that I felt the seat of my panties become slightly damp. He was so close to my face that what he exhaled, I inhaled.

"No."

As he was about to speak, a voice interrupted us. It was the voice of someone that I'd completely forgotten about and shouldn't have.

"Fuck is going on here, Yikayla?" Roscoe hissed, standing to the side of me and Waayil. His light caramel complexion was damn near cherry red.

"This must be the boyfriend." Waayil laughed as if Roscoe were the funniest joke ever. To make things worse, Waayil was still close as hell to me, clearly not fazed by my man being right here.

"You damn right I'm her fucking boyfriend! And she got my son, nigga!"

"Roscoe." I tried to diffuse the situation by placing one hand out to him, and one against Waayil's very hard and muscular chest.

"Aye, homie, you need to make yaself busy for a few moments while I finish this conversation up with Yikayla." Waayil rose up off the tree so that he was no longer leaning over me. His face was subtly knotted, making him look so good.

Laughing, Roscoe replied, "You got shit twisted."

"Nah, you got shit twisted, mane. I'm not gon' tell yo' ass again to step the fuck back while I finish saying what the fuck I got to say."

"Come on, Kay!" Roscoe barked, glancing from me to Waayil every now and again. They were pretty much the same height, but Waayil appeared to be a bit taller.

"Waayil, please," I begged when I saw his jaw tighten. People were starting to come over and see what all the commotion was, and I just didn't want that attention right now.

Waayil glared into Roscoe's eyes for a moment before chuckling and rubbing his perfectly trimmed facial hair.

"Aight." Waayil turned to me and kissed me on the lips three good times, sending everyone around, including Roscoe into a frenzy.

It happened too quickly for me to stop... okay, no, I didn't mind the kiss, but I pretended to be so surprised that I couldn't stop it.

"You bitch ass nigga!" Roscoe tried to run up to Waayil, but some dude stopped him. It was kind of embarrassing because Roscoe was acting all wildly and Waayil was just calmly standing there, arms folded and laughing at his expense.

"Aye, let his ass go, Phonzy," Waayil called out to the random guy. "Let me beat his ass real quick."

People around laughed at Roscoe's expense as they ate freeze cups and barbecue, clearly finding what Waayil was saying humorous.

"Baby, come on." I walked up to Roscoe who was still flailing wildly.

"And watch ya hands because if you mistakenly hit *my girl*, I'm beating yo' ass in front of all these people," Waayil tossed out seriously. His once lighthearted tone changed to a stern one and I guess everyone around felt it too, because the laughter and giggly facial expressions were no longer.

To my surprise, Roscoe calmed down, and started off to his car angrily, with me behind him.

"Roscoe!" I called out, still feeling weak in the damn knees at those sweet pecks Waayil gave me. I almost twisted my ankle going after Roscoe.

"For real, Kay!" Roscoe turned to face me once we got to his car and hollered.

"What? I didn't do anything!"

"You over here hemmed up on some tree like a hoe with this nigga! You know how that shit makes me look? I pull up and niggas telling me you don' followed his ass off somewhere!"

"We're friends, Roscoe, and we just wanted to talk for a little bit, away from the music!"

"Yeah right," he snickered angrily. "You fuck him?"

"No! Do I look like I've been fucked?"

"No, I mean have you *ever* fucked him! Has that nigga ever stuck his dick in you, or has it been platonic friends from jump!"

"Platonic!" I quickly answered, even though my heart rate sped up at the sound of the question.

"Yikayla, I don't want you talking to him no more."

"Roscoe, I—"

"I'm serious. Regardless of how you feel, he wants you, and I don't feel comfortable with you being around him."

As Roscoe spoke, he stared hard at Waayil who was across the park laughing and talking with his brother, Nusef; my sisters, Jonaya and Rori; his sister, Wednesday, plus some other people.

Roscoe always hated how close Waayil was with my family. And my sisters didn't really like Roscoe, because they shared the same views as my stepdad, that he wasn't worth the salt in his drawers, so he couldn't get close to them like Waayil had.

"Fine," I replied regrettably, watching Waayil right along with Roscoe at this point. Something told me that no matter what I said or did, Waayil wasn't gonna give up. That ridiculously made me smile on the inside.

"Let's go." Roscoe interrupted my thoughts. "We can get Lonan from yo' crib."

"Let me go give my keys to Rori."

8

____

JONAYA GOODE

As I bit into the last rib tip on my plate, I watched Yikayla make her way over to us. I rolled my eyes to myself because I could bet my money that Roscoe's ass wanted to go home. I so badly wanted to tell him to just let Yikayla be because Nusef told me that Waayil had already made it clear that he was getting her. He said that was one of the first things, along with the tattoo shop, that he wanted to take care of when he was released.

"Here, Rori." Yikayla handed her car keys out to our other sister.

"Where you going?" I quizzed, already knowing the answer.

"I'm tired, so I'm just gonna pick Lonan up from the house and then go to Roscoe's."

As Yikayla spoke, she tried her best not to look Waayil's way.

Before she turned away, Waayil gripped her waist in his hands, making both Rori and I raise our eyebrows as we watched, being nosey.

"You wanna leave?" he spoke lowly to her. "You ain't gotta leave just because he told you to."

"Waayil!" Alba barked as she jogged towards us.

"Yeah, I do." Yikayla threw Waayil's hands from her body and walked off towards Roscoe. Even though Alba was hugging Waayil from behind, he kept his eyes on Yikayla until she was in the car.

"I love my nephew, but I can't stand his weak ass daddy," I said, downing the juice in my cup as Wednesday nodded in agreement. I'd had enough alcohol for the night, and it was still flowing through my system.

"She really love that nigga, huh?" Waayil took a seat at the table, and Alba sat right next to him, latching her arm through his like the little puppy dog that she was. I'd never seen someone so possessive over a significant other. Alba didn't even want you standing next to Waayil.

"Who knows with Kay? Once she says something, she never wavers from it." Rori shrugged.

"Why do you care?" Alba chuckled, but you could tell she wasn't joking. She just knew Waayil was a little off and didn't want to upset him by interrogating him seriously.

Waayil ignored her and started to roll a blunt. Alba gave up that quickly and just laid her head on his shoulder.

"Where are the rest of these fucking shorts, Jo?" Nusef tugged the end of my booty shorts.

"In the trash, nigga." I giggled and pinched his chin.

Nusef and Waayil were fine as fuck, but I didn't see them like these other bitches did. I mean, would I fuck Nusef? Yeah, I would, but it would be weird. He was my best friend basically, and like an older brother. Plus, I highly doubted that he would even give me the dick.

"What's good, nigga?" Some sexy ass dude walked up on Nusef and dapped him up, before doing the same to Waayil and Sax. He then spoke to Wednesday.

"Jonaya." I stuck my hand out, and flashed him my smile that I knew would reel his ass in. I was bomb as fuck and everybody here in Memphis knew it.

"What's good, ma?" Old boy smiled. "I'm Marquise."

"Nice to meet you. How do you know my brother?" I pointed to Nusef.

"We went to high school together, but I do his tattoos and shit now," Nusef replied, bobbing his head to the Gucci Mane song blasting.

Marquise was grinning hard at ya girl, and looking oh so fucking fine while doing it. Tossing my hair back, I rose to my feet and started to move a little bit to the music. When I felt Marquise's eyes on my body, a small smile spread across my face. Got 'em!

"Aye, you wanna dance?" Marquise quizzed.

"Nah, man, you don't wanna dance with her crazy ass," Nusef responded, making everyone at our table chortle.

"Fuck you, Sef." I moved my chair out the way and said, "I hope you can keep up. Come on."

I walked off towards where most people were dancing, and grabbed one of the freeze cups from the table where they were sitting. I glanced over my shoulder to make sure Marquise was behind me, which he was, but I spotted Nusef looking over his shoulder at us. His eyes were squinted, but somehow, I could still see his bright hazel eyes even from afar. He licked his lips and then turned back towards his brother.

I stopped where I wanted, and Marquise got right behind me, gripping my waist in his hands. His hands weren't that big, which I found odd since he was sort of tall.

Moving my body to "T-Shirt" by Migos, I bent over a little bit, pushing my ass up against Marquise's crotch. Looking over my shoulder, I used my free hand to pin my hair down so it'd stop swinging and I could really show out.

As I continued to grind to the beat, I felt the rise in Marquise's jeans, which made me grin. That was always my goal, and if a nigga didn't get hard from dancing with me, he was probably gay. I pressed my back into Marquise's chest as I ate the freeze cup, and he hugged my body from the back as we continued to dance.

"You fine as hell." He whispered in my ear what I already knew, so I didn't feel the need to respond to it directly.

"So what that mean?" I quizzed, still moving slowly, surrounded by everybody else dancing in the grass.

"That I wanna do some shit to you."

"Like eat my pussy?" I inquired seriously.

"That and many other things."

"Let's start with that." I wasn't interested in getting any dick at the moment, plus, I wanted to see if his head game was good. If he could make me cum with head, then most likely his dick would be good too, I learned.

I led Marquise from the dance floor, as he chuckled like I was joking with his ass. He was for real about to eat my pussy, so I hoped he was ready.

As we passed the table I was sitting at, Nusef shook his head at me.

"Alright, bitch!" Wednesday shouted as Rori laughed.

"My car is right over there," Marquise pointed.

"You got your own crib?"

"Of course, ma. I'm a grown ass man, fuck I look like living at home with moms?" He palmed his chest and flashed his nice smile.

"Just making sure. I know plenty of *grown ass* niggas who live with Mommy."

We made it to his Lexus and he opened the door for me, which I was surprised by. He didn't seem like the chivalrous type, but it was cool.

As soon as I got in, the smell of weed hit me like a ton of bricks. I listened as Marquise hollered goodbye and some other shit to a few of his homies, and while he did that, I scanned his car for remnants of a bitch. I didn't see anything suspicious, so I relaxed and put my seatbelt on.

"You hot?" Marquise asked as he cranked his car once he got in.

"Nope, I'm good. Play some music though."

"Aye, you're bossy as fuck. I kind of like that shit though. It's different for me. I ain't used to a take charge type of bitch." He cranked up, turned on some music, and drove off.

"Well, get used to it if you want me around. No nigga runs me, and I don't care how many bodies he got or how much drugs he sells."

Laughing as he peeled down the street with some random rap blasting, he said, "So you think I sell drugs?"

"It's possible."

"Wednesday is ya sister?"

"No, the one in the red tube top is. Nusef is just my play brother and Wednesday is my friend."

"The chocolate one in the red top is ya sister?" He frowned, glancing from the road to me briefly. I nodded with a frown. "Why you light skinned?"

"Because black people come in all colors nigga. You need to get out more."

He laughed and nodded at my response.

I hated when people said that shit to me. When I was younger and gave a fuck, I hated going places with my mom and sisters because people always looked at me funny since I was the only light one. Or they would say some rude shit to me like I was adopted. It was a quick way to get your ass beat by my sisters too. Now, it didn't make me feel sad, it just annoyed the hell out of me. I still remember the nights I used to pray to wake up darker, or try to use lotions that gave me more color.

We made it to a cool little house on the Southside, and after Marquise parked, he came around to let me out. Once inside of his place, I eyed the living room, looking for anything that could belong to a female. It wasn't like I was expecting him to be my man, but just because I was single and ready to mingle, didn't mean I liked to deal with taken niggas. The last thing I wanted to have to do was fuck a bitch up over *her* nigga. It'd happened before, and it just wasn't my thing. Plus, I was too fine to be fighting over a man that wasn't mine.

"You drink Hennessy?" Marquise cut the lights on and lifted the bottle up.

"Yep, but I'm twisted enough, so what's up?"

Laughing and nodding his head, he replied, "Damn, I feel like you're using me or some shit, ma. I thought we were gon' get to know one another."

"And maybe we will, but it depends on how hard you make me cum." I moved closer to him, enjoying the smell of his cologne mixed with the weed he must have smoked before we met. "Ah ah ah." I pulled back when he tried to kiss my lips. "These first."

He stared down at me with a smirk like he wanted to say something, but instead, he took my hand in his and led me to his bedroom. He had a nice big bed but no headboard, which I had yet to see before. He sat me down on the edge, and then began to unbutton my shorts as I watched him. I lifted a little bit so he could get them down, and once he had them off, he reached for my panties but I stopped him.

"Just push 'em to the side."

Gripping my thighs, he trailed his tongue up my right one, which made me roll my eyes. Finally, he pulled my panties to the side and began to tease my clit with his thick tongue. His flicks turned to sucks, and soon enough, I was moaning softly at the feeling. Palming the back of his head, I pressed my pussy more into his mouth, and he took it like a champ. Tossing my head back, I lifted my leg a little to give him more access and he went in on my shit, had me grasping the sheets with my free hand.

"Fuck," I whimpered, feeling myself about to cum.

Marquise continued to attack between my legs, and soon after, my orgasm tore through my body. He ate me into another one, and then finally he pulled away.

"So what's good, can a nigga get a movie date and some conversation now?"

"Hell yeah," I panted heavily, prompting us both to laugh.

9
____

WAAYIL

"I cannot wait to get a text from Jonaya about her and Marquise." Wednesday smiled widely, clutching her phone as if the text would come through at any moment.

I noticed Nusef was a little tight, and I wondered why. I knew he couldn't possibly be interested in Jonaya's loud, ratchet ass. They were cool as hell, almost as cool as me and Yikayla, but shit, I guess that didn't mean anything because I for sure wanted my best friend.

"You don't need to be hearing no shit like that." I looked to Wednesday, whose smile faded. I hated to even think about her dealing with niggas, but shit, hanging with Jonaya, I'm sure she was.

"I live through her, Waayil, nothing more."

"Lies." Rori coughed, and Wednesday nudged her.

"Let me find out. I ain't Sef, I'll snatch yo' ass up, Wednesday."

"What you mean you ain't me? I don't let Wednesday do whatever the fuck she wanna do, my nigga. However, I got my own pussy to slide up in so I can't be a babysitter too." Nusef laughed and slapped hands with Sax.

"Y'all niggas' dicks are gon' fall off, bruh."

"That's why I love you, baby, you ain't like most of these niggas." Alba kissed my cheek, then the corner of my mouth.

"You ready to get up out of here?" I looked to her, feeling a little frisky since I had to cut the head she was giving me short.

Alba nodded, so she and I rose from the table. After saying our goodbyes, we were in my car and on the way to her crib.

I felt her looking at me as I drove, but I chose not to address it. All we did lately was argue and fuck, and frankly, I was tired as hell of the former. I hadn't been out that long and already I was stressing like a muthafucka. I ain't know why I thought being out would be calming, because while locked up, I did dumb shit. In my defense, I didn't think it would matter.

"I found some new movies on Netflix, wanna watch them until we fall asleep?" Alba smiled once I pulled into the driveway of her spot. "Waayil."

"Yeah, we can do that. I have to make a quick run though." During the drive, Yikayla entered my mind and suddenly busting Alba down didn't sound too good anymore.

"At 10 p.m.? What kind of run is it?"

"What the fuck I tell you about questioning me all the muthafuckin' time?"

"I can't know where my man is going this late at night?" she hissed, eyes squinted like she was about to hit me or some shit. "It's not like you're some fucking dope boy, so I can't understand why you'd need to go anywhere this late!"

"Maybe I need some fucking time alone! I been locked up for six fucking years, Alba. Maybe I wanna take a got damn drive around my city!" I closed my eyes and took a deep breath. "Aye, get up outta my car before this shit goes left, ma." My tone was calmer now. My mother's words, telling me Alba wasn't good for me if she got me this angry, circled my mind.

"Fine. Fuck you!" she spat just before climbing out and slamming the fuck out of my door. I had to grip my steering wheel to keep my hands from wringing her neck.

I swear I didn't understand how I could be so calm with everything else, except when it came to Alba. Sometimes I legit couldn't stand her ass, not even enough to smash.

Pulling out of her driveway, I picked my phone up from the cup holder. Once I got to a red light, I shot Yikayla a text.

Me: *You up?*

I didn't get a response for a couple streets, but eventually I did.

Kay: *Yes, but I shouldn't be.*

Me: *Let me see you.*

Kay: *You know I'm at Roscoe's.*

Me: *Fuck that nigga. He asleep?*

Kay: *Yes, Waayil.*

Me: *Let me see you then. If he wakes up, I'll just beat his ass.*

Kay: *No you won't… lol.*

I chuckled at her response, but felt a sense of anxiousness as I saw her text with the address come through. I was gonna keep that shit handy in case I needed to drop by there. I wasn't fucking around when I said Yikayla was gon' be mine, and I had a feeling I may be using this address more than once.

Because I was dipping through the streets like the police didn't exist, I made it to Roscoe's spot in less than ten minutes. Before I even found a park in the complex, I texted Yikayla to let her know I had arrived. When I saw her coming down the steps of the apartment across the small parking lot, I flicked my lights to let her know where I was.

"I hate that it stays hot damn near twenty-four hours." She shook her head as she slipped into the car. She had on some little dress that looked like sleepwear. I bit my lip at the sight of her thighs and her nipples poking through the thin fabric. "Don't talk about my shoes," she giggled.

Wasn't even looking at them…

"Aight, I'll leave you alone." I played along. Usually, I spoke my mind, but I didn't want her trying to run back up to Roscoe just yet. It seemed like as soon as I mentioned her and I sexing, she wanted to flee.

"So what's up? Why did you want to see me? You caused me enough problems with Roscoe."

"What he do to you?" My brows dipped. I was more than ready to bust off in his spot and fuck his ass up.

"Calm down, he just fussed at me."

"He know about us?"

"Us as in...?"

"That we're more than just friends like you let everybody think."

"Like *I* let everybody think? What about you?" She pointed at me with her weird colored nail.

"I *been* telling everybody how I feel about you since I got out. I ain't playing, Yikayla."

"Even Alba?"

"Answer my question."

"No, he doesn't know, just like Alba doesn't know anything." She fidgeted with the end of her dress thing before glancing at me briefly. "What happened, Waayil?"

"I'm sure you put two and two together by now."

I told my brother and Wednesday to keep what I did on the low and from everybody. Most people just used common sense, realizing I was in jail for murder and Uncle Harry was no longer. Typical Yikayla wanted details though.

"Yeah, I did, but I wanna know more. You refused to tell me in the letters we wrote, and putting two and two together isn't enough for me now that you're out."

"He was touching Wednesday and when I confronted him about it, he tried to get fly by the mouth and I reacted."

"Touching her like... molesting? Or just touching?"

"He raped her."

"Dang, poor thing. That's not like you to do something so horrific without thinking."

"I did think." I looked her in the eyes and she nodded slowly before looking away briefly. "The moment his name left her lips, I decided right then I was gonna kill him. Him talking shit to me just made it easier." I chuckled subtly.

"If you could go back—"

"I would do it again. I would just use the lawyer my parents offered me instead of the public defender. That nigga just wanted to get shit over with, so he didn't really try to get me off."

"Well, I'm happy Mr. and Mrs. Samuels didn't give up." She looked at me and then asked, "You went six years without sex?"

"You trying to ask if I was fucking on niggas?" I cheesed and she giggled before shrugging.

"No, I couldn't imagine you doing something like that. I'm just curious how you got by without any."

"I'll just say I made some connections, and that the right amount of money can get you anything you need, even in jail."

The prison I was in didn't allow conjugal visits, so even if you had a wife, y'all wasn't gon' be fucking. But I knew somebody with a heavy cash flow, who agreed to help me out, so I had a little shorty that would come through and let me fuck a few times a week. I was regretting that shit though now that I was free.

"I bet. Did you have to fight off big buff guys who wanted to sleep with you?" She burst into laughter when she saw my facial expression.

"There were definitely muthafuckas who were on that bullshit, but after my first couple of fights, niggas showed me respect so I was good. Weird ass."

She laughed.

"Sorry, I just had to know."

"Come here." I picked Yikayla's soft hand up and kissed the back of it.

"Come where?"

"Over here." I moved my seat back some more, even though it was already pretty far away from the steering wheel.

"Waayil."

I just looked at her, so eventually she climbed over into my lap to straddle me. I could for real hear her ass breathing, and after a few seconds, we were sucking one another's lips. My hands moved up and down her petite frame, before going up under the dress she had on, to squeeze on that ass she'd grown while I was away.

"I love you, Waayil."

"I know," I whispered back in between kisses, sliding my hand down into her panties.

With my free hand, I pushed down the top of her dress some to reveal her apple sized breasts, and then took her nipple into my mouth. I began toying with her clit until she juiced up enough, then I slid my fingers inside of her. I wanted to slide up in her with my dick badly as fuck, but I didn't want our first time since I'd been out to take place in a fucking car.

Yikayla began grinding her hips against my hand as I plunged my fingers in and out of her, enjoying the feeling of her juices seeping between my two fingers. I nibbled, sucked, and flicked my tongue over her nipples as her small hands gripped my shoulders tightly. I vacuumed her bottom lip into my mouth once I felt her pussy contracting around my fingers, and then I glided my lips down to her spot on her neck as I sped up my motions.

"Waayil," she whimpered, grabbing at my low-cut fade as if she could actually grip something.

"You're so fucking wet, Kay, damn," I mumbled, before sucking her nipple hard into my mouth.

Her body trembled slightly, just as a flood damn near came from her pussy. I continued to finger her slowly, making sure I got it all, then I removed my fingers from her panties to taste her. She watched me, eyes filled with lust, just before she gripped the sides of my face and kissed me roughly. My hands caressed and groped her smooth thighs, gripping her perfect ass in my hands before giving it a nice smack. I was so damn hard I could shatter a TV screen with one tap.

"Baby, I want you. I'm gon' have you," I told her as I sucked on her neck. She was so in the moment she didn't realize I was leaving a hickey on her.

"You can have me... if you let her go, Waayil. Then I will do the same. It has to be just you and me, nobody else."

"I got you."

After looking into my eyes for a bit, a soft smile gradually appeared on her face before she said, "Good. Now I have to go shower, so goodnight."

She fixed her clothes, excitedly pecked me, then pushed my door open, and raced back up to Roscoe's apartment. I watched her the whole time, low-key overwhelmed as fuck with emotions, but it was a good thing.

For a moment, I thought it would take me much longer to have Yikayla. Now as soon as I fixed a couple things, other shit would hopefully fall in line.

~

The Next Morning...

When I woke up, Alba was already out of the bed, and I was thankful as fuck. I didn't feel like hearing her mouth about me coming home so late. Shit, a nigga was only gone about an hour or two, and her ass was knocked out when I got here. I almost had a mind to go to my brother's crib to sleep, but since I needed to chop it up with her, I decided to kill two birds with one stone.

I brushed my teeth and then took a shower, feeling like a bitch over how my night went with Yikayla. A nigga was feeling way too giddy about the shit. When I stepped out and wrapped a towel around me, all the good shit faded at the sight of Alba fuming like she was about to run up.

Nonchalantly moving past her so I could get some boxers, I stayed silent because I was gonna let her speak her mind first.

"What time did you get here?" she finally asked as I pulled a wife beater over my head.

"Don't remember."

"I love you, Waayil, and I don't understand why you treat me this way! Is it because of Yikayla? Someone told me you kissed her at the barbecue! While I was right there making your plate, Waayil? Really?"

As I buckled my jeans, I replied, "We ain't really been clicking like we used to, Alba. You want something from me that I'm not ready to give you, ma."

"What? A ring? Don't you think I deserve one, Waayil!"

"Yeah, but not from me."

"Asshole! You are such a fucking asshole! I fucking hate you, I swear I do!" She hollered so loudly I swear I saw spit fly from her mouth. But as angry and as loud as she got, it didn't faze me because I was too ecstatic right now. Any other time I would have cut that bullshit short.

"So then maybe we should let this shit go."

She had her head lowered as she massaged her temples, but when I spoke, she paused and slowly picked it up to make eye contact with me.

"Excuse me?"

"I said we should let this shit go. You heard what the fuck I said, Alba." I yanked down my white t-shirt, then slipped on my shoes.

"No! No! No! No!" She screamed repeatedly, as she flailed her fists, trying to fight me.

"You gon' make me put hands on you!" I growled, gripping her wrists and pinning her to the wall. "The fuck I tell you about trying to fight me, huh? That ain't some shit you want, ma," I seethed, irritated that she'd hit me in the throat and now my shit felt like I'd swallowed a Popeyes biscuit with no butter or honey sauce. I was ready to knock the dog shit out of this bitch, on God.

Her chest rose and fell as she stared up into my eyes with fury in hers.

"What about our baby?"

It was like her wrists had the plague because of how quickly I released them bitches and backed away from her.

"What?"

"Our baby, Waayil. I'm pregnant."

"Nah." I shook my head, chuckling. "Get the fuck back before I deck the shit out you!" I barked when she tried to move closer to me and she jumped at the sound of my voice.

"I just found out and I was waiting for the right time to—"

"Shut yo' ass up. Don't you speak on this shit to anybody else until I get at you."

"Waayil!" she called after me once I snatched my hoodie up and left the bedroom. "Waayil!"

As I hopped into my whip, I saw her standing in the doorway, crying and shit like I was supposed to give a fuck. I knew it was wrong for me to hate her for being pregnant, but I did. If she was telling the fucking truth, this would derail my whole fucking plan. Not only would I be tied to her ass for life, but I knew for sure Yikayla wouldn't fuck with me.

My mind drifted right to the day I found out I was getting released soon. After I left court, one of the officers I became cool with gave me ten minutes with Alba in her car. I was already getting pussy elsewhere and wasn't hurting for any, but I knew if I turned her ass down she'd be bugging, so I hit.

I sped all the way to the tattoo shop, and got out before my car was even all the way in the park.

"Hey, Waayil—"

I kept it pushing towards the back, ignoring Chiara because I just needed a moment.

"Fuck!" I hollered when I got into my tattoo room, before punching a hole in the wall accidentally.

"Hey, you okay?" Chiara walked in and closed the door.

"Chiara, I just need a moment, baby." I plopped down into the chair. When I looked her way, I saw she was coming towards me.

"You look tense." She half smiled but let it drop soon after as she squatted down to look up into my face. "Anything I can do?"

I declined to respond because I wasn't in the fucking mood and there wasn't shit she could do to help me and she knew that shit.

Her small hands moved up my lap, and when she got to my belt, she began to undo it. I watched her, letting her do the same to my jeans. She kept her eyes on mine as she reached into my boxers to remove my dick, which was already semi erect from her touch.

Before I could say anything, she had my head hitting the back of her throat like a pro. Her mouth was filled with so much saliva that it made me frown in a good way. Gripping a handful of her soft hair, I began guiding her up and down, pounding her throat like it was a pussy and she took it with no problem.

"Damn," I mumbled as I listened to her slurp and hum while she sucked me up like a Popsicle on a hot summer's day.

Seconds later, it seemed, I busted down her throat.

When she got up to lift her dress, I put my hand up to stop her and said, "Nah, I'm good, but thank you."

Obviously embarrassed, she wiped her mouth and replied, "Oh well, I—"

"Go get me something to clean up with. Please."

She nodded and left my area, but promptly returned with something like I'd asked. She watched me clean myself, and after I fixed my pants and washed my hands, I had to tell her ass I needed some privacy so she'd leave.

Although I felt a little better, Alba's confession still fucked with me and I wondered if maybe God just didn't want Yikayla and I to be together...

10

NUSEF CHRISTIAN

I hugged Rebecca's body from behind and placed a kiss on her neck. Her plump ass sat right against my dick, and even though we'd just gotten that shit in, in the shower, I was ready to go again. Rebecca had that good good, and not only was it the shit, it was mine.

Hell muthafuckin' nah, we weren't in no damn relationship, and I made sure she knew that. She was the only bitch that I fucked with heavily though, and for a long period of time. Rebecca was what most niggas wanted out of a female. She could cook, she was loyal, sexy as a muthafucka, and she didn't nag me about dumb shit. However, for some reason, I just couldn't take that plunge with her. Not to mention, I liked to dabble with other females every now and again.

"Down, boy." Rebecca giggled and squirmed a little as I continued to caress her body and kiss on the nape of her neck.

"What you making?" I finally let her go.

"Fried chicken and hush puppies." She looked over her shoulder at me and smiled, before turning back to the food. See, one of my favorite things to eat were hush puppies, and here her ass was cooking 'em up for me after giving me some pussy. I had no complaints.

My eyes scanned her body that she had somewhat covered in little ass shorts and some kind of lacy ass top. I licked my lips at the sight of her ass damn near coming out the bottom of the shorts. Her sexy caramel complexion looked smooth as usual, and her long brown hair hung down her back, even though it was in one of them ponytail shits.

We made small talk while she finished up the food, and after she fixed our plates and cups of drink, she joined me at the table. We prayed over the food, and as soon as 'Amen' crossed my lips, I was shoving them hot ass hush puppies into my mouth.

"You had a lot of clients today." Rebecca broke the silence, and slowed me up from eating like a nigga in jail.

"Yep."

"A lot of girls, especially. I almost wanted to come back there and watch their asses for a little bit." She chuckled and sighed. "You know I love you, Sef."

"I love you too."

I wasn't lying; I did love Rebecca. But was it enough for me to make her my girl? Not one bit. As much as I liked to play dumb to what was holding me back, deep down I knew.

"Yeah, you tell me you love me, but do you really love me?" She cocked her head, nibbling on her full bottom lip as she waited.

"What's up? Why you asking me all this shit right now, ma?" I shoved another hush puppy in my mouth.

Squinting her eyes, with a small smile, she asked, "How long have we been messing around, Nusef?"

"For a minute." I shrugged.

I hated how women beat around the fucking bush all the mutha-fuckin' time. Just say what the fuck it is you're trying to say instead of making shit a damn guessing game. Niggas don't have a long enough attention span for that bullshit.

"Exactly... for a minute. We've been doing this for a while, you love me and I love you, so what's the next step?"

"Is this a quiz?"

"Nusef!"

"What? It sounds like a damn quiz, and right now I'm wondering when the fuck I agreed to take this shit."

"No, it's not a quiz, baby, it's a conversation. I just hate not knowing what we are to one another because it confuses me."

"Rebecca, I can't do the relationship shit right now. I told you that. I got my mind on other shit, and adding you on seriously ain't the move right this second."

"Okay." She nodded, and picked up one of her hush puppies.

Fuck...

I grabbed the chair she was in and pulled it towards me so that her soft legs were in between mine.

"Aye, but when I am ready, you already know who I'm gon' choose." I kissed her neck and when I pulled away, she was smiling. Thank God.

Rebecca was chill after that, and once we finished our food, we retired to her bedroom. As she lay next to me, knocked the fuck out, my mind was on one hundred. I didn't know if I was bored or just anxious, but I couldn't fall asleep for shit.

Tossing the covers off, I gently moved from up under Rebecca and snatched my phone off the dresser. I saw the clock read 10 p.m., so I dialed Jonaya's room phone. I wanted to see if her ass was home or running them fucking streets like a hoe, and the best way to do that was to see if she answered her room phone.

"For real?" I hissed lowly when her voicemail came through.

Sitting in the dark contemplating, I finally rose to my feet, slipped on some sweats, a t-shirt, and some socks and slides, before leaving Rebecca's crib.

I sped down her street once I was in my car, not even knowing where the fuck I was going. I didn't know where the fuck Jonaya was at this point, so I was literally just wasting my damn gas. And I didn't want to text her ass asking where she was because I felt like that shit would be suspicious.

After stopping at the liquor store for a few snacks, I drove to her crib in Midtown and parked along the street. Getting out, I hit the alarm on my whip and rang the doorbell. Jonaya's mama was cool, more like a fifth Goode sister than anything, so I wasn't worried about her getting in my ass about showing up so late.

"Yes?" Dree answered the door with her uppity ass.

"Man, unlock this shit," I tapped the screen door.

"For what, nigga? It's late as hell."

BAM!

"Open the fucking door, mane!" I slammed an open palm on it, making her jump before she quickly unlocked it.

"You better be glad I somewhat like your ass." She sucked her teeth before going into the kitchen.

I paid her ass no mind as I hit the stairs, headed for Jonaya's room. I wanted to be sitting there when her hoe ass walked in all late. Just thinking about what she was possibly out doing had me heated and I didn't want to admit why.

Jonaya and I had been cool for a long ass time, almost since Waayil and Yikayla became close. I always saw her crazy ass as a little sister, but the older we got and the more time we spent together, shit changed. We bonded over our love for the opposite sex, swapping freaky ass stories, and going to them ghetto ass parties together to pull. But lately, I found myself annoyed and disgusted by the shit she did or would tell me she did. I wanted to fucking choke her ass whenever she would call me up to tell me about the best head or dick she'd ever gotten. Like right now, I was gripping the fuck out of my phone just thinking about the shit.

When I entered her bedroom, I heard the shower running, and relief suddenly came over me. As soon as I took a seat on her bed, the water cut off.

"Oh shit!" Jonaya jumped once she yanked the bathroom door

open, ass naked and dripping water. Laughing, she said, "You scared me, Sef."

"Put some fucking clothes on!"

"I am, nigga. I forgot my dry off towel in here." She sauntered out, butt naked like I wasn't sitting here. I used to not mind her being naked in front of me, but now my dick couldn't take it. "What you doing here?" she inquired as she began to pat her body with the towel, just before covering it in lotion.

It took everything in me not to lick my lips at the sight. She wasn't that little girl trying to be grown anymore; she was a woman. Hips, thighs, ass, titties—she had it all—and it was perfectly placed right where it was supposed to be. My eyes drifted down her cinnamon complexion, admiring her shiny belly ring and her neatly waxed pussy just before she covered it with some shorts.

"Where ya panties?"

"I don't wear them to bed. But what you here for? And without calling?" She tied her hair up.

"Oh, now I gotta call? I ain't never had to call before."

Calm yo' ass, nigga, I had to tell myself when I felt like I was getting mad.

"Umm, no, but you usually don't come over this late, so I thought you would have let me know." She pulled on some little top that only covered her titties, and then came and sat on her bed by me.

"Where you was at?"

"Here."

"I called you."

"Probably while I was in the shower, Sef. Something wrong?" She touched my leg and my dick was hard again that quickly.

Her phone buzzed and I saw it was the homie, Marquise. That was my nigga, but right now, I couldn't stand his ass.

"So that's yo' new shit?" I chuckled like I didn't care, but it was really to hide my displeasure.

Shrugging, she replied, "Maybe. I know he can eat pussy like no other."

Don't choke her, Sef.

"Word? Y'all already fucking? That quick?"

"No, he just ate me out a couple of times. He gave me head the night of the barbecue and then this evening right out there in the driveway!" She laughed and I gave a fake one.

"You need to slow down with all that shit."

"Slow down with what? I like sex, and it likes me too."

"Yeah, but you need to maybe only fuck with one nigga for the long haul. That shit you doing ain't cute, Jo."

"When did you start caring so much about how many niggas I fuck? And do you only smash Rebecca? Or are there other hoes too?" I sucked my teeth and she said, "Exactly. Plus, you know you love my stories! And this will be even juicier because he's someone you know!" She grinned, and I just gave a smile back.

I needed to get my feelings in fucking order, ASAP.

11

———————

YIKAYLA

A Couple Days Later...

I checked my phone for the hundredth time today to see if Waayil had called or texted me back. Ever since that night we had in the car together, we hadn't spoken. Nigga had me wearing turtlenecks for the past two days because of that damn hickey, and had the nerve to be ignoring me.

I expected him to be ready the next day with the way he was acting, but I guess something went wrong. My heart started to beat out of my damn chest, thinking of all the possibilities. Maybe he'd changed his mind and realized he really did love Alba. If that was the case, honestly, it would break my heart.

"Yikayla, you have a table." My co-worker, Jodi, peeked into the back room and smiled. "You okay? You seem down today?"

"Yeah, I'm fine, just having cramps," I lied.

"The worst. Well, this table is small, only two people, so you should be good."

"Great, thank you."

I glanced down at my phone again, contemplating whether or not

I should send Waayil another text. I decided against it because I didn't want to seem too eager. He was the one who broke up what we were building, so he should be the one trying to put it back together. What the hell do I look like pressuring him and putting in the most effort? Plus, I still hadn't broken things off with Roscoe, and I think it was because I was not only afraid to, but I felt bad.

I washed my hands and then came from the back of my mom's Waffle House to see who I had in my section. When I spotted Alba and some other bitch, my hands started to sweat. Did she know what Waayil and I had planned? If so, I prayed she didn't come here to cause a scene because I was not trying to be fighting in my mom's business. However, if Alba got out of line with me then that would definitely be the case.

"Welcome to Natasha's Waffle House, ladies. Have you ever dined with us before?" I smiled hard as hell even though I wanted to turn my lip up.

"Yikayla, look at you in your little uniform." Alba cheesed.

I should have known this bitch was coming in here to antagonize me. In all the years this shit had been built, Alba never ate here unless Waayil did. And right now, he was nowhere to be found. On the bright side, it made me happy to know he wasn't somewhere laid up with this hoe.

"What can I get for you ladies?"

"What y'all got to drink?" her friend asked, patting her weave that was about five inches off her head. I didn't understand why someone would pay for their hair to look like that. I'd slap the shit out of a hairstylist if she tried to send me on my way looking like this bitch right here.

"We have orange, apple, pineapple, and passion fruit juice. We also have all Coca Cola products," I replied, trying to keep my attention on her eyes and not her sky-rise weave.

"We'll both have orange mixed with pineapple juice, and don't be giving us a lot of ice, Yikayla. I know y'all like to cheat people," Alba spat.

"Of course. And do you need more time to decide on food?"

"Umm, we did just get here." Her friend frowned.

"Of course." I smiled, giving myself a talk so I wouldn't react.

I went to make their drinks, and once I dropped them off, I couldn't help myself, so I dialed Waayil. He didn't answer and if I'm not mistaken, he sent me to voicemail.

"Asshole," I mumbled, coming from the back after washing my hands again.

"Hey, bitch, I need a stack."

"Who the fuck—" I calmed down when I saw Dree smiling and chuckling, while sitting down at the bar area. "Lisha can get your order, Dree, I'm busy."

"Whatever, I just need my waffles." She set her purse on the counter. "And who the fuck got your little panties in a bunch?"

"None of your business." I walked past her, back to Alba's table to see if they were ready. I wanted to get this shit over with. They were my last table of the day. "Ready?"

"Actually, nothing on here looks too appetizing and our drinks were rather warm, Yikayla. When I said not a lot of ice, I didn't mean no ice."

"There was ice in there, Alba."

"I sense a little attitude, Yikayla Goode." Alba giggled along with her friend. "You and Waayil are so different that I don't even see how you two were ever best friends. He's so sweet to me, and you're so mean." She playfully pouted before she and her friend laughed again.

"Opposites *attract*."

"Usually, but not in you guys' case. I know you have a little crush on him, sweetie, but give it up. Waayil has never and will never want you. I mean, come on, you've been trying since you were a minor, and he still never touched you. Plus, you have a kid."

"Is that what he told you?" I chuckled, making her smile slowly drop.

"Excuse me?" She shot me a look like she wanted to swing, and I was prepared if she did so.

"Is that what he told you? That he never touched me?"

"What the fuck are you implying?" She stood up slowly so that we were face to face.

"I think she's trying to say she fucked your nigga, girl," her homegirl chimed in, downing that so called too warm drink.

"I'm simply asking a question. You think you know Waayil, but you don't. Only reason he even got with you is because you begged and begged for some dick for months and he finally gave in. Then he needed companionship when he got locked up. So see, the only reason you have Waayil is because you're thirsty as fuck, and he's been using you."

I knew Waayil wouldn't want me spilling the beans, but this bitch had me mad as hell.

"You don't know what the hell you're talking about, bitch! If he was just using me, he wouldn't have made love to me all last night and this morning!"

"Watch your tone with my sister, hoe," Dree chimed in with her back still to us at the bar.

"Typical hoe, thinking a nigga sliding up in her means he loves her," I spoke candidly, but hearing that she'd slept with him made my stomach turn.

"Watch your back, Yikayla. Come on, Ashley!" Alba snatched her purse up and switched out with her homegirl on her heels.

Once they were gone, I wiped that smug ass expression off of my face and collected their glasses. I clocked out, and ignored whatever the hell Dree was saying as I walked past her.

As soon as I was in my car, I sped to Monarch Tattoo, hoping Waayil was there. If he was, he was about to get a piece of my fucking mind.

"Good afternoon, and welcome to Monarch. My name is Chiara, are you looking to get a tattoo? If so, I can schedule you for tomorrow since we're booked solid today. Unless you have an appointment." Some pretty girl with brownish red hair and light skin greeted me.

"No, I'm looking for Waayil."

Her expression changed and she cocked her head a little bit, almost like she had a problem with what I'd said. So in response, I cocked my head as well and raised my brow.

"Waayil? May I ask why?"

"No. Where is he?"

"He's busy right now, but I'm the receptionist and... you can't go back there!" She shouted the last part once I darted towards the back. "I said you can't—"

"Touch me, and it'll be the last time you're able to use your motor skills," I gritted when that bitch reached for my arm. She quickly pulled it back, and then slipped past me to knock on a door with Waayil's name on it.

"Waayil, you have—"

"Thank you. I can introduce myself." I slipped into the room and stared at this nigga with my arms folded and face knotted up.

He had on a black hoodie, which was pulled up over his head. He glanced up at me from his chair, and then went right back to working on the girl laid back in the chair with her thigh out. For a moment, I didn't know what to say because I was caught off guard by his reaction or lack thereof.

"Let me know if you need anything, Waayil." Chiara left the room.

"What's up?" Waayil finally asked, effortlessly using his machine to draw on the young girl.

"What's up? Shouldn't I be asking you that?"

"You seem mad, ma." He looked to me briefly before setting down his needle. "You can take your break, baby," he said to the girl who blushed.

"Okay." She got up and fixed her skirt, before leaving the room.

"Why you mad, Kay?" He started straightening up his things, giving me a whiff of his cologne every time he moved.

"Are you still fucking Alba?"

"Depends what you mean by still. If you mean within the last week or so, yeah, but not since we fucked around in the car."

I was relieved.

"So it's over then?"

"Kind of." He took his gloves off and trashed them. "You left Roscoe yet or are you waiting for me to fuck my shit up before you make a move?"

"Fuck your shit up? If letting Alba go is fucking your shit up then don't do it. Be with her and let me stay with Roscoe."

"Aight."

"Aight?"

He nodded as he dried his hands and tried to walk past me, but I grabbed his arm.

"Yikayla, get up out of here. This shit ain't gon' work, and it's about time we both stop trying to force shit."

"Waayil—"

"Yikayla..." He moved my hand from his bicep. "I got work to do."

I stared up into his beautiful eyes for a moment, and then bumped the shit out of him as I stormed towards the front, hitting ignore when I saw Roscoe calling. When I did get to the lobby area, I saw Chiara smirking, which pissed me off even more.

"What the fuck!" she hollered when I cleared the desk she sat behind, knocking every damn thing on the floor.

Fuck Waayil, fuck Alba, fuck Chiara, and fuck this stupid ass shop.

12

DREE GOODE

I danced in my mirror to my favorite song since forever, "It's All About Me" by Mya, feeling good as hell about today. The weather was nice, a little hot, but nice nonetheless, and today I'd be getting that much closer to my dream of becoming a lawyer.

Today I had to register for classes, and I was beyond excited. I just wished we could fast forward time and get this shit going already. People loved to tell me how hard it was gonna be and all this shit, but what they needed to realize was that I was Dree Goode and they weren't. Nothing was hard for me, especially not when it came to school. I always got good grades, the lowest being a B+, and that was only because I used to ditch all the time. By saying that, I knew law school was gonna be a breeze, and soon enough, I was gonna be in someone's courtroom, making them cry on the stand.

"Hey, can I ride with you? I need to use the computer in the lab. I don't wanna use mine." My little sister, Rori, came and stood in the doorway.

"Yes, but who is picking you up?" I placed my hand on my hip, liking the way my soft hair brushed against my back.

"Gavin. He's working though so he can't take me."

"Okay."

"Once you start classes, you have to tell me all about it, Dree." Rori grinned widely which made me do the same.

"Now you know I love talking about myself, so I have no problem filling you in on my life in law school."

We laughed in unison as we left my bedroom and descended the stairs. My mother was on the couch with her feet in her boyfriend's lap, getting them massaged.

I never understood how my mother could cheat on a successful man like Jasper, with some lowlife bum like Buddy. I usually never even learned her little side niggas' names, but this one had been here a while, since my stepdad was in New York. I'd have my popcorn ready once he got back in a couple weeks though, because I had a feeling Buddy wouldn't be so easy to throw away like my mom's others.

"You guys look cute. Where are you going?" my mother asked, popping an almond into her mouth. Say what you want, but my mother was a beautiful woman. I mean how else was she able to convince a man like Jasper to marry her and take care of her four kids?

"I'm going to register for my classes, but I'm gonna drop Rori off at the computer lab to do whatever it is that she does."

"Ohhh, you're in law school, right?" Buddy smiled, golds damn near blinding me. I was sure he was my age, a year older at the most.

"Yes. Bye!" I cut him off when I saw him open his mouth to speak again.

I wished my mom would tell him he was temporary so he'd stop trying to bond with us. I was too old for that shit anyways at twenty-five. The only reason I still lived here was because my undergrad counselor and my stepfather convinced me that it wouldn't be wise to work while in law school. But boy was it getting harder every day not to go find something just to get me enough bread for my own spot.

"You know I saw him in Jasper's robe, right?" Rori giggled once we were in my car.

I loved having a car, and it was something my stepdad promised us all upon seeing a college degree in hand, which was why only Yikayla and I had one. Rori would soon be there and as for Jonaya, I was sure she'd have to purchase her own shit.

"I hope he didn't leave his favorite scent of malt liquor in it," I replied, before we both burst into laughter.

Rori and I listened to music and chatted the whole way, and after I dropped her off in the area she needed to be in, I drove closer to the counseling office. I checked in, but because I was forty-five minutes early, I decided to step outside and just scan the area with my eyes. Plus, it was cold as a fucking meat locker in there.

"Dree?" I heard a familiar voice say as soon as I stepped out more into the sun.

I turned to look and saw the one person I never thought I would see again. He looked the same, but much more grown up and... somewhat sophisticated. He moved towards me with a smile, and I immediately recognized the attraction I still had to him. His caramel complexion, neatly trimmed beard, semi muscular and tall frame, and bedroom brown eyes had only intensified over the years. His hair was cut low, and looked freshly shaped too.

"Canyon, hey." I frowned in confusion. I knew his ass wasn't attending law school; he just wasn't that type of dude.

"Nah, I ain't in law school, or trying to be. I work in the counseling office for the undergrad, but they needed some help over here with the financial aid shit."

"*You* work in the counseling office? In a college? So you're an academic advisor?"

"Yeah, is that so damn surprising?" He laughed, making me lick my lips on the sly. Homie was looking good, smelling good, and sounding good too. "I ain't rich or nothing, but I'm comfortable. How are you?"

My words got stuck for a moment as memories of Canyon and I circled my mind. I met him in eighth grade, and ever since then, we'd been close. Him, his sister, Jupiter, and I were like the three amigos.

When I started feeling like Canyon had a crush on me, I got scared and basically did everything in my power to let him know I didn't like him. It was a lie, but being with him just frightened the shit out of me at that time, and I couldn't do it. Because of my actions, he did something that I could never forgive him for, and that was the end of us.

He never really knew why I stopped talking to him, because if I told him why, he would have known I had feelings for him. So instead, I just shunned him until he gave up and moved on with his life. That was five years ago, and it seemed, even now, I had some feelings for him.

"Dree?"

"Oh yes, I'm fine. I'm perfect, actually. I'm finally about to start law school. I took a break to travel for a year to just relax," I lied. Really, I didn't get into the law school I'd wanted and became discouraged, which lasted for a minute. I was just happy I'd gotten back on track, and in enough time to still pursue this.

"That's what's up, ma. So umm, maybe we should get something to eat one of these days." He stroked his beard and licked his plump lips, making it seem so much hotter out here than it was.

"I'll think about it."

"Lock yo' number in." He handed me his iPhone, and it was like my fingers started typing before I could respond verbally. "Aight, I'll check you later." He hugged me and I wanted to just cry tears of joy and gratefulness into his hard ass chest, but I refrained.

I watched him for a moment as he walked off with the most swag in the world, before taking my ass back into the counseling office to wait. Being out here with Canyon's fine ass was gonna give me a fucking heat stroke.

It didn't take long for me to get my classes because I was a first-year student and had a clean palette. I think my counselor attempted to scare my ass with the description of the courses, but she would soon learn that didn't shit scare me but God.

As I left the office, I checked my iPhone and saw that Canyon had texted me. Even though it was just to give me his number, I found myself smiling from ear to ear.

"Aye, watch where you're going, beautiful." A soft but masculine voice, accompanied by a firm grip to my shoulders, stopped me.

Looking up, I saw a nice, clean-cut chocolate boy, with luminous curly hair. His teeth were white as snow, and his features seemed to be perfectly picked out from a handbook. No facial hair graced his face, but he surprisingly didn't look like a newborn baby.

"Sorry."

"No worries," he responded and nodded, before slipping around me.

If I kept running into niggas that looked like him and Canyon, I wasn't too sure I'd be able to concentrate. But on the bright side, I loved this school already.

13

RORI GOODE

I stood outside for an hour after the lab closed, waiting on Gavin's ass. I swear this was like the tenth time he'd done this shit, and he always had some bullshit as reason as to why he was late.

"Ugh!" I grunted when his voicemail picked up yet again. I was stranded because Dree had left already, but not before me stupidly rejecting a ride home from her. I knew Gavin's M.O., but I stupidly believed he'd be here to pick me up yet again.

Feeling like I was about to blow a fucking fuse, I dialed his homeboy, Eko, to see if he would at least answer. He and Gavin were thick as thieves and usually wherever you saw Gavin, you saw Eko.

"Hello?" Eko's deep voice flowed through the phone. I could tell that he was driving because I could hear the wind and the atmosphere of the car.

"Hey, Eko, are you with Gavin right now? He was supposed to pick me up a minute ago."

"Nah, I'm on my way to the trap. He said he was gonna meet me there after scooping you from the lab but... shit, that was some hours ago."

Suddenly my anger subsided, and worry overcame me. What if

something had happened to Gavin? He was a dope boy, and them niggas got shot and killed every day. Regular men got killed every day in Memphis. My heart started to beat quickly as hell as I thought about all the shit I'd called Gavin, and he could possibly be dead somewhere.

"You want me to come get you?"

"I mean, if you don't mind," my voice trembled.

"Rori, that nigga is alright, trust me," Eko assured me. "Just probably got caught up in some shit, but he'll come through."

"Yeah."

"On my way to you."

About ten minutes later, Eko was pulling up in his silver Honda Accord with his music blasting. I rounded the front of the car and slid inside, falling back against the headrest and enjoying the air he had blowing.

"You aight?" He chuckled, turning his music down and whipping out of the school parking lot.

"No, I'm hot as hell and I'm worried."

Eko didn't say anything in response as he looked down at his phone. He read it, locked his phone, and then placed it in a cup holder.

"That was him. I told you he's good. He's handling some shit and then he'll meet us at the crib. You make that map for us?" Eko glanced at me as he came to a red light.

"Yeah. That's what I came here for."

"Thanks, ma."

Eko stroked his beard, before pulling off at the green light. He was an extremely good-looking guy with caramel brown skin, a built ass body covered in tattoos, and he was nice and tall too.

I met him around the same time I'd met Gavin, but I'd never really paid attention to his looks. And over time, as I became so enthralled in my relationship with Gavin, Eko just seemed to fade into the back.

But now that my relationship was starting to lose its spark, Eko was starting to look better and better every time I saw him. He was my man's best friend though, and I wouldn't dare touch him. Plus, Eko was loyal and loved Gavin like a brother, so he wouldn't even think of me that way.

As we headed towards the trap, I let my hair down and closed my eyes to enjoy the cool air seeping through the air conditioning vents. I placed my barefoot flat on the seat, so I had one leg up and one placed flat as I relaxed. I felt the car slow down, and when I opened my eyes, Eko was pulling into a Wendy's drive-thru.

"You want something?" He looked to me. As I was about to respond, I noticed his eyes drift all over my body. I had on a pink crop top, halter that showed my stomach, and some light blue jean shorts. I'd taken my hair down from its bun earlier, and that seemed to pull him in as well. "You got some nice ass skin, Rori." My coffee colored complexion was glowing under the hot ass sun.

"Thanks." I chuckled, trying to make light of the compliment. "I just want some nuggets; the six piece."

He nodded and then ordered the food. He got me a drink even though I didn't ask for one, and then we got back en route to the trap house. Every now and again, I could feel him glance at me, but I pretended that I was in deep thought and didn't notice. Once we got to the trap, we went inside and sat down on the couch after washing our hands in the kitchen.

"Whatever happened to Jenni, Eko?" I dipped my nugget into the barbecue sauce and bit down on it.

"She good, we good, but it's nothing like that." He sat back against the couch and sipped his drink. It was silent as we looked at one another, so I just turned away to dip my nugget again. "Nothing like what you and the homie got."

"Probably because you won't give it a chance."

"I don't waste my time. I know Jenni ain't the one for me like that, so right now, I'm just fucking until I find it."

"Does she know that?"

He nodded matter-of-factly. "I ain't in the business of being a liar. She knew from jump what it was, and she don't trip about it."

"That's good."

We finished our food and I noticed that not only had Gavin not showed up yet, but he didn't reply once to any of my messages nor did he return any of my calls. Just as I was about to vent, Eko's phone rang and I saw it was Gavin. They talked for a little bit, but I couldn't really get any information from eavesdropping.

"What he say?" I asked as soon as Eko hung up.

"Same shit. He got caught up but is on his way."

I nodded and balled my trash up. I took a sip of my drink, and then stood up. When I turned to get Eko's trash, I saw his eyes, yet again, cascading down my frame. Except this time, his teeth sank into his plump bottom lip as his right arm laid along the back of the couch. I ignored it again, and picked the trash up to go toss it.

"Going to the bathroom," I told him before heading to the back. Eko, for some reason, had me a little hot and bothered with his fine ass. I needed to take a moment.

KNOCK! KNOCK!

"Yeah?" I called out, wondering what the fuck he wanted.

Eko didn't respond, he just came into the bathroom and closed the door behind himself. Turning my back to the sink, I gripped the edges of it as his big hands gripped my waist. For the second time today, my heart was damn near beating out of my chest, and every time I inhaled to calm myself down, his sexy scent would damn near knock me over.

"Why you playing?" he questioned softly, eyes looking so deeply into mine that I was sure he could see my thoughts.

"P-playing about what?" I stammered.

He nodded his head up down as to say 'this', and then brought my body closer to his. He pecked me gently, then gave me a few more before I circled his neck with my arms and reciprocated. Before I knew it, he had picked my ass up and sat me on the sink.

Just as he was unbuttoning my shorts, I heard loud music

coming from Gavin's car as he pulled up. To my surprise, Eko kept going like we were really about to still fuck now that Gavin was here.

"Move, E!" I shouted in a hushed tone. I had snapped out of the trance he had me in and was now wondering what the hell I was thinking for trying to sleep with my man's best friend.

Eko chuckled, kissed me once more, and then backed away. He slipped out of the bathroom, and I fixed myself.

As I stared in the mirror at my reflection, I heard the screen door to the house creak, before Gavin and Eko began talking. I walked out of the bathroom to see them in the living room, and when Eko saw me, he grinned sexily.

"Hey, baby, I'm sorry about earlier. I had to handle something," Gavin explained.

"Whatever. Just take me home, Gavin."

"The map though," he replied.

I glared up at him for a few moments and then went to my bag to dig out the map of all the traps and areas they planned to work with.

Since I'd met Gavin, I'd always assisted him in his work shit, and at first I thought it was dope. I felt like we had a Bonnie and Clyde type relationship. But now, I felt like he saw me more as his bottom bitch or something, than his woman. All we talked about was his work, and the only time he hit me up was to ask me to handle something for him. The only boyfriend and girlfriend thing we did was fuck. He'd sometimes take me out, but only when he thought I was on the verge of leaving his ass.

"Here." I smashed the paper against his chest and stormed out.

"Let me handle that real quick and then I'll be back through here," Gavin told Eko.

His car was open, so by the time he came to get in, I was already inside. Gavin sucked his teeth when he saw how angry I looked, and then he pulled off. I didn't look at him or say anything for the first half of the ride, and when I did look his way, I saw something I didn't want to see.

"What is this?" I picked up the piece of golden brown curly hair on his shirt.

"Shit, I don't know!" He shrugged. "Can barely see that shit!"

"What bitch were you with? Did you seriously have me helping you with your street shit while you fucked some hoe?" I grimaced, dangling the thin ass strand in his face.

"No! Fuck I look like making you wait while I get at some junt, Rori! I was handling business!"

I plopped back against the seat, trying to think of every golden-haired bitch I'd ever seen or met. I was furious, chest heaving, and blowing air out of my nostrils.

"Calm yo' pretty ass down, baby."

When Gavin pulled up to my house, I quickly yanked the door open, but he gripped my arm to stop me.

"Let me go," I sniffled, on the verge of crying.

"Baby, I wasn't with no bitch. I don't know where the hair came from." He leaned over and tried to kiss me, but I turned away.

Snatching my arm, I got out of the car, ignoring his calls for me. I saw he started calling my phone, so I hit the ignore button on my iPhone and continued inside. Part of me wished I had just fucked Eko.

14

────────

WAAYIL

My personal life was in fucking shambles, so I stayed in the shop, taking client after client. On the bright side, my money was piling up, and soon enough, I'd be able to get my own spot. For now, I was going back and forth between staying in hotels and at my brother's spot, so I was beyond ready to have my own permanent space, at least for more than a damn night.

"All done." I set my needle down and began removing my gloves.

I'd just finished tattooing one of the homies from way back named Canyon. I knew him through Yikayla's sister, Dree, because they used to be attached at the hip. I thought when I got out shit would be the same, but the few times I did see Dree, Canyon was nowhere to be found. That wasn't like their asses at all, so I knew some shit was up.

"Looks good, my nigga. Thank you." Canyon stared into the mirror at the bird I'd tattooed down his bicep.

"Yo' job ain't gon' trip, bruh?" I fucked with him and laughed when he sucked his teeth as I patched him up.

"I'm the best thing that ever happened to them niggas. I could walk in that bitch shirtless and they wouldn't say shit."

"Aight then, shit." We chuckled in unison as we made our way to the front where Nusef and Sax were.

We were closed at this point, so all the other employees had gone home. I was happy not to see Chiara's ass because ever since she sucked me off, she'd been on me like white on fucking rice. It was like she thought we were tight now, but to me, she was still some bitch that worked the front desk. Only now, I knew what her head game was like.

Canyon took a seat next to Nusef, and I sat down on the couch next to Sax. They had some Hennessy open, so Canyon and I poured some into a red cup for ourselves.

"You decide what you gon' do about, Alba?" Nusef inquired as Sax and Canyon stared at me.

"Alba? Damn, you still fucking with her? I just knew that shit was gon' fall apart eventually, but I guess not." Canyon chuckled.

Shit, I wish I had let that shit fall apart. I kept Alba for companionship after I cut ties with Yikayla, but after the first year and half of my sentence, I didn't really need that shit anymore; at least not from her. I slowed up my responses to her letters, but she didn't. And because she would put money on my books and come see me at least once every couple months, I felt obligated to call her.

And don't get shit twisted, I didn't completely *not* give a fuck about Alba. How could I not when I'd been with her so long? I just wanted to care from a distance. Being her nigga just wasn't what I wanted anymore. I hadn't wanted it even before I got locked up.

"Nah, she's pregnant." I shook my head and ran my hand down my face. Speaking those three words almost made me vomit.

I missed the shit out of Yikayla, and right now I didn't have the strength to let her know why we couldn't be. The excitement and happiness in her pretty ass face when she thought we were gon' be together was some shit I didn't want to take away from her again.

This would be the second fucking time I'd gotten her hopes up—shit, *my* hopes up—and that bugged the fuck out of me.

"Tell this nigga how dumb he is." Nusef shook his head and drank from his cup, making Canyon and Sax laugh.

"Nigga, worry about Jonaya getting fucked by Marquise," I retorted. A smirk spread across my face when I saw the anger in that nigga's eyes. He could pretend with everybody else, but I knew his feelings towards Jonaya had changed.

"I don't know how you did that shit with Alba though. She got yo' ass for at least eighteen years now," Sax interjected. "The pussy was that good?" Sax grinned and I couldn't help but to smile.

Pussy is good as fuck, but still...

"I wouldn't even care, if it wasn't for the fact that I know Yikayla will not be okay with it. I just wish I could convince her ass that the baby wouldn't fuck our shit up."

I wanted Yikayla badly, but I knew I would have to choose, and of course, my child would come before any and everybody; even my baby, Yikayla.

"Yeah, she gon' try to kill yo' ass when you tell her," Nusef added, and I just gave him a look. I hadn't told Yikayla yet, but I needed to. I knew it was fucked up for me to just end what had barely even started without telling her why.

"You still talk to Dree?" I questioned Canyon, even though I kind of already knew the answer.

Canyon sighed and said, "Nah, we haven't talked in almost six years. I saw her the other day though and got her number. You ain't seen her with nobody, have you?"

Sax, Nusef, and I all said "no" simultaneously.

"What happened to y'all?" Nusef questioned.

"Shit, you tell me. Everything was going good, until I started showing that I had feelings for her. When she started kind of making it clear that she didn't feel the same, I started fucking with my baby mama, and Dree just cut me off after."

"She was jealous." Sax sighed.

"I mean, I don't know. It didn't seem like it. It was like she was angry with a nigga for no reason." Canyon looked off like he was thinking.

The four of us chopped it up for a little longer, but then I decided to get up out of there because I wanted to talk to Yikayla.

I left straight from the shop and drove to her house, and once I was parked, I dialed her number. She didn't answer the first time, which was expected, so I called her again. I wasn't leaving until she let me explain myself. I got no answer the second time, so I got out of my car and jogged across the street to her crib. Ringing the doorbell, I waited until I heard someone unlocking the door.

"Oh, hey, Waayil." Rori half smiled, but I could hear in her voice that she'd been crying.

"You good, Rori?" I frowned. Rori was a pretty tough girl, so to see her ass crying had caught me off guard. For a second, I'd forgotten what I'd brought my ass over here for.

"Yeah, I'm fine."

I could barely hear her response because after she let me in, she started off towards the big ass den, plopped down on the couch, and pressed play to resume whatever she was watching. I grew up with all of the Goode girls, so Rori was like a sister to me. I wanted to ask her more questions, but Yikayla was my priority right now.

Making my way up the stairs, I saw Yikayla's door was closed, so I knocked lightly on it. I could hear the TV going in her room, but she didn't say anything. I just walked in, and there she was, deep into some TV show that I'd never seen before. Upon seeing me, she paused it and looked at me like she'd seen a ghost. Her room was dark, so the TV lit it up just enough for me to see where I was going, which was to check on her son and then to sit on her bed.

"What you watching?" I questioned.

"Waayil, what do you want?"

When Yikayla said she wasn't the same person anymore, she was right. I was used to the shy version of her, and now that wasn't her style at all. This new Yikayla clearly played no muthafuckin' games, and I low-key liked that shit. It only made me want her ass even more.

"I came to talk to you."

"Oh, now you want to talk." She chuckled and sighed. "So that's how you work now? When you wanna talk, we talk, but when someone else wants to, they have to wait?"

"No."

"Well it sure seems like it."

I closed my eyes and ran my hand down my face. I looked her way and she had one eyebrow raised with her arms folded like if I didn't start talking, she was gon' light into my ass again.

"Yikayla, I love you and you know that. I may not have acted like it over these past years but I do. I—"

"Then what's the problem, Waayil? I thought we said we would do this." I noticed her voice was softer and didn't have as much anger and bass like it did before.

Looking at her, it was like my words got caught in my throat. I kept going back and forth between telling her what was good and not telling her. I knew once I said what I said, she and I would be over with, and that shit cut deep to even think about.

"Alba is pregnant, Kay."

"By you?" Her voice trembled. I nodded, and she immediately looked off to the side with an expression I couldn't read.

I gripped her chin and made her look my way. As I was about to speak, a lone tear traveled down her cheek before she sniffled lightly.

"Yikayla, please."

"Why would you do that!" she sobbed, and damn was this shit fucking me up. She had me even angrier with myself than before.

"I didn't do it on purpose, Yikayla, and you know that! This shit was just as unexpected for me as it is for you right now. If I could go back in time to when it happened, I swear to God I would."

"I don't think we should talk anymore, even as friends."

"Yikayla—"

"You need to leave."

"Baby, I didn't do this shit on purpose, and it's not—"

WHAM!

I made the mistake of trying to kiss her and she slapped the shit out of me. Slapped me so damn hard, I had to remind myself who she was before I knocked the shit out her ass. A part of me wanted to look in the mirror and see if I was still dark skinned, because I was sure her muthafuckin' ass had slapped the black off me.

"Leave, Waayil!" She pointed towards her bedroom door as tears skied down her smooth brown cheeks. When I didn't move fast enough, she tried to shove me out of her bed with all her might, but I didn't budge.

Having nothing else to say, I just got up and walked slowly to the door. Once on the other side of it, I heard Yikayla break down, which had me tempted to go back in there. Everything was telling me to just take my black ass home like she'd asked me to, but I couldn't, so I walked right back inside.

Her back was to me, so I removed my shoes and got in the bed behind her. She was crying so hard that she didn't even say anything as I hugged her body from behind and kissed the nape of her neck.

"I'm sorry, baby." I spoke lowly against her neck before delivering another kiss.

We fell asleep just like that.

15

———————

ALBA MICEL

I'd been calling Waayil since I told him I was pregnant, and the nigga didn't answer the phone once. I texted him and he never responded, and when I dropped by the tattoo shop a few sporadic times, they claimed he wasn't there.

This was not what the fuck I'd expected from him when I told him I was pregnant. I thought for sure he would change his ways and be more devoted to me. After all, I did deserve it. I stuck by him through a jail sentence that I thought was gonna last a lifetime, and the way he's treating me now is unacceptable, considering that fact.

"Girl, stop hitting him and give him some time." My friend, Tammy, rolled her eyes at me.

"Time for what! That nigga better man up!" my other homegirl, Ashley, chimed in, and I nodded towards her.

"Thank you!" I agreed.

I knew Waayil was acting this way because of Yikayla. My inside source tells me everything, and God am I thankful for Sax. Sax was good friends with both me and Waayil, and he had a hard time choosing who to be more loyal to. By saying that, he felt bad enough for me to tell me the shit Waayil said in what he thought were their private conversations.

He told me how Waayil had planned to be with Yikayla, but my pregnancy halted that. I guess my confession did do some good in that case. I smiled at the thought.

Sax may have even had a little crush on me, but who didn't in Memphis? That's why I didn't understand what Waayil's problem was. All these niggas got on their knees every night and prayed to King Jesus for a chance with me, and Waayil had me.

I hated that about him, ever since we got together. He didn't seem grateful that I chose him out of all these niggas in my face. He acted like if I left him, he would be perfectly fine, and that shit has bothered me for years. So why did I love him? Because Waayil was fine as fuck, sweet when he wanted to be, and the dick was hands down the best that I'd ever had. And those eyes, don't get me started on those beautiful hazel eyes he had.

"I mean, the man just got out of jail, and now you're pregnant. I'm sure he needs time to think about all of this," Tammy kept going.

Tammy was my best friend, like grew up together and everything, but she got on my nerves sometimes with her know-it-all ass. That's why I recruited Ashley. Ashley did whatever the fuck I said and agreed with everything I did. Some days I didn't want to hear what Tammy said since it was the truth, so lately it was rare that we hung together.

Ashley was my go-to because I could convince her to do anything, go anywhere, and say or think whatever. And she needed the guidance I provided for her anyway. She wasn't half as pretty as me, and she didn't have anything going for her like I did. She looked up to me, so whatever I said was facts in her eyes, and I liked that.

"Well, his fucking time is up!" I spat, before rising to my feet and grabbing my purse. I came over here to Tammy's to help keep my mind off of Waayil, but it wasn't working. "Come on, Ash."

"Y'all leaving already?" Tammy frowned, setting her wine glass on the coffee table in her nice ass home.

That was another thing; Tammy didn't look up to me. She had a good job, a nice little home, and a man who would jump for joy if she got pregnant. Ashley just got hired at Checkers and lived with her sister, so you could see the vast difference between them already.

"Yeah, we're out." I yanked her door open and switched outside.

Ashley and I hopped into my Lexus, and I peeled off with all kinds of shit going through my mind. Waayil was making my ass crazy, and I didn't like it one bit. As I made a left turn, my phone chimed.

"Who is that?" I asked Ashley. I listened as she picked my phone up and looked at the screen.

"Gavin."

As soon as she said his name, it was like a lightbulb went off in my head. I smiled at my thoughts as I gunned it down Ashley's street so she could hurry the fuck up and get out of my damn car.

"Okay, get out, I have to go."

"Where?" she asked.

"None of your business, Ashley. Now go!" I saw the sadness in her stupid skinny face so I said, "I will tell you about it later. Just make sure you answer the phone when I call or you won't know."

"Okay." She giggled and I gave her a smile before rolling my eyes to her back.

I picked my phone up to read the text from Gavin.

Gavin: *I miss you.*

Me: *I miss you too. Busy?*

Gavin: *It's your lucky day. You caught me at a good time.*

Me: *Meet at the apartment?*

Gavin: *Yep, be there in 10.*

I checked myself out in the mirror and grinned widely at what I saw. I was beautiful as hell with my long golden brown hair, smooth vanilla complexion, and a body that spoke for me when I walked through anywhere. I can't remember a time where I wasn't pulling niggas in with just the switch of my hips. Waayil just didn't realize how lucky his stupid ass was.

After parking at Gavin's apartment complex, I shut the engine off and searched the parking lot for his car. When I saw it, I got out and headed up. He'd gotten this apartment because his young little clingy girlfriend didn't know about it. I think he loved her, but I didn't really care; I was just using him for dick while Waayil was away.

Because he was involved himself, Gavin didn't say too much about me claiming Waayil while he was locked up, but I knew it bothered him. On more than one occasion, he talked to me about us leaving our significant others. I would never, I repeat, never leave Waayil Christian, especially not for some dope boy. Dick was good, but not that good.

"Damn, I've been missing you." Gavin yanked me in his spot and kissed my lips.

He was a very handsome guy; brown skinned, low cut fade, and minimal chin hair with a thin mustache. He always looked clean, had a nice amount of cash that I sometimes used to put money on Waayil's books, and he treated me nicely. He treated me how I wished Waayil did sometimes.

"I missed you too. I've been thinking about what you said the other day." I dropped my purse onto the couch and sat down. This nigga had slipped up and said he loved me.

"I know you don't feel the same—"

"I do, baby, I just didn't know how to tell you." When his eyes bucked slightly and he came to sit next to me, my heart rate sped up with excitement. "I love you, Gavin Peace."

"Shit, I love you too. So what's up? Let's do this shit together." He was way too anxious. It was kind of cute but sad at the same time.

"Remember what else you said to me? When we were fucking that one night?" I snickered, straddling him and placing a soft kiss on his neck.

"I wanted you to have my baby."

"Mhm," I nodded. "We should do that too. I'm ready to have your baby."

The way his naïve, love sick ass stared up at me was priceless. I wanted to snap a damn picture of it.

Without another word, Gavin stood up, holding me, and started carrying me to the bedroom. All I needed from him was to get me pregnant, and then I would have Waayil in the palm of my hands. I couldn't get Waayil to impregnate me because he never wanted to do it raw. He did it once, the day he found out he was getting out of jail, but I didn't get pregnant. My damn period came two days later.

So once Gavin gave me what I wanted, I would send him back to whatever little bitch that thought he was about something.

16

———————

YIKAYLA

"I'm about to come get you," Roscoe said into the phone as I rubbed my baby's soft hair. He was fast sleep, looking so adorable.

"I'm not feeling well, Roscoe."

"I told you I'm gonna be busy all day tomorrow, so if I don't see you tonight, then don't be trying to bug me and shit at all tomorrow."

For a few moments longer than I'd intended, I was silent. I was on the verge of telling him that I didn't want to be with his ass anymore. Ever since I found out about Alba's pregnancy, I felt dead inside unless my son was awake. I didn't even want Roscoe anymore. I'd rather be alone than laid up with him every night, being more miserable than I already was.

"Hello?" he pulled me from my thoughts.

"I just... that's fine. I don't have to see you tomorrow."

"See, now you got a damn attitude."

"No, honestly, Roscoe, it's okay."

"Nah, I can tell—"

I hung up the phone because I just didn't wanna hear his voice anymore. I hated that it seemed like I was perfectly fine with our situation until Waayil came home, but honestly, that wasn't the truth. Yes, I loved Roscoe, but I think I loved him because I wanted to and felt like I had to. We have a baby together, and being a family was something that I've always wanted. So me admitting that Roscoe wasn't the one I wanted anymore, was a little hard for me to do.

It was late as hell and I wasn't tired at all, so I got out of bed and slowly dressed my son in some really warm clothes. While he slept, I changed into a casual dress, and slipped my feet into some sandals before picking him back up. After buckling Lonan into his car seat without waking him, I got in on the driver's side and headed to my destination.

I made it to the hotel I knew Waayil was staying in. He'd been texting me a lot, even though I gave him no response, and he told me where he was. I smiled thinking about how he let me know his where-abouts every night just in case I wanted to 'get something off my chest' as he'd say. I assumed, over time, I would get back to normal, but I could barely concentrate knowing that he and I were finished.

"Okay, here we go," I said as I got my baby out of the car and went inside. Once I got to Waayil's room door, I took a deep breath then knocked lightly.

It didn't take long for him to answer, and when he did, I hated myself for smiling. I couldn't help it though because he was cheesing too. To my surprise, he took Lonan from me and then carefully carried him to the extra bed to lie him down. I couldn't remember the last time Roscoe held our baby, and here Waayil was acting like his daddy.

"I'm happy you came." He sat down on the other bed wearing basketball shorts, boxers, and socks. His tattoo-covered chest was exposed and covered in the perfect shade of chocolate.

"Are you?" I was moving slowly into the room, looking around for earrings or anything belonging to a woman; namely Alba.

"Yeah. Come here." He grabbed my hand and pulled me into his lap.

I was straddling him and I could feel his solid ass dick pressing against my pussy. I was all of sudden so horny for him. I still fanta-sized about the night we had together before he went to jail, even while Roscoe was on top of me sometimes.

"Waayil," I stated sternly when his large hands began to glide up my thighs under my dress.

"I love the fuck outta you, Yikayla." His eyes were so serious. I believed him. I already knew that anyway. "I know this baby shit fucked everything up, shorty, but I want you to know I didn't do this shit on purpose. If I was gon' get anybody pregnant on purpose, that would have been you."

Like a dumb hoe, I grinned widely at his admission.

He pressed his lips against my collarbone and began to deliver soft sensual kisses while groping my ass and thighs. The lights were low, so the mood had been set since I stepped into the room. Feeling his hands on me was like an aphrodisiac.

"I want you bad, Kay."

"I don't care about the baby, Waayil," I moaned, as his hands trav-eled up my back slowly. His touch was something else.

He stopped upon hearing my statement, and scanned my face with his eyes. Placing my hands on the sides of his handsome mug, I leaned down to kiss him gently a few times before our tongues tangled together. Our breathing pace picked up as he laid me on my back and yanked my dress over my head. Getting in between my legs, he continued to caress me while sucking my lips. His dick was hard as a rock, as he pressed himself against me. That feeling alone had me wetter than I'd ever been.

I watched as he dipped down to suck my nipples hungrily, while tugging down my panties. I'd been dreaming of us making love again for years, and it was finally happening.

Waayil trailed his lips down my stomach, sucking in various areas, which almost made me cum. His thick lips grazed my skin, which was burning up from the anticipation of feeling him inside of me. Placing my thighs on his shoulders, he latched onto my clit with his mouth and began to suck slowly. He spread my legs a little further when he buried his face between my hips, and teased my bud with his tongue.

"Shit, Waayil," I whimpered. I had completely forgotten how good his head game was.

I rubbed his freshly cut fade as he went to town on me, slurping, groaning, and sucking like this was what he'd been dreaming of. My body trembled as I came hard as hell, but Waayil ignored it, gripping my thighs roughly and sucking the life out of me.

"Oh my gosh," my voice trembled. I was breathing heavily, and had stiffened up as he made sure his mouth and my pussy were one.

Abruptly pressing my thighs into my stomach, Waayil dug deeper with his tongue, lapping me up like a dog did the water in its bowl. My nails scraped the sheets, and my head fell back into the pillow as he yanked another orgasm out of me. It was so strong that my moan came out stammered yet high pitched, as my body became temporarily paralyzed.

"You better wake yo' ass up," he stated seriously, once he came up for air, sucking parts of my thighs. I was beat already just from the head, and was ready to go to sleep, sucking my thumb.

"I'm up," I half lied as he removed his bottoms. He was bigger than I remembered, and I was a bit afraid.

He nodded to tell me to come to the edge of the bed, so I did. I quickly glanced over my shoulder to see my baby was still on his back, knocked the hell out.

When I turned back towards Waayil, he was looking down at me with the sexiest expression ever. His bright honey eyes beamed right through me, as his dick stood at attention. I started to lick and suck on the tip, while looking up at him. When he moaned and tossed his head back for a moment, I took him deeper into my mouth.

"Fuck, ma," he grumbled once I had most of him in my mouth.

I used my hand and some of my saliva to take care of what I couldn't deal with, then continued to please him. He palmed the top of my head, taking control of my speed, as his moans became more frequent. Hearing the pleasure in his voice turned me on like crazy.

Suddenly, he pulled me off of him and tongued me down hard, as he laid on top of me on the bed.

"Baby, you know how fucking sexy you are?" He whispered against my lips before kissing me nastily.

Before I could answer, he placed my legs onto his shoulders. While gazing hard into my eyes, he pressed the head of his thick dick against my opening. He pushed hard, and finally got a little of himself inside, which prompted a moan to burst through. It was a little painful, as he moved in and out, opening me up to welcome more of his length and thickness.

"Shit." He let out a breathy moan once he got all the way inside of me. "You okay?" he asked lowly, stroking me with precision and passion.

"Mhm." I nodded, since the pain was starting to subside.

With my legs still resting on his shoulders, he leaned down to kiss me roughly while plunging deeply inside of me. I whimpered into his mouth, feeling him damn near in my stomach. The curve in his manhood was tapping my spot every time he made the slightest move, so I knew I was on the verge of cumming and hard.

"Don't you ever let another nigga get in this again," he ordered, as he pounded me at a slightly faster pace. "You hear me?" he asked, knowing I could barely talk. "Mmm," he grumbled against my neck before sucking it, which made me cum. "This shit is mine, Yikayla."

I guess to prove that his words rang true, he lifted up off of me a little bit and began to pound me hard. My pussy was sopping wet, so you could hear him fucking me loud and clear. Our skin was sweaty as hell, and our moans were now in competition with the loud sound of our lovemaking.

"You love me?" he inquired, staring down into my eyes while sucking my inner thigh, which sat against his chiseled chest.

"Yeah," I sniveled, knowing I was about to cum again. "Aaah!" I called out uncontrollably, once he began hammering me while keeping eye contact with me.

My mouth was open, and my right hand was pressed against his six-pack as he fucked me senseless. While lightly choking me, he delivered some long, hard pumps that made me cream, just before he let loose inside of me. He moved my legs off of his shoulders, and laid down on top of me to kiss me hungrily.

"You sure you okay with this shit?" He was still inside of me as I throbbed around his girth.

I nodded and replied, "Yes. I love you," before he dipped his tongue back into my mouth.

Alba would have to do more than get pregnant to keep us apart.

17

———————

JONAYA

"**D**amn, baby." Marquise breathed heavily as he rolled off of me. Like I had suspected, the dick was really good, so I was definitely enjoying my time with Marquise.

"Be right back."

I got out of the bed and grabbed a tissue so I could take the condom from him. Once I flushed it down the toilet, I turned the shower on and hopped in. I cleansed my body twice, and then stepped out to dry off and use the lotion I brought when I came yesterday afternoon. I then brushed, flossed, and rinsed my teeth. I went back to the bedroom to get my panties out of my bag, and I felt Marquise watching me closely.

"I think we should make this shit official." He lit the blunt hanging between his fingers.

"Official?" I giggled, hoping he was joking. I was not ready to be in a relationship with anyone at all.

"Yeah." He ashed the blunt then patted the area of the bed that I was just in. "Sit down."

Once I had my tube top and tights on, I walked over to the bed and sat down like he'd told me to. He pulled me closer by my arm, and draped his arms around my shoulders so that he was hugging me from the side. He kissed my forehead gently, and then sighed.

"I know you're not the type of girl to get tied down and shit, neither am I, but I'm man enough to admit when I want something more with a woman, Jonaya."

"We've only known one another a couple weeks now, Marquise. You don't think that's too fast? What if you see another girl you like better?" I looked up at him and smiled.

"Nah, I won't. I see bitches every day in my line of work, and none of them compare to you, Jo. Is this not what you want?"

I contemplated on what I did want. I'd never really had a boyfriend unless you count the guy I dated in second grade for a couple days. I liked having no strings attached for some reason, and I wasn't sure if I was ready to take that relationship plunge. However, I did like Marquise a lot, and unlike the other niggas in the past, I didn't mind talking with him or doing other things outside of sex. Maybe God was telling me that I needed to get a grip and change my ways. Even Nusef told me to, and he's the king of not being in a relationship.

"Yeah, I do want it," I whispered slowly, making sure I agreed with each word I spoke as it flowed from my mouth.

The most adorable grin covered Marquise's face as he leaned down to peck my lips a few times. A rush of awkward feelings came over me knowing I was someone's girlfriend now, but I was hoping that it would soon pass.

"Where you headed?" he inquired as I climbed off the bed, suddenly feeling like I didn't want to be near my new boyfriend. I needed a moment alone to process it all.

"To the nail shop with my friends, and then I'm going to dinner later with my mom and sisters, so I will probably see you tomorrow."

"Damn, you can't come through after dinner?"

"School is starting soon, Marquise, and I need to get my sleep schedule back on track for classes," I quickly half lied as I packed up.

School *was* starting, but I never cared about my sleep track. My stepfather always tried to get me to prepare myself by gradually changing my summer sleeping times to my fall sleeping time, but I never listened.

"Aight. Tomorrow morning then."

"Yep. Bye, baby."

I started out of his room, but then stopped, turned around, and walked over to him to kiss his lips. I wasn't used to this stuff, but I would try.

Wednesday and my other good friend, Leighton, had texted me ten minutes ago saying they were outside of Marquise's house, so when I came outside and got into the car, they were complaining.

"Sorry. This nigga wanted to have a heart to heart and then he asked me to be his girlfriend. It messed up my get ready flow for a moment." I zipped my duffle bag which I'd forgotten to, due to me trying to hurry my ass out of there.

"He did? Oh my gosh, you're so lucky, Jonaya. I wish my brothers would let me have a boyfriend." Wednesday turned to look at me in the back seat. "I can only have short flings because of them."

Nusef, and especially Waayil did not play when it came to Wednesday. I sort of felt sorry for her, and on multiple occasions tried to convince Nusef to ease up on her, but he wouldn't budge. She'd had a few little relationships here and there, but they never lasted because the guys would either be too scared of Nusef, or couldn't take the tight grip she was on. She'd had her fair share of dick though for sure.

Wednesday was only a year younger than Leighton and I, but it didn't seem like it. She was my best friend, and had been since we were ten and eleven years old. I then met Leighton in eighth grade, and eventually we all became a trio.

"Girl, you just have to start rebelling," Leighton chimed in and ran her fingers through her fresh curly weave as she made a left turn.

"Well, I don't know about all that. I just say find a guy that isn't too bitch made to stand up to your brothers, and put your foot down, Wednesday. Stop letting them control everything you do. I sure as hell wouldn't," I scoffed.

Wednesday nodded as she stared out of the front windshield, like she was soaking up everything being said to her.

We made it to the nail shop, and after being seated in the spa chairs with our feet in the nice warm blue water, Leighton gave Wednesday a look. Since I was in the middle of them, I looked at Wednesday as well to see what the hell was up.

"Ask her." Leighton bucked her eyes at Wednesday.

"Alright, alright." Wednesday adjusted herself in the seat. "So, Leighton has a little bit of a crush on Nusef, and she was wondering if you could set something up."

"Okay, two questions: one, why couldn't you have asked me that, Leighton? And two, Wednesday, he's *your* damn brother, you set something up."

"Yeah, he's my brother, but you're his best friend, Jonaya. If I try to talk about his dating life, he's gonna ignore my ass or just nod and not take what I say into account. But you, you can convince him," Wednesday replied.

"Exactly. I'm too scared to chill with him alone, but now that you and Marquise are an item, maybe you can set up a double date instead of a single date," Leighton suggested.

Laughing as I glanced back and forth between the two, I said, "You want the four of us to go on a damn double date?"

I'd never been on a date really. Trust me, niggas have asked and have tried, but that was never the tip I was on. The closest I'd ever been to a date, was making a nigga take me to get something to eat, or drive me around town when I needed him to. Marquise and I, to this day, have never been out on a date, and he's been begging to take me to dinner or something plenty of times. And now that he was my man, I felt obligated to agree to one, so maybe this double date actually was a good idea. At least he and Nusef were homies, so that was a positive.

"Yeah, I do. Please, Jonaya; Nusef is fine as fuck. I just need you to get the door open for me, and after I warm up to him on the double date, I can take it from there."

"Okay. Alright, I will see what he says. But you know his main thing is this girl named Rebecca, right? So your chances may be slim."

"She's his main thing, meaning he ain't looking to make it official because if was going to, he would have already done it," Wednesday chimed in, and I, unfortunately, had to nod my head to agree.

"But question, what made you choose Nusef instead of Waayil? They look exactly the same?" I chuckled.

"Waayil is a little off and I don't do crazy. Nusef is funny and he likes to turn up, which is more my type," Leighton answered.

I laid back against the spa chair, smiling at her reasoning because it was so true. Waayil was the quiet mixed with *a lot* of crazy, and Nusef was just the life of the party. They were both cool and funny as hell though.

Sighing, I glanced over at Leighton as she told the lady what design she wanted. I hoped to God that Nusef agreed to come on this double date. Leighton wasn't the only one who needed it.

Later That Night... Around 7 p.m....

My sisters, mom, Buddy, and I had just come home from having dinner, and I was stuffed like a Thanksgiving turkey.

"Kay, heeeyyyy." I stopped my sister as she ascended the stairs, holding my adorable sleeping nephew.

"What do you want?" She smiled. She'd been smiling a lot lately, and I wondered if it had anything to do with Waayil.

"Can I use your car? I—"

"For what, Jo?"

"To run them streets like a thot," Dree chimed in, making Rori and Yikayla laugh.

"Haha, bitch. Actually, I'm going to Nusef's because I have to talk to him about something. That's all, I swear."

Yikayla moved to the side to let Rori and Dree pass her up the stairs, and made a face like she was thinking.

"Fine, Jonaya. But you go to Nusef's and bring your ass right back in my car."

Ever since I took Dree's car to some dude's house in the Highland Heights area and some nigga stole the battery out, no one wanted to let me use their car. I had zero chance with Dree, but at times, Yikayla gave in.

"I will. Thank you." I kissed her cheek and then my nephew's before rushing out of the house. I was tired as hell and wanted to get this over with. I could have called, but Nusef was a face-to-face person and this would take some hard convincing.

I made it to his spot in no time it seemed, since I was grooving to the radio the whole way. They were playing some back-to-back shit that I liked, which was a rarity.

I parked in the lot of Nusef's apartment, and then rushed up to his door. I had a key, so I just slipped it in and entered. The TV was on in the bedroom, so I made my way back there to see him sitting in the bed with his back against the headboard and playing the game. He was in a wife beater shirt, and basketball shorts, showing his toned muscular frame. My best friend was fine, just like Leighton said.

"So you just popping up now?" He laughed as he pressed a few buttons on the controller before groaning.

The room was dim, only being lit up by the television, and smelled like his cologne.

"I'll only be here for a second." I removed my Nike slides and climbed into the bed to sit next to him Indian style. "So I have a favor to ask of you."

"Jo, I'm not following you to a nigga's house to make sure he ain't crazy."

I laughed heartily, thinking about the few times I'd asked him to do that.

"No, no, nothing like that. This is something you will like." He stopped the game and looked at me, licking his full lips as he waited for me to continue. His bright honey colored eyes pierced through me, as the TV light illuminated his dark cocoa skin. "You know my friend Leighton."

"Unfortunately."

"What? Why unfortunately, Sef?"

"I'm joking. But what's up?"

"She really likes, I mean really, really likes you, Sef, and I was thinking that maybe you, her, Marquise, and I should do like a double date thing."

He squinted his eyes for a moment like he was trying to see if I was joking, and then he burst into laughter, flashing his perfect white choppers.

"No." He shook his head repeatedly while still snickering.

"Please! Leighton is so pretty, and what would be the harm in it?"

"Leighton is aight at best, ma, don't play me. I got bitches that look ten times better than her, ready to suck my dick without me having to spend a dime."

"Do this for me?" I pouted and straddled his lap. I always did that when I had to beg him for something.

"You care that much about Leighton?" He frowned but not angrily, almost like he couldn't believe it.

"Well yes, because she's my best friend, but Marquise and I made things official today, and I think this would be a good first date for us. You know I'm not the dating type; it's weird for me, and a double date with none other than my two besties would make it easier."

I noticed his face changed to a serious expression when I mentioned that Marquise and I had made things official.

"So y'all are an item or some shit?"

He almost sounded angry.

"Yeah, pretty much."

"You just met this nigga and y'all fucking and becoming boyfriend and girlfriend! What the fuck is wrong with you?" he hissed, catching me off guard.

"Nothing, Sef! Didn't you just tell me to slow it down? Well that's what I'm doing!"

"Aight." He tried to move me off his lap but I stayed put.

"Please just do this for me. Plus, I think you would really like Leighton." He didn't say anything so I got more comfortable in his lap while holding his face and pouting. "Pleeeaaasssse!"

"Fine, aight, mane! Just one got damn date and that's it. Now move."

I noticed his dick was hard as a brick under me. I'd straddled him plenty of times and jokingly moved on it, and it never got that hard. Maybe a little because he was a man, but this was like he wanted to fuck.

"What the hell is going on in here?" I heard Rebecca's voice just as I was climbing off of Nusef.

"Hey, Rebecca." I smiled.

"Don't hey Rebecca me. What the fuck are you doing straddling my man while—"

"Hold up, ma. For one, this ain't your man, so let's stop with the theatrics. Secondly, I do that shit all the time and he *never* complains. Maybe you should call before you come over and you won't get ya feelings hurt." I slipped my feet into my shoes and like the little punk she was, Rebecca didn't bust a grape. "Bye, best friend, and thank you again."

He nodded to me so I left.

Before I closed the front door behind me, I heard them start to argue. Maybe Leighton would be just what Nusef needed.

18

DREE

I rolled my eyes for the tenth time at the hundredth speaker that had come on stage to talk. I'd been excited about everything having to do with law school, except this boring ass orientation. Half of the time I wasn't even listening, and from the looks of it, no one else was either. I so badly wanted to hop my fine ass up and walk out of here, because I had other shit I could be doing, but I felt like it would be too obvious. Plus, we had to take our school I.D. pictures afterwards, and I definitely didn't wanna miss that.

As I ran my freshly done nails through my freshly done press, my phone buzzed in my purse. When I retrieved it, I smiled upon seeing Canyon's name. We'd been texting and talking on the phone here and there, and he was the same person he was five years ago. Only now, he was more of a man, which turned me on.

Tonight we were going on our first date since linking back up, and to say I was excited, was definitely an understatement. I hadn't realized I missed Canyon as much as I did until now. I was a fool for not taking the chance to be with him back then, but I wasn't gonna let that happen this time. I was gonna lock his fine ass down and never let him go.

"Finally," I mumbled once they made the announcement for us to line up according to the first letter of our last name. After I took this I.D. photo, I was going home to get my beauty rest for the night.

"So I guess our last names are close," a familiar voice spoke to me. It wasn't familiar like Canyon familiar, but one I'd heard before. I looked over my shoulder to see the adorable dark-skinned guy that I'd ran into when I had to register.

"Oh, I guess so. Mine is Goode."

"Ike. Sean Ike." He grinned widely and reached his hand down to me.

"Dree."

I turned back around, but I guess he wasn't done talking to me, so I glanced back over my shoulder to listen.

"This your first year?" he inquired.

"Isn't it everybody's? I mean, this is first-year orientation."

"True, but it's not my first year. I'm actually in my last. I take the bar and shit pretty soon."

"Then why are you here?"

"Because I had a feeling you would be here." He grinned, making me blush slightly. "After I saw you by the counseling office, I couldn't get your pretty face out of my head."

"Boy, please," I giggled.

"I'm serious."

I chuckled and went into the booth after placing my signature by my name on the clipboard. After making sure what the photographer had was something I liked, I stepped out to wait for my I.D. Once they handed it to me in some thick plastic holder with a lanyard attached, I was on my way to leave.

"Where you headed?" Sean caught up to me.

"Oh, I'm gonna go home. I have an engagement to attend tonight so I want to get my rest. But it was nice meeting you, Sean."

"You have to leave now?" He playfully pouted, and I just sighed with a smile. He was so cute, and although he was trying way too hard, I kind of liked it.

"I umm... I'm really tired. I've been here since 8 a.m. and it's a little after 1 p.m. now."

"Can I get your number then? Call you sometime? I'm sure we'll have a class or two together and we may need to help one another out."

"I thought you were a senior."

"I lied. You just look like the type of girl who only dates the older niggas, so I had to do what I had to do."

We laughed in unison as I shook my head.

Staring up into his soft brown eyes, I contemplated on whether or not I should give him my number. I was dead set on Canyon, but there was no harm in me talking with other guys. Plus, Sean was gonna be a lawyer like me, so he was a very qualified back-up nigga.

I gave him my number, and we made a little more small talk before going our separate ways. I admit I was a little excited about getting to know Sean. I didn't know if it was because he was so cute, or if it was because he was in the same field as me. Who knows, but I was smiling at the thought of finding out more about him.

That Evening...

After hours of trying to decide what to wear, I'd finally chosen a red halter dress with a plunging neckline. It was classy enough for dinner, but just the right amount of sexy to make Canyon drool like a puppy dog. The red looked perfect against my dark chocolate skin, which had a slight sheen to it from my perfumed lotion. I was looking fabulous, smelling fabulous, and I felt even better than that, if possible. After tonight, Canyon would be proposing to me.

"Canyon is downstairs." My mother walked into my room and smiled.

"Thank you. I'll be down in about ten minutes."

"You're not ready *yet*?" She leaned in my doorway with her arms folded. Her face was frowned up as she scanned me, looking for something else that needed to be fixed.

"No, I'm ready to walk out of the door, but I always keep my men waiting, so by the time I come down there, he'll be extra anxious for me." I was making sure my edges were laid as I looked in my full-length mirror.

My mother just tittered at my response, then sighed, "Okay, Dree."

I passed the ten minutes easily by snapping photos of myself for social media. I was looking way too fine for Canyon to be the only one to see it tonight. The patrons in the restaurant didn't count.

My red peep-toe booties clicked against the laminate flooring of my house, as I made my way to and down the stairs. I followed the sound of laughter and conversation, which landed me in the den. Canyon, my mom's boy toy, Buddy, and Rori were talking about something that I didn't care about, I'm sure.

"Damn, shorty," Canyon spoke lowly as he took me in.

He looked good too in his ¾-sleeve button up with gray jeans, and some gray and white Adidas Samoas. His wrist was adorned with a nice watch that wasn't too flashy, and a chain laid against his broad chest. The sight of his strong arms sent me damn near begging for a hug with my arms out.

Canyon rose to his feet, allowing the den's lights to beam on his deep caramel complexion. I admired his fresh fade as he pulled me in for a much-needed hug.

"You don't look so bad yourself," I finally answered since I had myself together. These red thongs wouldn't last much longer if I kept salivating below at the sight of this man.

We said our goodbyes, and Canyon took my hand into his big one to lead me outside. I was anxious to see what kind of car he had. Yes, I was smitten with Canyon, but I still liked and preferred nice things. When I saw he was pushing a Nissan Armada, I nodded my head discreetly. That was okay I guess. It wasn't an expensive car, but it wasn't cheap per se.

Canyon opened the passenger side for me, and then came around to get in as well. We exchanged shy smiles, as we both buckled up and he cranked the car.

"This is nice," I half lied. I mean it was nice for what it was.

"Thank you. It's a good truck too." He nodded.

We ended up at this restaurant downtown named Bleu, across from the FedEx Forum. It was inside of a big building, and pretty crowded tonight. I think that was mainly because it had a bar inside, and the drunks were definitely out to play tonight.

We were seated outside at a nice table so we had a view of the Gibson Guitar center. The air was nice outside since it was the tail end of summer, so I was very comfortable.

As Canyon scanned the menu, I surveyed what I could see of the inside and outside of restaurant. It wasn't upscale, but it wasn't some hole in the wall either. I was starting to see that Canyon's tastes were a cut below mine.

"See anything you like?" he inquired.

"Oh, I haven't been looking." I giggled and turned my attention down to the menu.

I ended up ordering the honey truffle salmon, and he got the ribs. We ordered crab cakes for the appetizer, and I got a Blue Lemon Drop for a cocktail while he got an Old Fashioned.

"You look so damn good tonight that you got my mind on some other shit, Dree. I came here trying to be on the respectful tip, but damn, ma."

We both laughed at his words as I pushed my hair behind my ears.

"I had to show you what you'd been missing all of these years."

"You did a hell of a job, baby." He licked his lips, which made my nipples hard. He wasn't the only one with his mind in the gutter. "So other than you looking sexy as hell, what else have I missed?" he asked, as the waiter set down our drinks and appetizer.

"Well," I sighed and sipped my drink. "Not much, I guess. I've just been getting ready for law school is all."

"So no nigga is around that I'd have to put the paws on?"

Chuckling, I shook my head 'no'.

"I mean the few I've dated may still hold a torch for me, but I have nothing to do with that." I cheesed before we laughed together.

"Your pretty ass is still a piece of work."

"I must say, Canyon, I didn't expect you to turn out like... this. I'm pleasantly surprised."

Canyon, years ago, was a senior in college, but he acted like he was gonna drop out all of the time. I never expected him to get his degree and then go on to get a Master's Degree as well. I hated to say it, but I just knew if I ever ran into him he'd be some low-life drug dealer living off of his fifth baby mama. I didn't want to think like that, but it seemed to be the road he was headed down... back then.

"Shit, me either. But once my son came, I knew I had to shape the fuck up. Life ain't yours no more when you have a kid, Dree. I had to make sure that I could always provide for him."

Whenever he mentioned his son, my stomach churned and my body began to perspire. I loved kids, I did, but Canyon having a son still bothered me to this day.

19

CANYON DENNIS

I noticed Dree get quiet as fuck at me mentioning my son, like always. Every time we spoke over the phone or texted one another, when my son came up, she would take long pauses or forever to text back. I didn't wanna believe that me having a kid would be a problem, but I couldn't deny the obvious.

"What did I say?" I leaned forward, trying to look deeply into her damn eyes. Dree was the queen of pretending shit was fine when it wasn't. She'd been that way since I met her, and I learned some shit had yet to change.

"Nothing, I was just thinking about orientation earlier."

"Dree, every fucking time I mention, Cade, you clam up. If me having a son is a problem, you need to say that shit now."

I was getting a little upset at her bullshit; not only because her having a problem with my kid was stupid as fuck, but because she *knew* about him. My baby mama, Luna, got pregnant with him when Dree and I were still tight, so for her to be acting like shit was too much was some bullshit in my eyes.

"It's not a problem!" she shouted, but quickly stopped herself to take a deep breath. "It's not a problem, Canyon, I just have to get used to it. I've never dated a guy with a son before so this is new to me." She sipped her drink, polishing the shit off, which made me raise my brow. "I'm happy that you decided to change your way of thinking for your son."

I simply nodded, exhaling heavily because I didn't know how to feel. I'd been hella fucking excited at the thought of picking shit back up with Dree, but if she was gon' be acting like this all the damn time, then we wouldn't work at all. Yeah, I had major love for her fine ass, but my son was first before any and every damn body except God. And even that was hard for me to admit.

The rest of the dinner was aight, but Dree still seem to be bothered. That's why I was surprised that she wanted to go home with me. Shit, I figured she was gon' run her ass in the house and cut me off again, like she did way back.

So a little while later, we were at my apartment, which was literally walking distance from the school I worked at. I got a slick little discount on it since I worked for the university.

"You live alone, right?" Dree smiled as I let her into my spot.

"Sort of. When my son is with his mama, yeah." I hung my keys up and shoved my hands in my pockets as she surveyed my living room.

While Dree looked around it, I took the time to take in how good she looked. Her body was stacked like a muthafucka under all that sexy mocha skin that I wanted to travel with my tongue. Her nice round ass sat up nicely just like her titties, and her long legs had not an imperfection in sight. I honestly didn't know how she'd gone unclaimed all this damn time. Ever since I knew Dree, she'd been every nigga in Memphis' dream, including mine. She wasn't with it then, but I was hoping all that shit had changed.

I trailed her around my spot, enjoying the soft feminine scent of her perfume. She was driving me crazy and hadn't even done shit yet. When we ended up in the kitchen, where there was a little more light, I could barely hold myself together.

"I would love to have my own place." She turned in a circle as she stood in the middle of my kitchen. "How much—"

She couldn't finish her sentence because I had backed her sexy ass into the wall and pressed my lips against hers. I didn't care if that red shit got on me. She was tense at first as my hands moved across her body, grabbing at her plump ass, but eventually her body relaxed and she hugged my neck. Our tongues came together as she cupped the back of my head, pressing my mouth further into hers. I had never fucked Dree, but as many times as I'd dreamt about the shit, you would think I had.

My hands glided up her smooth thighs until they were under her dress and tugging on the waistband of her panties. I trailed my lips from her mouth, down her cheek, and to her neck, where I began sucking that shit like a vampire eager for blood.

"You know how long I've been wanting you, Dree," I whispered against her neck as she moaned softly.

I felt her lifting my shirt, so I pulled away to help her get it off me, before going back in to suck on her sexy lips. I kissed down her collarbone and pushed open the slit of her dress to reveal her breasts. I hungrily sucked her nipples, while using one of my hands to toy with her clit. Her pussy was soaking, making my dick brick the fuck up even more.

"Ah!" she squealed when I brought her ass to the kitchen floor.

I roughly shoved her dress up, and ripped her panties like they were plastic wrap to a new video game. The way her pussy glistened made me lick my lips, so I dove right into that shit, sucking her clit gently but flicking my tongue over it feverishly.

"Canyon, fuck," she sniveled, spreading her legs wider as they sat on my shoulders.

I closed my eyes to enjoy the taste of her, and before I knew it, she was releasing right into my mouth. I kissed her pussy a couple times, and then trailed my lips up to the part of her stomach that was exposed. I quickly turned her over, gripped her hips so that her ass was in the air, and then I hurriedly released myself.

I had never fumbled with a condom so damn long in my mutha-fuckin' life. It seemed like an hour had passed before I was rolling that shit down. I was sure Dree's pussy had rolled its eyes at me.

Once I had it down, I pressed myself into Dree and we both let out a throaty moan. I had to sit in that shit for a bit. It was so snug and wet that I had to shake my head as I started to move in and out of her.

"Mmm," she cooed, scraping her nails against my kitchen tile.

I kept plunging in and out of her slowly, holding tightly onto her waist. When she looked back at me with one of her sex faces, I almost busted early. This was the prettiest bitch in Memphis and it wasn't up for debate. I began pounding her harder, liking the sound of my dick entering her, in combination with her sexy ass moans.

"Can— Can— ahhh!" she attempted to call my name, but I'd gripped her shoulder and started fucking her even harder. She came hard, making her pussy even more wet, which almost sent me over the edge.

"Fuck." I threw my head back, not slowing up my strokes one bit. I used to pray every night for the chance to beat this pussy up the way that I was right now.

She tried to run, so I pressed her up against the wall so that she was facing it, and continued to drill her hard from behind, while grasping her hair with one hand and holding her waist with the other. Her smooth ass bounced against me every time I slammed her, and the sight along with the feeling of her sopping walls gripping me, yanked my nut right out of me and into the condom. I came so hard I trembled a bit and let out a deep moan against the side of her face.

Still hemming her up against the wall, my hands assaulted her sexy body for a few moments as we both attempted to catch our breaths. I kissed all over her shoulders and the nape of her neck as I sat inside of her.

"Give me a kiss," I demanded. She turned her face to the side, and leaned her head back a little so I could plant a nasty one on her.

If I died right now, I would die a happy ass muthafucka.

After we cleaned ourselves up in the shower and went for round two, where I got the best head of my life, I gave Dree one of my t-shirts and we climbed into my bed.

"I so did not plan to fuck you tonight." She chuckled as she laid on my chest. Her delicate fingers danced around my abs as she spoke.

"I'm just smooth like that."

"Nigga, please!"

We laughed in unison.

"Nah, but I didn't expect it either, ma. I mean back in the day when I told you how I was starting to feel about you, you was on some other shit, so I didn't think tonight would go as planned either." I looked down into her eyes and she gave me a closed mouth smile.

After letting her eyes scan mine for a little longer, she whispered, "I always felt the same, Canyon, I was just afraid."

That shit caught me off guard, so I moved back a little so that I could really look into her face.

"Why?" I frowned in confusion.

"Because I knew that if we got together, what we would have would be real, and I wasn't prepared for that. I liked not caring about the relationships I was in. But I knew with you, everything would be legit and I would have been vulnerable."

"Fuck is wrong with that?"

Shit still wasn't making sense to me.

"I just wasn't ready to deal with that. But I'm different now, more mature. I want something real at this point in my life."

Hearing her talk like this got my shit hard again, so I dipped my tongue into her mouth and climbed on top of her.

I know this shit made me sound like a bitch, but a nigga was happy as hell to have the one woman I never thought I would.

20

WAAYIL

"Mmm," Yikayla cried softly.

I had her arms pinned behind her back as I pounded her hard from behind. Her pussy was sopping wet, coating my dick completely every time I plunged deeply inside of her. The way her shit choked my dick should have been illegal. I licked my lips at the sight of her perfect round ass jiggling against me like Jell-O. Sweat covered her sweet cognac complexion, as she whimpered and sniveled like a wounded animal.

"Fuck," I grumbled, feeling myself on the verge of busting.

I couldn't get enough of this shit, and it made me wonder how I'd gone so long without it. Keeping both her wrists in one of my hands, I used my free one to smack and grip her right ass cheek roughly, while still plowing her like the shit was going out of style. The sound alone of my dick plunging into her snug wet walls was enough to make me let loose of the load that I'd been holding onto. Our skin collided together so forcefully that the sound began to bounce off of the hotel room walls.

"Ahhh, oh my— mmm," she whined, releasing her nectar for what felt like the tenth time this afternoon. Her son was with her mother, so I was able to turn her ass out like I'd been wanting to since we'd rekindled.

"Shit," I groaned, knowing I didn't have much longer.

Gripping a handful of her hair, I yanked her head back and sped up, thrusting into her forcefully while sucking hard on her shoulders. Letting her wrists go, I reached around the front of her body to toy with her nipples. After a few moments, I couldn't take it anymore, so I bit down on her shoulder, while groping her breasts, and continued to beat my pussy up from the back until I busted inside of her.

Even after I spilled my seeds, I didn't want to pull out just yet, so I stayed inside, enjoying the feeling of her hot middle pulsating around my dick. I pushed her lightly so that her face was back into the pillow, and then I slowly pulled out of her. The sight of my dick glistening with her juices made me bite down on my lip, so I lowered and kissed her pussy from the back a few times as she panted heavily.

I climbed off the bed and then picked Yikayla's ass up so we could go shower together. She sighed dejectedly, so I knew she wanted to lie there and pass the fuck out like she always did once I dicked her down. We'd been out earlier today so we'd already showered, brushed our teeth and shit, but that was one hell of a muthafuckin' session, so I felt we needed a re-up.

"My legs feel like noodles." She smiled lazily as I helped her get into the shower.

"Means I did my job." I got in with her and crushed my lips against hers as the showerhead wet up our bodies. "Look what you do." I nodded down towards my dick, which was rising back up.

"No, Waayil—"

"Calm yo' scary ass down, Yikayla. And shit, you better get used to this muthafucka wanting to be inside of you all the damn time."

She gave me that innocent ass smile that I fell in love with years ago, before starting to lather her body.

After we showered, we both got dressed and left the room. I took Yikayla home so she could get her son and run her errands that she needed to before we met back up later. We'd spent every damn night together, because I was refusing to let her sleep without me.

She tried me the night she went to dinner with her peoples, and I had to show up to scoop her and little man. Call it crazy, obsessed, clingy, whatever the fuck you want to, but I didn't give a fuck. Yikayla was mine, and if I wanted her up under me all fucking day, then that's what the fuck I was gon' do.

I shut the engine off once I was outside of Alba's crib, and just stared at the front door. I'd been avoiding her ass ever since she sprung that fucking news on me.

At first I thought it bothered me, just because it was gon' fuck up what I had with Yikayla, but now that Yikayla and I were good, I was realizing that I just didn't wanna be tied to Alba's ass anymore.

I was angry as fuck with myself for letting our relationship drag on so damn long. It started off with me not giving a fuck if she was my bitch or not, then onto me needing companionship, and then back to not giving a fuck. Now I was about to be stuck with a woman I didn't love and was having my kid.

I knocked on her front door, and before I could even step back from it, I heard her unlocking it. I knew she was off today because she'd had the same off days since I was in jail, reading her letters that only talked about her and how many niggas were trying to get at her but how she'd stayed loyal. It was almost like she was trying to force me to admit that I was grateful for her hoe ass. I sucked my teeth at thought.

"Hey." She spoke dryly and turned on her heels to saunter into her house. I followed behind, closing and locking the door behind myself. Before I could even sit down on her couch good, she snapped. "Where the fuck have you been, Waayil!"

"Aight, so listen. I need you to pee on this shit right here." I dropped the brown paper bag on the coffee table.

"Excuse me? Wait, hold up." She chuckled in disbelief as I sat back on the couch. "I tell you that we're having a baby, you disappear, and then have the nerve to come up in my damn house asking me to prove it?"

"Smart girl."

"No. I'm not peeing on shit, nigga."

"Then we don't have shit to talk about, Alba." I stood up and so did she.

"Why! This is your damn baby, you asshole!"

"Is it? So the whole time I was locked up, you wasn't fucking with nobody else? And think long and muthafuckin' hard before you lie, ma. What, you thought I was cut off from the outside world once I got locked up?" I frowned, hoping she didn't think a nigga was that fucking stupid.

I had plenty of homies that told me Alba was in the clubs and flirting with all types of niggas. I didn't give a fuck, because like I said, I was using her for what I needed at the time. What pissed me off was her stupid ass trying to pretend like she was on her nun tip while I was away. The least her hoe ass could have done was be honest. Shit, I was supposedly in jail for life; I didn't expect her retarded ass to stick by me anyway.

"Waayil, I wasn't!" She started to cry, which made me laugh. "Seriously? I tell you I held you down and you laugh at me crying?"

"Yeah, because yo' ass is full of shit. Either you pee on this mutha-fuckin' stick I don' brought you, or we don't have shit to talk about. If you comply, once I confirm that ya ass is pregnant, we can see about a DNA."

"This is because of that Goode bitch! She was the one fucking and sucking while you were lock—"

I gripped the shit out of her jaw as she whimpered with worried ass eyes.

"Make that the last time you run yo' mouth about Yikayla, ma. If I'll kill for Wednesday, just imagine what the fuck I'll do for my girl," I gritted, finally letting her face go. "Next time, I'm gon' snap that shit."

She moved her jaw around a little bit while glaring at me.

"She's not even your girl," she said like she knew.

"Who you think I been with this whole time I been dodging yo' simple ass, Alba?" I squinted my eyes at her as her mouth twisted up.

"So what about our family! What will this baby think, knowing its father just left us to go be with his bi— girl!"

I gave her ass a look so she could save herself from calling Yikayla a bitch again.

"Until you pee on that fucking stick with me present, don't ask me shit else. Don't hit me up about no fucking baby, don't come to my place of business with yo' bullshit, and most importantly, don't say shit to my girl either. Do any of the above, especially the latter, and you'll be on an episode of *First 48*, on everything I love, ma."

I wasn't fucking around with shorty. I hated to say it, but committing a murder changed me in a lot of ways I hated to acknowledge. Before, I couldn't even imagine taking someone's life, but actually doing it and spending time in jail had fucked me up in the head a little. So if Alba wanted to gamble with her fucking life, then so be it. It was in her best interest to prove that my kid was actually in her belly, because it'd be the only muthafuckin' lifeline she had if she didn't come correct.

Tired of having a staring contest with her ass, I made my way out her crib and back to my car. Once I got in, I just stared out at the passing cars, silently praying that my suspicions about the baby Alba was supposedly carrying were true.

As I got ready to crank up, my cell phone rang, and a number I'd been ignoring since I got out flashed across it. Didn't even know how they got my shit. I ain't wanna answer that shit, but if I wanted to have my life in order so I could move forward with Yikayla, I had to face the fucking music.

"Hello?" I answered, sighing dejectedly.

"Damn, I thought I was gon' have to get one of my niggas to take yo' head off, Waayil."

"Nah, you ain't crazy. Don't get one of ya niggas murked from trying to fuck with me, Neo." He laughed loudly as I stayed silent, waiting for his amusement to dissipate. "What you need, man, I'm busy?"

"What I need is for you to hold up your end of the deal."

"That was a deal I made under different circumstances, my nigga. Shit has changed, and therefore the deal is no longer."

"See, that's where you're mistaken, Waayil."

"Nah, I'm not. Get ya old ass off my phone, bruh. You got some shit to say to me, you know where to find me, my nigga. I don't do the telephone gangsta shit."

"Waayil—"

I quickly hung up and dropped my phone in the cup holder. When they say your past comes back to haunt you, that shit is true as fuck.

21

NUSEF

Rebecca's ass was still mad as fuck about catching Jonaya in my lap, and the fact that I didn't defend her ass. But for one, I told her stupid ass about popping up at my shit unannounced, and secondly, Jonaya was right about Rebecca not being my bitch. Technically, I could fuck whomever I wanted, and she couldn't say shit about it.

I didn't have the energy nor did I care enough to chase after Rebecca and deal with her bullshit. I was too busy trying to suppress these stupid ass fucking feelings that I had for Jonaya. Unfortunately for Rebecca, at this point, I cared more about pleasing Jonaya than her, so I wasn't about to reprimand Jonaya for what she did. Shit, maybe if Rebecca hadn't have shown up, I might have gotten some pussy.

As I fastened my watch on my wrist, my front door opened and closed. I knew it wasn't Jonaya because we'd already agreed to meet at the movie theater.

Tonight was that fuck ass double date that I'd agreed to, and the plan was to do dinner and a movie. Only reason I wanted to go was because I needed to keep an eye on Jonaya and Marquise. However, I wasn't too sure how well I would react to seeing them together tonight. My feelings for Jonaya only seemed to get deeper, and the more I tried to stay away from her, the worse they got.

"Going out?" Rebecca inquired, dropping her big ass purse on my bed, and plopping down as well. She looked good and thick in them tights she had on, making me lick my lips at the print of her pussy. I may have had Jonaya on my heart, but sliding up in other females was still on my brain.

"Yeah."

"You're so busy going out that you don't have time to make shit right with me, Sef?"

I pulled my hat down lower on my head and checked myself out in the mirror. I kept it simple with a navy-blue Polo shirt, blue jeans, and some navy blue Nike Roshes. My hat bore the same blue color as well.

"Rebecca, I'm not in the mood. How many damn times are we gon' argue about the same shit, ma? I don' told you that's just how Jonaya is. It's how we both are."

"You need to tell her it's not okay!"

"No, I'm not gon' tell her that bullshit." I frowned at the fact that Rebecca even thought that shit would happen.

"Because you wanna be with her or something?"

"No, because I knew her before you, Rebecca. She been doing shit like that since we became close, and I'm not gon' tell her to change just because you want me to. She was around first. You knew what our friendship was like from day one."

"Yeah, but now it seems like y'all are fucking, Sef," she whined.

Turning to face her as she stood from the bed, I pulled her body closer to me. She locked her arms around my neck, and I pecked her lips lightly before speaking.

"Baby, I swear to you I have never fucked Jonaya. She is my best friend and nothing more. She and I will never become anything." I was telling this shit to myself more than Rebecca. "But, shorty, I need you to relax for me. This is exactly why I told you I can't be in no exclusive shit."

"I know, I know, but I can't help how I feel about you, Nusef. I get jealous when girls act a certain way towards you because I love you."

I wanted to make shit work with Rebecca; not only because I wanted to forget about Jonaya as far as a relationship goes, but she deserved it. She'd been my fuck buddy, turned a little more for a couple years now, and she was better than that shit. What I should have been doing was letting her go so a nigga that deserved her could have her, but I couldn't. I needed somebody here with me to keep my mind off of who I really wanted to rock with, as fucked up as it sounds. Yeah, I could fuck other hoes and let Rebecca bounce, but I had a bond with Rebecca, which made my nights without Jonaya a little easier.

"And I love you too, baby, so relax."

I did love Rebecca. I did love her. I loved her, I did.... Fuck... but I was on some bitch nigga lovesick shit when it came to Jonaya. Had me on the verge of writing poems and shit; a big damn difference.

She nodded and asked, "Where are you going? Can I come?" Smiling, I squinted my eyes at her and she did the same. "Where the hell are you going, Nusef Christian?"

"A double date, but relax, shorty, I'm just going with one of Jonaya's bucket head ass friends so Jonaya will feel comfortable around her new boyfriend."

"She has a boyfriend?"

"Yeah, she does, another reason why you need to fall back on ya bullshit." I pecked her lips a couple times then let her go.

"And why couldn't she have asked to double date with us, instead of you going with one of her little homegirls." Rebecca folded her arms as I spritzed my cologne on.

I just gave her a look to drop it. I was tired, and she was lucky I gave her ass what little she got out of me tonight. She threw her hands up in mock surrender, and then followed me through my crib to the door. I really didn't want her to be here when I got back, but we'd just gotten back on good terms so I kept that shit to myself.

Thankfully, Jonaya said she and Marquise were picking Leighton up, because otherwise, it would have just been the three of us. I didn't know that bitch like that, and I wasn't about to be using up all my muthafuckin' gas just to scoop her.

By the time I parked at the theater, I had a text from Jonaya telling me they were outside waiting for me. I took a deep breath, gave myself a silent pep talk to behave, and then got out the car. As soon as I started towards the front, I saw Jonaya, Marquise, and unfortunately, Leighton.

Jonaya had on this white dress that was tight as hell, showing just how good her body looked. Her long, dark hair was hanging down, and her smooth vanilla complexion looked like it'd been dipped in butter. I swear to God I saw a light shining around her pretty ass as she smiled upon seeing me.

"You came!" She laughed and reached up to hug me. I basked in the perfume she always wore, and took my time letting her out of my arms.

"Sup." I nodded my head up to Marquise who then dapped me up.

"Sup, mane."

I could feel Leighton staring up at the side of my face, so I turned to look at her.

"Leighton, this is Nusef. Nusef, this is Leighton. Y'all know each other already, but just not well." Jonaya introduced us.

Shorty was looking alright. She was light skinned like Jonaya, had blond curly hair, and an alright body that she covered up in a dress as well. I could tell she thought she was fine as fuck, but she really wasn't. She had no ass, but her titties were nice. Would I fuck? Probably, but I can't say for sure.

"Thank you for coming tonight." Leighton smiled as the four of us approached the ticket window.

I was too busy watching Jonaya and Marquise who were ahead of us. He had his arm draped around her, saying little shit in her ear that had her laughing. Her ass was looking right as hell, to the point where I had to adjust myself.

I honestly didn't know what we came to see. Leighton told the box office cashier what we wanted, and I just paid the fee. Like I said, I was more focused on what Marquise and Jonaya's asses were doing. I felt bad for neglecting Leighton so far, so I offered to buy her some snacks, even though I hadn't planned to. She of course took me up on my offer, and while I got her stuff, I got Jonaya some candy too, her favorite.

"Does that girl you always hang with know where you are?" Leighton quizzed as we entered the theater, looking for where Jonaya and Marquise were.

"Yeah. Why wouldn't she? Ain't like that's my girlfriend."

"I was just making sure. I didn't want any problems over you." She smiled and I gave her one back as I let her go down the aisle first in order to sit next to Jonaya.

"Jo." I got Jonaya's attention and handed her the candy.

"Thank you, boo bear!" She squealed as she took the candy. I used to hate when she called me that shit, but for some reason, it had me grinning like a bitch at the moment.

Leighton and I made awkward eye contact, just as the lights in the theater went down. I tried to keep my eyes on the screen for the previews, but I kept seeing Jonaya and Marquise out of my peripheral. I heard kissing, and that shit caused me to inhale and exhale sharply.

"You okay?" Leighton inquired.

"Yeah, I'm good, you?"

"Great." She shoved some popcorn into her mouth. "I've been wanting to see this movie for the longest."

"Word? Me too," I lied. I ain't even know what the fuck it was still. Jonaya giggling lowly was pissing me the fuck off, especially because this nigga was gnawing on her neck and shit.

Leighton moved the armrest in between us back, and then scooted closer to me. It was weird, so I just put my arm around her shoulders. Finally, the movie started, and I realized it was *The Fate of the Furious*. I did kind of want to see that, so I relaxed a little bit to hopefully enjoy it.

Jonaya and I made eye contact when she looked to check on Leighton and I, and when she saw us all cozied the fuck up, she smiled widely. Fuck, she was beautiful.

By the middle of the film, I was doing aight. Leighton was kind of cool, and the little corny ass jokes she made about the movie were kind of funny. I realized she was actually pretty cute, and I was enjoying myself. That was until I got a glimpse of Marquise kissing on Jonaya's neck as his hand started to move up her thigh and under her dress. I felt a sickness in the pit of my stomach like I was about to throw the fuck up, but I also felt a sense of anger flowing through my veins.

"Can y'all pay-a-fucking-tention! Damn! I can't hear for all that kissing and shit!" I barked loudly as hell, making Marquise, Jonaya, Leighton, and a few other movie goers jump.

"Nusef—"

"Fuck this shit." I cut Jonaya off.

"Nigga, what's wrong with you!" I heard Marquise yell, and boy did it take a lot for me not to go back and mop the floor with that bitch ass nigga.

I left the theater, ignoring Jonaya and Leighton calling after me. By the time I got outside into the parking lot, I looked over my shoulder to see Jonaya racing after me, hair blowing in the warm air, looking all good and shit.

"Nusef!" She turned me to face her just as I got to my car, so I leaned up against it and ran my hand down my face. "What happened back there?"

"I'm just... I'm not in the mood for this tonight, Jo." I shoved my hands into my pockets as I leaned back against the car.

"Why? What did she say to you?"

Staring down into her questioning face, I went back and forth with myself, wondering if I should tell her ass the truth. The shit was eating me up at this point. I decided not to. I decided I could get rid of what I felt for her ass in order to save our friendship.

"I just don't wanna do this."

"Why, Sef! Why are you doing this?" she whined. "I ask you to do this one thing for me and this is how you act? Is this because of Rebecca? You're gonna do this to *me*, because of *her*?"

"No, I'm doing this shit because I love you, Jonaya. Damn!" I grunted, angry that I had admitted the shit aloud and to her.

"Right, so if you love me then you will go back in there and finish the date."

I closed my eyes and sighed. Taking my hands from my pockets, I pulled her into me and held the sides of her face. She was confused as she stared up into my eyes, waiting for me to say or do something.

"Baby, I love you like on some real-life shit." My voice was now much lower, low enough so that only she and I could hear.

She frowned at first, but then her facial expression softened once my words had registered.

"No, Nusef, you don't—" She shook her head repeatedly as I held it in my hands.

"Yeah." I nodded. "Yeah I do." I spoke closely against her lips before kissing her slowly. The light pecks we delivered to one another soon turned into lip sucking, and then our tongues came in contact. She held my wrists as I held her face, while we kissed hungrily as hell. I never wanted this shit to stop, but unfortunately for me, she suddenly pulled back.

"Nusef, no. You don't love me. You just... just being here with Leighton—"

"You think I just figured this shit out?" I furrowed my brows. "I've been struggling with this bullshit for months, Jonaya! I can't take it no fucking more, ma."

She stared at me, breathing a bit heavily as she listened.

"I umm, I will tell Leighton that you weren't feeling well," was the last thing she said before she turned around and walked her ass back into the theater. I watched her until I couldn't see her anymore, then got my ass back into the car.

A part of me knew that I'd ruined a friendship that meant a whole fucking lot to me.

22

———————

YIKAYLA

My mother and Buddy were out tonight and wouldn't be back until tomorrow, so my bedroom door was locked, my baby was knocked out, and Waayil and I were lying in my bed. He hated to come over here and lounge in my bedroom because he said no grown ass man should ever do such a thing, but I was tired of him spending his money on hotel rooms when he needed to be saving it for an apartment.

"I've been so caught up in this shit we got going, Yikayla, that I didn't even ask you about your bum ass baby daddy." Waayil sighed as he laid on my stomach. We were naked, in the dark, with only Lonan's mobile providing very minimal light in the room.

"What about him?" I pretended not to understand.

"Did you tell him what's good? I mean, you and little man have been spending every fucking day with me and that nigga hasn't made a peep."

"He's out of town right now, but when he comes back tomorrow, I will tell him."

Roscoe did go out of town for a couple days, but before that, I'd been telling him I was too busy to see him. Even though I didn't want to be with him anymore, the fact that he hadn't popped up over here or at the Waffle House to find out why I hadn't seen him in a minute, alarmed me. And worse, he hadn't seen Lonan either. Something was off and it gave me a weird feeling.

Waayil picked his head up to look at me, pressing his chin into my stomach. His eyes were low as he licked his lips slowly.

"Yikayla, I'm not fucking around with you, shorty. You tell that nigga what's good, or I'm gon' do that shit for you. And if I have to, that muthafucka may leave the crib in a body bag."

"Don't talk like that, Waayil. He's Lonan's father."

"Sure and the fuck don't act like it. Nigga ain't seen his kid in a cool muthafuckin' minute." He laid his head back on me. "He don't even cry for him."

Those six words resonated with me. I never noticed it, but it was true; Lonan had never cried for his daddy. Hell, he didn't even call him daddy. Yet, whenever I left him with my sisters or mother for more than a couple hours, he would always cry for me. The realization of the fact that my baby and his father had no connection gave me a sharp pain in my chest. The simple fact that neither of them missed one another when apart was hurtful. Roscoe was supposed to love our baby just as much as I did.

"I'm sorry, baby, I ain't mean what I said." Waayil interrupted my epiphany, placing a soft kiss on my stomach.

"No, it's okay. It's the truth."

Taking my hand into his, he kissed the palm of it and said, "Don't trip off that shit though. Lonan deserves way better than that nigga. And no matter what, I'm gon' always be here for the both of you, ma."

I blushed at the sound of his words as he kissed my palm again. He rose up and got between my legs, while adjusting the covers over us.

"Got me wondering if... I could swim in your ocean, girl. Silhouette of your hips... got me thinking 'bout stroking, girl..." He sang lyrics from "Malibu Nights" by Eric Bellinger with his beautiful voice as he kissed down my body sensually.

Something about Waayil's velvety vocals always got me in the mood. I loved when he sang and especially when he sang to me.

I closed my eyes and bit down on my lip as the vibrations from his voice passed through his lips and poured out onto my skin. He kept crooning all the way until his mouth was against my pussy, and my thighs sat comfortably on his shoulders.

~

The next afternoon...

Waayil had taken a shower, brushed his teeth, and gotten dressed using the bathroom within my room, and then he got out of here. He said he was booked solid today at the tattoo shop, and usually that would make me sad, but I had a few things of my own to take care of.

I wanted to get in touch with Roscoe so we could have a conversation, and then I had to meet with this lady who owned this fashion house. I wanted to see if I could get some work there, and I didn't mind what it was. I would work my way up.

I showered, brushed, flossed, and rinsed my teeth, then once I got dressed, I cleaned Lonan up and put his clothes on.

"You look so handsome." I smiled and kissed his plump cheek. He was talking my ear off in his own native baby language as I placed him to his feet so he could run wild in my room.

While keeping my eyes on him, I dialed Roscoe and listened as the line trilled... and trilled... and trilled... until finally his voicemail came through.

Roscoe always answered my calls, so I tried again but got the same result. I sent him a text that Lonan and I wanted to see him and to let me know what was a good time for him.

After about two hours of me tidying my room, Roscoe still hadn't responded, so I packed Lonan up so we could go to the grocery store in order to get what I needed to cook for the house tonight since Waayil agreed to eat here with us.

"Have a ball, cutie." I handed Lonan his snacks while I pushed the shopping cart, and he dug right in, stuffing his face, which was hilarious and adorable.

For the first time in ages, I was able to get what I needed without Lonan causing me too much trouble, so after only forty-five minutes, we were back in the car with the groceries and on our way home. My meeting wasn't for another four hours, so I was hoping Roscoe called before then. I checked my phone at a red light but saw nothing.

Just as I was pulling off since the light turned green, another car came from behind me but in another lane, and sped through the intersection. My eyes squinted as I drove behind it, because the car looked just like the one Roscoe bullied his mama out of, and the man in the driver's side looked just like Roscoe. I picked up my phone and dialed him again, but I got no answer, so I followed the car like a crazy person.

I didn't know where he was headed, but wherever we ended up, I planned to let him know what he and I had was over. I would rather wait and let it be in a calm setting like his mother's house, but I didn't want to risk he and Waayil running into one another before I got the chance. I believed Waayil when he said he would kill him.

We pulled onto a residential street, and I slowed down to see where Roscoe would stop. He pulled into the driveway of a home, and then got out of the car to walk to the door. I slowly crept down the street and pulled over into the closest park I could get. I assumed this was a friend's home until Roscoe slipped his key into the screen door to unlock it. Confusion came over me, because I knew his mother hadn't moved this quickly. And if Roscoe had moved, why hadn't he said anything? Plus, how the fuck would he have paid for this spot?

I got out and then unbuckled Lonan before approaching the home. I knocked hard because I wasn't only baffled, I was angry as hell.

"What the fu— Yikayla." Roscoe surprised me when he stepped outside and closed the door behind himself.

"What is this?" I hissed.

Looking from side to side, his eyes landed back on me before he said, "How did you get here? What the hell you doing here, shorty?"

"Roscoe, whose home is this?"

I was ready to slap fire from him.

"It's mine."

"Yours," I repeated skeptically.

"Yep."

"Let me see then—"

"Nah, back the fuck up, Yikayla." He stopped me from trying to go around him and get into the house. Now I was really wondering what the fuck was going on.

"I can't come in? Your son can't see your house, nigga?"

"Baby, I'll get up with you later. Right now, I'm busy with some shit, aight?"

My chest heaved up and down as I stared up at him, wondering how I could sock the shit out of him without possibly harming my baby. I wanted to get inside of this damn house and see what the hell he was hiding.

"Roscoe, if you don't let me in this house... nigga, I swear to God..." I ran my free hand through my hair.

I didn't even know what to say or what violent act I wanted to do at this moment. I just knew I was filled with fury and anxious as hell to knock his ass down like an NFL linebacker. This was the one time I was angry that my son was with me.

"I promise you, it's nothing." He gave me a smile.

Suddenly an idea hit me. I reached into the mailbox and yanked out the stack of letters. Roscoe panicked as I turned my back to him so I could sift through them. I only had one free hand, so I just dropped each letter into the grass once I was done looking. They all were addressed to Roscoe Cousins, but the very last one had a Shamaria Lopez on it.

"Give me my shit!" Roscoe yanked the letter from me and then began picking up the other letters in the grass.

Adjusting Lonan on my hip, I said, "Oh, so you live here with another bitch, Roscoe?"

"No. This is my aunt's house on my father's side, Yikayla. Come on now."

"Right. Sure it is." I nodded. "Well now that you've got *Shamaria Lopez*, I'm free to be with Waayil. I don't feel so bad now that this whole time I've been laid up with him."

"Fuck you say?" Roscoe walked up on me, clutching the letters in his hand and crushing them.

"I said that I've been *fucking* Waayil this whole time, nigga." As he glared down at me, I glared up at him, not flinching at all so he'd know I wasn't scared. "What, you gonna hit me, Roscoe? Go ahead, and then Waayil is gonna beat your ass. Probably kill you too."

Roscoe looked at me like he wanted to punch me, but clearly a part of him was afraid of Waayil because he backed down some.

"You ain't about to play house with my son and that nigga! And you're only fucking him because I've been busy trying to get this bread! You ungrateful ass bitch!"

"No, I fucked him before I even knew you too. He was the one who took my virginity, not some high school boyfriend like I told you." I fake smiled and then started back to my car with Lonan.

"Yikayla! Yikayla!" Roscoe hollered after me with mad bass in his voice. I ignored him all the way to my car.

I buckled Lonan in his seat, then climbed into the driver's side to see Roscoe going back into the house.

I was in love with Waayil, and happy to be with him, but I'd be lying if I said what I'd just *possibly* found out didn't bother me.

23

———

RORI

Gavin and I hadn't talked much at all since I found that piece of hair on his shirt. He'd tried texting and calling me a few times, but I never responded and never answered. I tried to make myself believe that I was ignoring him because of that hair, when in reality it was because I couldn't stop thinking about my and Eko's encounter. Granted, I was suspicious and a little peeved about a female's hair being on my nigga, but with all the people Gavin encountered on a daily due to his line of work, that could have come from anyone.

It seemed like every time I closed my eyes, I thought about Eko and the way his lips felt against mine, or how his strong hands groped me. I didn't understand why I was so on him, when I'd seen and been around the man for a couple years now. It's almost like I was seeing him for the first time, and I hated it.

"You're gonna miss out on your tip if you don't snap out of it." My co-worker, Jodi, smiled and nudged me.

See, I was standing here, coffee pot in hand and not paying attention. I'd cleared it with my mom to work a couple hours this week because my cash was running low now that Gavin hadn't been paying me to handle shit for him.

"Sorry about that. Is there anything else I can get for you guys?" I quizzed my table after serving cup number eighteen of coffee.

"No, just the check, sweetheart." The older man smiled and sighed once his kids started to make a little bit of noise.

I nodded to say "okay" and went to fetch his check. When I did, I heard loud voices of men come into the establishment, and my heart dropped at the sight of Eko and two guys I'd seen before. They worked with Gavin and Eko; I just didn't remember their names.

I watched Eko closely as he surveyed the restaurant looking way too sexy. He was dressed simply in dark jeans, a white t-shirt, and white Nikes, but everything was so fresh and well put together. His hair was tapered on the sides, with a little bit of length at the top. I swore I could smell his scent from all the way over here.

As I watched him, frozen at the computer where I was supposed to be closing out a check, he and I finally locked eyes. I quickly turned my attention back down to the computer, and finished what I was doing.

As I walked the check towards my table, I couldn't help but to watch this waitress named Lisha approach the guys since they were in her section. She, of course, had to gravitate towards Eko, touching his shoulder and laughing way too damn loudly like she wasn't supposed to be professional.

"Have a good day." I spoke to my patrons, and then made my way to Eko's table. "Lisha, they need you in the back to help with dishes," I lied.

With confusion spread all over her face, she replied, "Really? I was just back there."

Not knowing what to say really, I just smiled and patted her back before saying, "I guess Jodi was mistaken."

I could feel Eko checking my body out in my uniform, making me shift from one leg to the other nervously. I gave him a quick glance, then went towards the back because I needed to take a breather. Since my mom owned the place, I had the privilege of being able to sit in her office sometimes, because I knew she wouldn't mind.

KNOCK! KNOCK!

"Yeah?" I called out, rolling my eyes in the process. If this was one of my co-workers bugging me, they were about to get cursed the fuck out.

No one answered, but the door came open and I saw Eko in all of his fine brown-skinned glory. He was looking like a tall glass of water, and I was beyond parched. That same devious smile he gave me the day we kissed, crept across his face as he closed the door behind himself and locked it. He leaned up against it, checking me out as his tongue glided across his bottom lip. I felt my clit throb at the sight of him, and at the memory of what we did last time, even though it wasn't much.

"You look good all dressed up and shit." He grinned, looking around my mom's office at all the stuff that she had on the walls. I admired the smooth way that he strolled towards me as he did so.

"Well, that's the first time I've heard that." I chuckled awkwardly, tensing up as he got closer to the chair I was seated in.

In one motion, he scooped me up and sat me on my mom's desk. Standing in between my legs, he let his hands glide up and down my thighs as he began to kiss on my neck. It suddenly felt like it was 100 degrees in this damn room, and I could already feel my sweat starting to pour a little.

"Eko, we can't. I'm working," I moaned, as he started to pull my thong down slowly. The way his lips pressed against my neck had me ready to burst.

"I've waited too long for this shit, Rori."

His voice was deep and his tone was begging me not to stop him.

We made eye contact and began kissing soon after, as I helped him unbuckle his pants. We only stopped kissing so he could release himself and slide a condom down, then after that, it was on.

He lifted my right leg over his forearm, and brought me closer to the edge of the desk where I could feel the thick head of his dick poking around at my opening. I tensed up slightly, because he was definitely more blessed than Gavin. Eko snickered against my lips at the feel of my body tightening up, and then he pushed his way inside of me.

"Damn," he grumbled, slowly easing more of himself inside of me.

I could feel myself getting wetter and wetter every time he moved in and out. Gripping my body with his free hand, he pulled me closer to his torso and continued to stroke me so good, I thought my eyes would roll to the back of my head. Maybe they had. His kisses were rough, but in a perfect manly kind of way.

"Ahh, ahh," I cried, just before shivering slightly at the feel of my first orgasm.

He pushed my body back some, and I propped myself up using my elbows, as he placed my other leg over his forearm as well. He started slowly fucking me, biting down on his lip as he stared me in the eyes. This nigga knew he was fine, and I could barely take looking at his sexy ass while he did these things to my body.

Yanking me closer to him, he started slamming into me so hard I could barely finish one moan before another interrupted it. As he pounded me with force, subtle moans began to escape his sexy lips as he tossed his head back for a moment. Our bodies crashed together as we cooed and groaned louder than either of us wanted to.

"Uhh, ahhh!" I whined way too loudly, but I didn't care at this point.

Eko leaned down on top of me and kissed me nastily, while continuing to pound me nice and hard. I let out my snivels into his mouth, and he grumbled here and there into mine. Not long after, we were both exploding and yelling out like wild animals.

We laid there kissing for a few moments, and once he raised up and pulled out of me, guilt came pouring over me like a rain shower.

"You have to go." I jumped down off the desk, but then collapsed to the ground because my legs were not ready.

Eko burst into laughter as he cleaned himself with a damp paper towel.

"You sure you don't need my help, shorty?" He cocked his head, licking his lips slowly as he buckled his jeans. How was I around this fine ass specimen for so long and able to control myself?

"No, I don't." I pulled my thong back on while on the floor.

I used my mom's swivel chair to slowly stand up, and then I went to unlock her office door as Eko washed his hands.

"I'm gon' call you," he said, standing in the doorway and towering over me before tossing the paper towel he'd dried his hands with into the trashcan.

"Eko—"

He kissed me slowly a couple times, and I felt my knees buckle a little bit. I watched him walk away, scoping the scene with his fine ass, before I went into my locker to retrieve a feminine wipe. I rushed to the bathroom, ignoring Jodi attempting to scold me, and cleaned myself up after using the bathroom. As I washed my hands in the sink, I shook my head at myself in the mirror.

What the fuck did I just do?

Some Hours Later...

I was finally off work, and the sun had completely set. I was feeling like a straight up and down hoe, so I couldn't wait to get out of the Waffle House and to my bathroom for a hot shower.

"Hey, what were you and that guy up to earlier?" Lisha quizzed me as she got her shit from her locker.

"What guy?" I frowned as if I didn't know.

"The sexy brown-skinned one."

"He knows my boyfriend, so he was just keeping me company on my break." I rarely lied, so this one rolled off my tongue fairly easily.

Lisha nodded, threw her purse over her shoulder, and then closed her locker door.

"I was wondering if maybe you could put in a word for me. I tried to do my own flirting while serving his table, but either I wasn't doing it right or he wasn't attracted to me. I doubt it was the latter." She made a face saying 'yeah right.'

"I will see what I can do." I fake smiled before slamming my locker closed and heading out to leave.

I waved bye to the ladies working the night shift, and stepped outside. As soon as I hit the alarm to unlock my mom's car, my phone rang and Gavin's name flashed across.

Did he know? Eko is such a fucking snitch!

"Hey," I answered, putting my seatbelt on.

"You still mad at me?"

I was caught off guard, thinking he was about to go off on my ass about fucking his best friend. Oh my gosh, I actually fucked his best friend! And in the back of a restaurant! I was one of those girls I tried all my life not to be like. I was another Memphis hoe.

"Rori."

Snapping from my self-ridicule, I replied, "No, no, I'm not mad anymore, Gavin."

"Good. Can I see you tonight?"

"I'm really tired, baby. I just got off work, but tomorrow I'm yours the whole day, okay?"

"You're lucky I love you."

"I love you too."

24

____

EKO BENNET

I inhaled on the junt I was smoking, as I looked myself over in the mirror. I couldn't help but smile at the fact that I had finally busted down Rori's fine ass. I'd been low-key watching her since the day Gavin brought her ass around me. The shit was baffling as fuck to say the least, because I didn't understand what someone like Rori would want with Gavin's ass. Every nigga in Memphis had their eyes on one of them Goode sisters, and the fact that Gavin had somehow came up on one, puzzled the whole crew, not just me.

For years, I stayed in the background, leaving Rori alone because Gavin was my nigga and I wasn't about to step on his toes with one of his bitches; even if they were as fine as Rori. And believe me, Rori was at the top of the food chain when it came to bitches out here. She had deep smooth Hershey skin, shoulder-length curly hair that always looked soft as fuck, and them lips that she always covered in too much muthafuckin' gloss, were perfectly plump. Her body was on some other shit too, and this summer she stayed in short shit that accentuated her ass and thighs. Got damn... But physical attributes aside, Rori was smart as hell too, when it came to school *and* street shit. She was the exact type of bitch every nigga wanted by their side, hood or not.

Anyway, I left Rori alone for years, but when I recently found out that Gavin was trying to play me and have some side deals with other niggas, all that homie shit got thrown out the fucking window. So not only was I about to pull everything that nigga thought he was about to get in this drug shit, but I was gon' take his girl too. I've wanted her ass for this long so I might as well. Plus, he didn't deserve her ass anyway, I did.

I ashed the blunt then went to brush, floss, and rinse my mouth before hopping into the shower. Once out, I wrapped my towel around myself and dialed Rori. She didn't answer, but I called again.

"What, Eko?" She sighed into the phone. She tried to sound upset like I was bothering her, but I could hear the smile in her tone.

"That's how you talk to the nigga that made you cum like that?" I swiped my deodorant on as I waited for her response.

Giggling, she said, "I was hoping to act like it never happened. You know it wasn't supposed to happen, E."

"If it wasn't supposed to happen, it wouldn't have." She was quiet, so I added, "And it's gon' happen again too."

"What? No!"

"Yeah. Tonight. I let you get a couple days to recuperate, but my dick has been asking about you and shit."

We laughed in unison.

"Oh my gosh." She exhaled to herself and then sucked her teeth. "I—"

"What you got on?"

"Eko."

"Tell me. Start from your outfit and then tell me what's under." I licked my lips and leaned up against the dresser in my room as I waited.

"Well... I have on a white dress with no straps—"

"Damn, so no bra?"

"Eko, I could have on a strapless bra."

"But do you?"

"No."

"Your panties, are they like the ones I took off you at the waffle house?"

"Oh my gosh, boy. No, these are solid white thongs."

"Mmm," I moaned subtly to myself, keeping my lips tucked in as a visual of her fine ass entered my mind. "So, tonight. I gotta deal with some shit, and then I can come pick you up to bring you over here."

"You think you can just pick me up to fuck me?"

"Yeah, that's exactly what I think. I'll text you when I'm on my way to you, aight?" There was silence, letting me know she was pondering, so I repeated, "Aight?"

"Yes, Eko."

The way my name sounded in her voice had my dick waking up that easily. I finished getting dressed and when I checked my phone again, I saw Jenni had called me four fucking times.

Jenni was this lil' junt I'd been fucking with pretty heavily, and even went as far as making her my girl, but on the low though. Everything was straight until I found out her ass fucked the homie. She claimed she was sorry and only did the shit because I worked a lot, but I wasn't feeling that bullshit not one bit.

Jenni not being one to give up, worked on my ass for almost a year and finally, I decided to start fucking with her ass again. I wouldn't say she was my bitch because I just didn't see her like that anymore, but she was damn close. My pride just wouldn't allow me to let her get back to where we were, and she knew that shit.

I decided not to call her back because I wasn't really in the mood to deal with her ass. But it was just my luck when I walked outside to see her car parked across the street from my crib. As soon as I stepped out, her homegirl, Kina, got out the car and started switching her thick ass over to me.

"Kina, not today, ma." I put my hand up, not in the mood for any bullshit.

"Why you ain't answering the phone, nigga!" Kina hissed and pointed to Jenni's car. Jenni was in the driver's seat, watching like a little bitch.

That was another thing that made me not want to fuck with Jenni; the bitch let her friends overstep their boundaries, especially Kina's ass. Whenever she had some shit to say to me about what I did that she didn't like, she always sent her guard dog, Kina. Usually how it went is, once Kina said everything Jenni's ass was too scared to say, Jenni would step in.

"I didn't answer because I didn't. Neither one of y'all have the authority to question me, ma, so get the fuck back so I can go."

Kina was blocking my way, and in a minute, I was about to fling her ass into the grass. I was trying to give this hoe a chance to step the fuck out my way, but she was acting like she ain't want that chance.

"What kind of nigga goes two days without hitting his girl up, and then doesn't answer when she calls!"

"Kina, back yo' stupid ass up before I knock the shit out you! I got shit to handle and if I'm late fucking around with you, I'm fucking you and her ass up!" I pointed to the car that Jenni was sitting in.

Jenni got out the car and after glaring at me for a moment, Kina made an about face and sashayed back across the street.

"Girl, he's probably cheating on you, fuck him," I heard Kina say as she got back in the car, while Jenni started towards me.

"Where are you going, Eko?" Jenni whined, jogging up to me. I couldn't stand a meek bitch and Jenni was just that. She was the total opposite of Rori Goode, and now that I'd had a taste of that pussy, Jenni was the least of my muthafuckin' worries.

"I got some work to do. Move," I demanded when she leaned on my car door. She hopped off it quickly as if it were diseased.

"What time are you coming back? I can stay here and clean up and cook and stuff. I'm off work today and—"

"Nah, I'm gon' be late, shorty. But look here, don't bring that bitch 'round here no fucking more, Jenni. Let Kina speak for you one more time, just one…" I put up one finger, "and I'm gon' be done with yo' ass."

She nodded and then smiled before saying, "Give me a kiss."

"Jenni, take yo' ass home."

As I got in my car, she stood there like she was paralyzed or some shit. Some days she annoyed the fuck out of me trying to pretend like what we had was perfect and normal. She fucked up when she let the homie hit, and she needed to act like it. She could go be with that nigga for all I cared.

It was around noon when I left my crib, and I wasn't done making moves until around 6 p.m. Today was about me and taking care of my own shit since Gavin wanted to play games. He was trying to get this plug that *I* fucking found, to work exclusively with his ass, and was trying to get the few dudes we'd recruited to do the same. I honestly didn't know what this nigga's issue was, but I'd get to the bottom of that right before I killed his ass.

I wasn't even interested in this drug shit no more, and was only slanging dope so I could save my cash to buy the barbershop I managed. The owner was old and selling, and he agreed to hold it for me. I got the damn dope plug *for* Gavin's ungrateful hatin' ass, but since I found out he was trying to scheme on a nigga and kick me to the curb before I could bow out gracefully, I was gon' take it all just because.

I'd texted Rori about ten minutes ago, and was hoping her ass wasn't trying to flake or have me waiting too long. I could barely work from thinking about her all day, and I didn't want to be waiting too much fucking longer.

To my surprise, when I pulled up in front her people's crib, she was sitting on the porch with her older sister, Yikayla. I smirked when I saw a smile creep across her face. She couldn't see me because I had some dark ass tint on my shit, but she knew my whip, and the fact that seeing it made her react, had me feeling myself.

"I can't believe I'm about to go to your house." Rori got in and immediately put her seatbelt on. She looked good in that white dress, so I just let my eyes dance all over her for a minute.

"Get used to it. You about to be at my spot all the time." I pulled off down her street and lowered the volume of my music.

"I am?" She was smirking when I glanced over at her.

"Yeah, you are."

"Gavin—"

"Gavin ain't gon' do shit but nod his head and say 'okay'."

She gave me this look that I loved, and then got comfortable in my passenger seat. I guess she'd have to see it to believe it; and trust me, Gavin wasn't gon' do or say shit to stop me from snagging Rori.

25

WAAYIL

"**W**as the pussy good or not?" I laughed as my brother told us some story about this new bitch he'd met. Rebecca's ass had stepped out to handle some errands for the shop, so he took that opportunity to let us in on the shit while she was gone.

"Hold on my nigga, I'm getting there." Nusef put his hand out as myself, Sax, and the homie, Eko, listened in. I knew Eko from back when I used to sell drugs, which was before getting locked up. We used to work for the same nigga, and over time we became somewhat tight.

"Well get there, shit. As fine as this bitch sounds, I need the damn details," Eko chimed in, making us all chuckle.

"Aight, aight. So we get to her crib and shit, and I don't kiss her ass because I'm not no kissing ass nigga—"

"Fast forward, please," Sax interjected.

"Nah, see that's a pivotal part, mane; the fact that I didn't kiss her. Aight, so look. I got the condom on, she riding my dick like a true professional. Then..." He dropped his head and shook it in disappointment.

"Aww shit." I smiled, damn near on the edge of my seat. I knew my brother, so I was sure that whatever he was about to say was somehow a deal breaker for this hoe.

"The bitch leans down in my face to talk that nasty shit, and I swear to God her breath almost took a nigga out. I think I for real passed out for a second."

"What the fuck!" Eko shrieked as we all roared with laughter.

"Nah, for real! The bitch was *literally* talking shit to me. Breath smelled like she'd had a bad case of diarrhea out her mouth, mane."

We were laughing hard as fuck, while Nusef stood there with his lip turned up.

"I would have knocked that bitch off my dick, on God, bruh. No fucking way she'd be riding my dick with funky ass breath. Pussy probably stink too." I shook my head. Hell nah!

"But listen... her body was crazy, pussy was aight, and at the end of the day, I still hit, so." Nusef shrugged.

"I don't think I could have busted, bruh." Eko frowned. "Pretty sure my shit would have gone limp as soon as I got a whiff of that shit."

"Like I said, her body was looking good, so..."

"Did she suck yo' dick?" Sax inquired, and it was silent as we waited for Nusef's response.

"Thankfully no, but I almost asked for some head. I'm glad I didn't though. Would have had my dick smelling like an adult diaper."

"Damn, an adult diaper? Not even a baby's diaper?" I chuckled.

"Fuck no. The shit on that breath was mature as hell."

The four of us laughed loudly as hell at this nigga, just as Rebecca returned with Chiara on her heels. Nusef had finished that damn story just in time. Even though Rebecca wasn't technically his bitch, she took every chance to act like it. In my opinion, he just needed to let that shit go and get Jonaya's ass like he really wanted.

"What's so funny?" Chiara inquired as she came and stood next to me. She would still flirt here and there, I guess hoping to top me off again.

We all said "nothing" simultaneously.

"Aye, I need to holla at you right quick, Waayil." Nusef started towards the back so I followed him, wondering what this was gon' be about.

We got into the back-office area, and he closed the door behind me. He then opened the brown cabinet containing the safe, and put in the combination to unlock it. He retrieved a sealed envelope, then turned around to hand it to me.

"I been meaning to give you that shit but I kept forgetting."

"Fuck is this?" I frowned at the envelope. It was thin and flat as hell, so it couldn't have been no cash.

"Open it, nigga."

I gently ripped the envelope open, and looked inside of it to see a check. When I retrieved it, I saw it was for $30,000 and made out to me. As my eyes scanned the document over and over, I tried to figure out what this shit was for.

"What's up, Sef?"

"That's your cut from the earnings and shit this place made while you were locked up, Waayil." He leaned back against the desk after locking the safe back.

"Nah, man, I can't take this. I didn't even do shit." I reached it out to him.

"You put up half the money for this place. I made $60,000 as the owner, and since you're co-owner, you get half. Waayil, this ain't a handout, this ain't some shit I'm throwing you because I'm balling, this is yo' damn money. If you hadn't agreed to give me your inheritance to invest in this shit, I wouldn't have gotten that $60,000."

I stared at my brother for a moment, letting his words sink in and contemplating whether or not I wanted to take this money. I didn't like getting shit from nobody, not even my own family. I hated when I was locked up and had to depend on people to put money on my books, but I had to quickly get over that shit. But now that I was out, I was determined to get back to how I was, doing shit on my own.

"Aight." I finally nodded and his ass smiled widely as hell before trying to hug me. "Get back, nigga."

"You better give me a hug, nigga. What you think we was doing in the womb together?"

"The fuck?" I laughed. "I damn sho wasn't hugging yo' ass, my nigga. I was doing my own shit, chilling."

"Nah, we was in that muthafucka cuddled the hell up and you know it. Bring that shit in, Yil." He yanked me to him for a hug, but I quickly pushed his ass back.

"So what's up with you and Jo?"

Shaking his head and sighing, he said, "Nothing, bruh. I umm, I told her how I felt and she reacted just like I knew she would. Jonaya ain't the relationship type."

"Neither are you, Sef."

"Yeah, but I was willing to try that shit with her. But it's whatever, I'll get over that shit and just umm..." He looked off. "I'll be good, and she'll be good."

"So you gon' be with Rebecca?"

"I don't know."

I talked with my brother for a little longer and then decided to leave while it was still light. I didn't have many clients today, on purpose, because I wanted to check on my peoples. I was glad I did that because now that I had this check, I wanted to see about getting a bank account. Nusef said he had all the records and receipts to account for this money, so if me spending it raised any red flags, we'd have the proper documentation to prove it as legit money I'd made. I was happy to know that shit because I needed to get on an apartment or something, ASAP.

"Heeeey... so are we like not okay anymore?" Chiara caught up to me outside of the shop in the parking lot.

"Why wouldn't we be?" I moved my hand from hers and she chuckled lowly at my movement.

"Because of stuff like that. It's almost like you're okay until you get your dick sucked. Is that how you do every girl you have a sexual encounter with?" She was cute when she was mad, which made me smile. She returned the gesture, and then rolled her eyes like she was disappointed in herself for doing so. "Those dimples and that smile get me every time, Waayil."

"We straight, Chiara, but you don't know me, ma. I'm not the most talkative muthafucka; that's my brother. Not to mention, I got a girl and I don't really want her knowing what we did and that we still interact and shit. So just be easy, shorty. We ain't gon' ever be best buddies."

"You had a girl when I did what I did?"

"I had a girl, but she ain't the one I'm with now. I was working on the one I'm with now when it happened."

"So you completely skipped over me." She pointed to herself and I shrugged.

"If that's how you see the shit."

"Can I at least have a hug before you go."

Licking my lips, I took in the damn near perfect shape of her body in that dress. I was low-key kicking myself for not smashing before I got with Yikayla. It wasn't worth it now, but damn was I tripping for not seeing what that pussy was about.

"Yeah, come here."

She damn near knocked me back as she moved closer to me.

I put my arm around her shoulders, but she stopped me and said, "No like this." She hugged my neck, and then used one of her arms to put mine around her midsection. "If this one doesn't work, don't skip over me, okay?" she whispered before I let her go.

She turned and switched back into the shop, and I was pretty sure she didn't have on any damn panties. Her ass was jiggling way too much... in a very good way.

I left the shop and went straight to my parents' house since I was gon' pick Yikayla up in a minute anyway. When I walked inside, I saw them sitting on the couch together. My mom was watching television and my pops was reading the paper.

"Y'all still doing the same shit?" I chuckled and my mom turned to look at me before smiling.

"Yes we are."

I leaned down to kiss her cheek, and then I hugged my pops before asking, "Where is Wednesday?"

"Oh, she's in the backyard with her friend."

I headed towards the back and when I pushed open the sliding door, I saw Wednesday sitting on the pool chair with some nigga, and they were kissing as if they were about to fuck in a minute.

"Ah!" The nigga yelped when I snatched his ass up by his collar and tossed him onto the ground by the pool.

"Waayil, what are you doing!" Wednesday shouted as she stood up and wiped her mouth.

"Fuck you doing back here, Wednesday? You think you about to fuck this nigga?" I pointed to his weak ass. "Man, get the fuck up and get yo' ass out of here before I fuck you up!" I barked and he scrambled to his feet.

"Wednesday, I—"

The sound of me taking the safety off my piece cut that nigga's sentence off real quick.

"Fuck I just say, bruh?" I pressed it to the back of his nappy ass head and he threw his hands up in mock surrender.

"Waayil!" my mother shouted as she rushed into the backyard with my father right behind her. The look in their eyes at the sight of my gun made me feel bad, but I didn't care enough to put it away. I was protective as hell over my baby sister, and I'm sure everyone had gotten that damn message by now.

"Okay, okay, I'm leaving," the little nigga all but whimpered.

My mother gently placed her hand on him, and started escorting him back towards the house. I finally put the safety back on my heat, and locked it into my waist.

"Stop all that fucking crying, Wednesday! Fuck you want with some bitch ass nigga like that anyway, huh?" I hissed as she sobbed uncontrollably.

"Waayil, what is wrong with you?" My father's brows dipped.

"Nah, what the fuck is wrong with yo' ass? She back here about to get fucked and y'all inside chilling like it's nothing!"

"We didn't know!"

"Just like y'all didn't know about bitch ass Harry!" The shit came out before I could think, and even though I didn't mean to say it, the shit was true. My parents were too fucking lax sometimes.

"Waayil, she doesn't need that brought back up again."

I shook my head and then squatted down to be eye level with Wednesday, who was sitting on the lounge chair crying hard as hell.

"Aye, aye, listen, baby, I'm sorry. You know how I feel about you, right?" I asked, and she nodded before sniffling. "You don't need to be doing that shit with these dudes. You need a nigga that's gon' have respect for you and one that ain't gon' run instead of standing his ground."

Wednesday nodded somberly, so I kissed her cheek and then hugged her tightly. She finally hugged me back.

"You're crazy." She giggled in between sniffles.

"Just about you. I love you, and I'm sorry, aight?"

She smiled and nodded again as my father rubbed her hair back.

26
———

ALBA

It'd been almost a month since I'd last talked to and seen Waayil. I didn't know what to do with myself, and I honestly was surprised. I loved him more than anything, but I'd been without him for way longer than a month before and didn't feel this sick. I guess it was because at least I was talking to him then. Now, we hadn't said a word to one another, and I felt like I had an empty space somewhere inside of me.

In the meantime, Gavin and I had been fucking like dogs in heat so that I could get pregnant. I would usually get some dick from him, make small talk so he wouldn't complain, and then send him on his way to his little girlfriend. Honestly, I was hoping I was pregnant already because I was dead tired of fucking him and listening to his weak ass go back and forth about how much he loved his girlfriend and didn't want to hurt her. It took so much for me not to just tell him I was only using him and that he could stay with her for all I cared.

"I got my fingers crossed." Ashley exhaled nervously as I read the packaging of the pregnancy test. This was the first one I'd bought since Waayil threatened me, and I definitely felt like I needed a prayer at this point.

"Here we go."

I sat on the toilet and then peed right on the stick, eyes closed, praying God came through for me. He knew how much I loved this man, and how badly I needed a baby to be growing inside of me. I was on a time limit, and if I didn't get pregnant soon, Waayil would know my child wasn't his by the timeline. I knew if I was a few weeks or even a month off I would be fine, but any more than that and Waayil was as good as gone.

"Won't he be suspicious that you're just now agreeing to take a pregnancy test?" Ashley frowned as I washed my hands.

"I'm just gonna tell him I was angry with him for thinking I would lie, but now I've realized our child needs a father so I will do what he has asked."

I had already thought up that part of the plan. I mean, Waayil was no dummy, so I knew I couldn't just walk up to him willing to pee on a stick a month later. So, I got my reasoning together and rehearsed it in the mirror until *I* damn near believed it.

"Damn, well I hope he believes—"

"He will believe it, Ashley! Damn! Stop being so fucking negative! It's almost like you don't want me to have Waayil!"

"What? No! Of course I want you to!"

"Bitch, I better not find out that you're running your fucking mouth about my plan or I swear to God I will have you handled," I gritted in her face as she stared at me with wide eyes.

"Alba, I swear I wouldn't do that to you!"

I opened my mouth to throw out another threat, but my iPhone timer beeped, letting me know the test was ready. I quickly turned around and leaned over the sink to look at it. My heart started to beat rapidly as I saw the word pregnant bright as day in the window.

"Oh shit! Oh my gosh!" I screeched.

"You're pregnant?" Ashley moved further into the bathroom smiling.

"Yes! Thank you, Jesus!" I put my hands up in the air, holding the test in one of them. "Do you think I should take another just in case?"

"False positives are rare to impossible, so I think you're good."

I nodded in agreement as I stared down at the test, before placing it into my medicine cabinet.

"Looks like my plan is in motion, Ashley."

Later that day...

I stayed home most of the day, way too damn nervous to approach Waayil. I kept going over everything in my mind, making sure I didn't have any loopholes in my story. If Waayil caught me in a lie, especially one of this caliber, we would be over for good. Not to mention, I honestly think he would whoop my ass. I'd seen Waayil fight on many occasions, and I would never want to be on the receiving end of his punches.

"What time is he coming?" Ashley bit into her piece of chicken.

"In like ten minutes." I paced the living room. "When he gets here you need to leave or... no, I guess he and I can go talk in the bedroom or something." I was beyond skittish, and if Waayil saw me like this, he would know something was up. "I need a shot."

"Alba, you can't. What about the baby?"

"It's not even a fucking baby yet. It's like a damn pumpkin seed!" I spat as if I really knew. I hadn't the slightest clue about what the baby looked like in this stage. I didn't even know how long I'd been pregnant.

"Still, you should start eliminating your habits now so you won't have to go cold turkey, you know?"

"I'm sorry, what kind of doctor are you?" I poured the Patrón into a shot glass and tossed it back, not bothering to look at Ashley when I spoke. I heard her exhale in response.

KNOCK! KNOCK!

"Shit!"

I hurriedly looked for a place to put the Patrón and shot glass, while Ashley hopped up and rushed to the back with her food. I shoved the liquor bottle and shot glass behind one of my plants, and then tested my breath to make sure it wasn't potent.

"Hey, baby." I smirked as I opened the door for Waayil.

Damn did he look good. He had on basketball shorts, a hoodie, socks, and slides, and he smelled so good. His coffee colored skin looked so vibrant and clear, and his thick lips made me lick mine from thinking about kissing them. Hopefully after my news, I would be.

"What's good? Let's make this shit quick." He handed me a plastic bag containing a pregnancy test.

I grabbed his hand and tried to lead him to the back, but he snatched from me. He continued to trail me to the bathroom, and stood in the doorway as I ripped open the packaging. I urinated on the stick, and then set it on the counter before washing my hands.

"I've missed you," I said while we waited. Typical Waayil didn't respond, he just looked me dead in the eyes with no enthusiasm whatsoever. "I umm, I took so long to do this because I was angry with you for thinking I would lie about this. It hurt my feelings. But I finally came to my senses and realized that our baby needs us both, and I can't shut you out—"

"It's been five minutes."

I stared up at him, wanting to slap him for cutting off the speech I'd taken so damn long to prepare.

I picked the stick up without looking at it, and showed it to him.

He simply looked at it and then said, "Come in here and let me get at you for a minute."

Nervously, I checked the test and breathed a sigh of relief when I saw the two pink lines. Cheap ass couldn't even get the digital test like I had.

I followed him to the living room, and we both took a seat on my couch. Pushing his hood off his head, he exhaled and then looked at me. His pretty eyes seemed to shoot right through me as he nibbled on his lip. Why was this man so unbelievably fine? Jail seemed to only enhance everything that he already was.

"To be honest, ma, I don't know whose baby this is that you're carrying right now, but because it could be mine, I'm gon' help you out here and there. Don't be expecting the works because like I said, it could be the next nigga's child and—"

"Waayil, no it's not! I have only been with you since we got together almost eight years ago!"

Ma, stop," he pleaded with a frown like he was annoyed as hell. "This is me, Alba. You honestly think I'm gon' believe that while I was locked up away from you, you weren't getting dick from the next muthafucka? Come on, shorty."

The fact that he didn't believe me angered me. So what if he was right, it still pissed me off. I bet he wouldn't think this way of Yikayla if she had been his bitch when he got locked up.

"Whatever, Waayil. You're only saying this because you've always thought the worst of me."

"Anyway, like I said, I'm gon' help you a little and then when shorty gets here, we gon' have a DNA test ran on it. If it comes back as mine, I'm gon' step all the way up, I promise. If it's not, I suggest you leave me the fuck alone afterwards because I'm bound to snap yo' fucking neck if you don't."

"Waayil, the baby needs to see us together."

"Nah, it doesn't, and it won't. Alba, I love Yikayla, and I always have, well before I went to jail. That's who the fuck I'm gon' be with, and I don't wanna hear shit else about it. I'm sorry for making you think otherwise because that shit was wrong of me, but stop making it seem like we had this great love because we didn't. You don't love me, Alba, you love the idea of being with me, and that's totally different."

His words were making me angry, so angry that tears began to spill from my eyes. I felt defeated, like there was nothing I could do to convince him to be with me. I did love him. I mean what was love anyway? I wanted to be with him even when I thought he'd be in jail for the rest of his life, isn't that love?

"You don't know what you're talking about, Waayil. And you can leave now since I so called don't love you." I pouted and sat back against the couch.

Like always, he didn't say a word, he just rose to his feet and left.

It frustrated me to no end that I couldn't make him love me or treat me the way I wanted him to. I have never wished to control somebody so much in my life. Some nights, I'd even contemplated having someone do something to Yikayla, but I was way too fine and sexy to go to jail. Plus, she wasn't worth me never seeing the outside again. I just didn't know what to do.

At the same time, the two most annoying ass people interrupted my thoughts. Ashley came from my bedroom looking like a deer in headlights, and Gavin was calling me.

"What happen—"

"Hello?" I cut Ashley off when I answered my phone.

"Sup, ma, I ain't talk to you in three days," Gavin replied.

"I've been busy. What do you need?"

"To see you, to feel you. We can work on that baby some more. You ain't pregnant yet, right? I wish you were because—"

"No, Gavin, I'm not pregnant. I think you have a low sperm count or something because I *should* be pregnant by now."

"Fuck does a low sperm count mean?"

Rolling my eyes, I said, "Gavin, I'm tired, okay?"

My eyes followed Ashley as she came and sat on the couch next to me.

"Maybe because you're pre—"

"I'm not pregnant, alright!" I shouted at the top of my lungs. "Give me some space and spend time with your girlfriend! I need to rethink if I even wanna be with you."

I hung up in the middle of his sentence. Now that I was pregnant, I didn't need him anymore. I wasn't gonna give up on Waayil, and by the time I had him wrapped around my finger, the DNA test would be the least of his worries.

27

———

JONAYA

"**S**hit," Marquise groaned as he wound his hips between my legs. I laid there, not even in the moment, as Nusef danced around in my head. What happened at the movie theater was still fresh on my mind, even though he and I hadn't really talked. I felt like I could barely function in my relationship with Marquise because my mind was now on someone else.

I didn't know if I loved Nusef the same, or what, but whatever it was, we couldn't let it ruin a friendship that we'd built over the years. I wasn't even used to not talking to him for this long.

"Jo." Marquise got my attention.

I was staring up at the ceiling as he lay on top of me, so I shifted my head a little to look into his eyes. He just stared at me for a few moments before pressing his lips against mine.

"What's wrong?" I quizzed.

"I'm doing this and you're acting like it's not happening." He chuckled but I could tell that me not moaning and acting like he was rocking my world bothered him. Like I said, the sex with Marquise was good, great even on occasions, but I wasn't really in the mood to do anything with anyone, which was a first for me.

"I'm sorry. It feels good. Keep going."

He did as I asked, kissing on my neck and jaw as he moved in and out of me. I tried to keep my mind on the task at hand, and when I succeeded in doing that, it did feel good. When Marquise began to go faster, getting my spot with every stroke, Nusef reentered my mind yet again, but I was instead imagining what it'd be like to experience this with him. My eyes shot open, hoping that the sight of Marquise would remove such disrespectful thoughts of the man who was supposed to be like my brother.

"Oh fuck," Marquise trembled violently as he let loose into the condom.

He panted heavily with his left hand pressed against the headboard I'd convinced him to buy, and then finally, he rolled off of me. After lying there for a few moments, breathing like a bear, he removed the condom and went to the bathroom to clean himself up. When he returned, he tried to clean me, but I stopped him and went to the bathroom alone. I peed, and was about to clean between my legs but decided to just take a shower. I was hoping Marquise would be knocked out by the time I finished.

When I returned to the bedroom to slip on my nightshirt, I caught a glimpse of my iPhone. I picked it up, contemplating whether or not I should send a text to Nusef, but I saw he had sent me one. I couldn't believe the immediate smile that graced my face upon seeing his name.

Boo Bear: *If you're wondering, I still love yo' ugly ass.*

I chuckled a little too loudly, because I heard Marquise stir in his bed.

I was gonna reply, but I knew he meant real love and not best friend love, so I didn't know what to say. I just locked my phone and slipped it into my purse.

"Who was that?" Marquise questioned as soon as I slid into the bed.

"Wednesday," I quickly lied.

"You ever talk to Sef about how he came at me?"

"Aren't you guys friends? You knew him before you knew me, so why can't you talk to him?" I frowned even though my back was to him. I was tired and didn't want to discuss this.

"Because the nigga acts like he don't fuck with me no more. Ever since I started fucking with you, his ass is either too busy or he don't respond to texts and calls."

"Well, he has been pretty busy now that his brother is back. And the shop has been booked like crazy."

"So you don't think he wants you and is hating on me?"

"No, Marquise. For one, if Nusef wanted me, he could have been made a move. Secondly, Nusef doesn't get jealous of any nigga."

"You sound like you're defending his ass, and I don't know how to feel about it."

"Feel however you want. He's like my brother, so of course I'm going to defend him. He's not the jealous type, especially of another man. Plus, I've told Nusef about guys I've been with and he never cared or got mad."

I was really going to bat for Nusef even though what Marquise was saying was true.

"Humph." Marquise sighed. "I'll let his ass slide this time, but if I feel like he's coming for me over you or anything else having to do with fucking up what we got, I'm beating his ass."

I snickered lowly by accident at the thought of Marquise beating up Nusef. He knew damn well that wouldn't happen. I'd never seen Marquise fight, and I'm sure he did well for himself, but the Christian twins were nothing nice, and I'm sure he knew that as well as I did.

"Goodnight, baby," I said before shutting my eyes.

I hope all of this soon passed.

～

The Next Morning...

I woke up to the smell of some kind of food, so I knew Marquise was making breakfast. I was overjoyed because I was definitely hungry.

Climbing out of bed, I immediately grabbed my phone from my purse to check and see if I had any messages from Nusef again. When I saw there were only texts from Leighton, Wednesday, and my sister, Dree, I exhaled. I don't know why I expected Nusef to hit me up again when I hadn't responded to his text from last night.

Placing my phone down on top of my purse, I went to the bathroom so I could pee, then brush, floss, and rinse my mouth. I showered again, and once I was finished putting on my lotion, I returned to Marquise's bedroom with my things. I didn't want to spend the night tonight again, because I wanted to be away from him. He hadn't done anything per se, but I just wasn't in the mood for his company.

"What are you doing?" I marched towards Marquise who had my iPhone in his hand, scrolling and reading something. I snatched my phone from him and shoved the shit out of his ass.

"I knew that nigga wanted you, and you up here pretending like I'm the muthafucka tripping!" he barked.

"Why the hell are you looking in my phone, fool?" I glanced down to see where he'd gotten in my messages, and it wasn't far, thankfully. He only really saw the message from last night.

"I looked in that shit because I knew yo' ass was lying for that nigga. But I'm gon' holla at his ass and get shit straight."

"Marquise, Sef and I say we love each other all the time. Him sending this is normal, so there is no point in you talking to him about anything." I slipped my panties on, then dug in my bag for the short dress I was gonna wear.

I wanted Marquise to think I was trying to protect Nusef, but really, I was trying to save him from an ass whooping and embarrassment. I can't say with confidence that I would still be attracted to him after watching Nusef fuck him up, so it was best I attempt to prevent it.

"Well we gon' have to see." He slammed his drawer closed after pulling out an all-black t-shirt.

It was like we were racing to see who could get dressed the quickest. By the time he had his jeans and shoes on, I had my purse and duffle bag thrown over my shoulders. As he snatched his keys from the dresser, I slipped my feet into my Fenty Puma slides, and raced after him. My hair was still up in a bun which was basically half ponytail too, but I didn't really care.

"I will never forgive you if you don't take me straight home." I pouted once I was in the passenger seat of his car.

"And you expect me to think that you don't have feelings for him? You're threatening to not fuck with me no more over another nigga, ma? Really?" Marquise frowned as he sped down his street, headed towards the tattoo shop.

God, please let his tire bust or drain all of the gas from his car. Amen.

"Because he is my best friend! I don't want you guys arguing or fighting!"

"Well too bad! And if nothing is going on with his ass, then it won't be a fight or no damn arguing. He just gon' hear me out and tell me straight up that nothing is going on."

I wanted to claw his fucking face right now as he continued on to Monarch Tattoo. In no time, he was pulling into the parking lot of the shop.

As if God had hit the snooze button on my prayer, Nusef was posted up outside of the shop with one of the tattoo artist girls named Venus. Nusef looked good as hell in only a wife beater, some jeans that weren't too baggy, and some Nike Huaraches. Tattoos covered his strong cognac tinted arms, and that wife beater was holding onto his chest and abs for dear life. He looked so fine and gangsta.

Oh my gosh, am I really looking at Nusef like that?

He lowered his lids upon seeing Marquise's car pull up, and I could see the beautiful honey color of his eyes brighten once he saw me in the passenger seat. Venus was watching too, and I guess it was because of how ferociously Marquise had whipped up into the lot.

"Marquise!" I hollered as he and I both got out of the car. He already looked dumb as hell because he was storming up to Nusef who was still calm. He didn't even feel the need to prepare himself for an obviously angry Marquise.

"Why you sending 'I love you' texts and shit to my girl?" Marquise hissed.

"Marquise!" I pulled on his arm.

"Because I felt like it," Nusef responded nonchalantly. He licked his sexy lips as he leaned up off the wall he was on and said, "What you gon' do about it?"

Marquise, face twisted into a knot damn near, shoved Nusef back hard, and before I could even say anything, Nusef socked the shit out of him.

"Oh shit!" Venus commented, backing up some so she wouldn't encounter whatever else Nusef had in store.

Marquise damn near hit the ground as blood poured from his lip and nose. How the fuck did Nusef get his mouth *and* nose with one hit? Shit, I don't know. This whole scenario was baffling as hell right now.

"Get up, bruh. You got a problem with what I text yo' girl, then do something about it, bitch." Nusef moved slowly towards Marquise who was clearly still dazed and confused.

WHAM!

Marquise dumbly swung on Nusef, and then got punched again, sending him flying onto the hood of somebody's car.

"Uh uh! Y'all niggas need to get a damn grip!" Some woman ran out of the beauty shop next door with foil in her hair. "Fighting by *my* damn car," she fussed as she inspected her vehicle. By this time, a few people from every establishment in this shopping center were outside, commenting, snapping pictures, filming, and chuckling.

Marquise slid down off her car onto the ground, groaning like a weakling. He had my pussy so dry it was ridiculous. I knew this was gon' happen. When I saw Nusef inching closer, but slowly to give Marquise time to gain some composure, I hopped between them.

"Move, Jonaya." Nusef gritted angrily, hazel eyes shooting through me like a million knives. The sun had his dark skin looking like fresh fudge ready to drizzle on a sundae.

"No, just stop this! He and I are gonna leave!"

"Y'*all* gon' leave, huh?" Nusef chuckled and stared off for a moment before regaining eye contact with me. "So the fact that I love you don't mean shit, huh?"

"Sef, I—"

"Nah, take yo' little bitch of a boyfriend and get up outta here before I kill his ass."

I nodded graciously and helped Marquise to his feet. I was scared to pass Nusef in fear of him hitting Marquise again, so Nusef backed away and went back inside the shop. I continued on towards Marquise's car, and put him in the passenger side before rounding the car and getting in on the driver's.

As I changed the gear shift into reverse, I shook my head at all the people who had come out of the surrounding businesses to watch my man get his ass whooped.

28

YIKAYLA

"I'm gonna need these five racks finished come Tuesday afternoon. Do you think you can do that for me?" my boss, Jerica, explained and inquired.

"Of course."

"Thank you, Yikayla. I'll be in my office for the rest of the day, so just let me know when you leave, okay?"

After meeting with Jerica about possibly working for her design house, she hired me right on the spot. I didn't know if she would at first because when she found out that I didn't go to fashion school, she seemed a little turned off. I think my book of designs is what kept her interested, even though that wasn't part of my job.

Here at Jerica Rose Fashion, all I did was steam dresses. I knew I would have to work my way up, and I just hoped I wasn't doing this shit for too long. On the up side, I made a nice amount of money, $500 a day, which was due to my experience with fashion and my degree.

The only thing I didn't like about that, is that it was a fixed rate. I got $500 a day no matter how many hours I worked, which wasn't good if a long day hit me. Jerica required that I work at least four days a week, and at least five hours. That wasn't too bad at all, especially because literally, all I did was steam the dresses she designed, and some days I would make drop offs if her assistant was too tied up.

"Do you like hot chocolate? It's Mexican style." This girl named Brynn smiled and held up a hot coffee cup.

I couldn't really call Brynn my co-worker because she didn't do what I did, and since I've been here, which has only been a week, we hadn't had any jobs together. All she did was make calls and book appointments for Jerica to meet with clients. And she told me she made $300 a day, which was obviously less than me.

"What's Mexican style?" I smiled, placing the steamer down gently. It was really expensive and I didn't need any parts of it having to come out of my damn check.

"Just with cinnamon and spices. Here, try it. I ordered one, but the guy at the coffee shop likes me so he gave me two. I'm not sure why he thought giving me two drinks would get him my number."

"Poor thing." I giggled before sniffing and then taking a sip. It was pretty good, so I gave her a nod and then set it on my desk. I expected her to leave, but she walked further into my area.

"So how did you get this position?" She folded her arms and leaned up against the wall.

"Excuse me?"

"Well I mean, I applied to work with Jerica and I get stuck making calls and booking appointments, while you get to do this. And you make more money than me. You know, some of her clients are big deals, and you get to meet them when you do drop offs."

"The people I have dropped off to, have not been anybody important. Just old rich women, or young girls who have wealthy parents."

"Yeah, that's because you haven't been here long."

"Well you get to talk to them when they call."

"No I don't. I speak to their *assistants* and nothing more. I've been here for a month and I honestly don't think it's fair that you get this position."

"Well, Brynn, I have a lot of work to do, and that sounds like something you need to discuss with Jerica, not me."

She stared at me, with the tip of her tongue hitting her molars like she was appalled before saying, "Am I sensing attitude, Yikayla? I'm simply trying to have a conversation."

"One, I don't care to have with you. And I don't care what you sense. Like I said, I have work to do. And in order for me to collect my *bigger* check, I need to handle it, so please." I gestured for her to go.

She rolled her eyes and snatched back the hot chocolate she gave me off my desk, before storming out.

I had a feeling her ass wouldn't be here much longer, so I wasn't gonna sweat that little encounter one bit. If she had a real problem, she could see me away from the work place.

I closed the door of my office area, and then got right back to work. By 6:30 p.m., I had three of the four racks done, which I was happy about. Since Jerica didn't need them until Tuesday, I would just take the rest of the weekend off to look into some fashion classes, and then do the last rack Monday.

After picking up my daily check from Jerica, and explaining my plans, I went to deposit the check in my bank account and headed home.

Tonight, there was a house party in Orange Mound, and everybody was gonna be there. This was the type of house party where niggas got caught up by their main chick and their side chick, where bitches and niggas handled their beefs, and where people who had been eyeing one another for a minute fucked around in the bathroom. It sounded messy as hell, and sometimes I wondered why I even bothered, but they were just so much damn fun. I couldn't wait to let loose.

When I walked into my house, I heard "Mobbin" by Adrian Marcel blasting from Jonaya's room, so I knew that meant she was getting ready.

"Be quick, because all the shit will be picked over if we get there too late." Rori passed me in the hallway to her room, wearing a little dress.

"I see you're taking the hoe role tonight," I joked, and she looked over her shoulder at me, frowning playfully.

I knew I didn't have much time, but I was a mother before anything, so I got my baby from my mom then fed and bathed him. By the time I had him in his onesie to sleep in, I had made up in my mind what I was gonna wear, which saved me time.

"Stay right here until Mommy finishes her shower, okay?" I placed Lonan in the middle of my bed. He ignored me as he kept his eyes on the movie I'd put on for him to watch.

I showered in my bathroom with the door open, and once out, I quickly spread lotion all over me while keeping my eyes on my baby. Once I was done dressing, he was sprawled out in the middle of my bed with his pacifier damn near hanging out of his mouth, so I placed him in his crib and took the baby monitor to my mom.

"That outfit is cute, Yikayla. I may have to borrow that." My mother took the monitor from me and turned it up. Buddy was knocked out, still clutching one of the biggest beer cans I'd ever seen in his hand.

"Then I'll be hiding this as soon as I take it off," I joked, and she and I laughed in unison. "Bye, Ma." I kissed her and then left out, but not before checking myself out in her full-length mirror.

I decided to wear a long-sleeved crop top, with matching pants of the same material. It was a deep green, so I threw on my Fenty Puma Creepers in green to match. I let my hair hang freely like I always did.

"'Bout time, bitch." Dree sucked her teeth once I made it to the den downstairs where all my sisters were.

"Dree, you're not even going." I laughed at her.

She shrugged with a smile and sipped some of her water.

Jonaya surprised me by wearing jeans and a tube top. She usually always went for the shortest item in her closet, but I guess she left that to Rori this time.

The three of us left, and I drove us to the liquor store to get our own drinks just in case. Most times these parties had closed bottle drinks, but sometimes punch was all they had and I wasn't trying to get slipped something, even though my man was gonna be there. I could see it now, some nigga trying to sneak me to his car and Waayil shooting the place up.

We were dancing to "Naked in the White House" by Eric Bellinger when I pulled up to the party, and luckily, I found a park not too far from the house. People were all up and down the street, and the house the party was in had the door wide open. You could hear the music loud and clear, and I knew it wouldn't be long before people complained and got it shut down. But until then, it was time to have fun.

We could barely get to the house because of all the can-I-get-a-hug ass niggas outside. We ignored most of them except the guys we knew, and then went right inside. The house was already hot as hell, full of smoke, and people were grinding against one another as "Bounce Back" by Big Sean blasted.

My sisters and I held hands as we moved through the crowd, not wanting to lose one another. When we found a good spot, the three of us began to dance as well. A few guys approached me trying to dance, but I was too afraid for their lives to accept.

Just as I shooed the last one away, I heard a bit of ruckus and saw Waayil, Nusef, Sax, and Eko walk through the door. Waayil looked so sexy, scoping the party with a frown. I knew he was looking for me, as he and his crew made their way further into the party. Nusef and Jonaya made awkward eye contact, which was weird. They usually always embraced or said something slick to one another, but they barely spoke before Nusef kept walking to greet some other people.

Eko led Rori off somewhere, and her ass followed with no questions. I was sure that Gavin wouldn't appreciate that, but maybe that's where Eko was taking her to. Then again, I'm pretty sure that was his car she'd gotten into that night we were out on the porch. Rori wasn't the type to cheat or mess with someone so close to her man, so

I was trying to figure out what the hell was going on, because it couldn't have been what it looked like.

"Hey." I smiled way too widely as Waayil threw his arm around my shoulder and kissed me.

His big hand gripped my waist as he pulled me closer to his body. He smelled so good and looked so perfect. The music was loud as hell and people were rowdy, but my attention was on him as we delivered sweet pecks to one another like it wasn't a damn zoo in here.

We walked over to where Nusef was along with Sax and some other guys and girls. Jonaya followed, and her boyfriend Marquise walked right up as well. He kissed Jonaya on the lips and then draped his arm around her.

"Get from over here, my nigga," Waayil spoke as I sat in his lap. I looked back at him to see he was staring right at Marquise.

"What?" Marquise and Jonaya said together.

"I said get the fuck from over here by us. Didn't you just square up with my brother? Don't come trying to kick it." Waayil frowned deeply.

"Waayil." Jonaya gave him a look.

"If I have to move my girl from my lap just to handle you, I'm gon' be real upset." Waayil spoke calmly, and after a few short seconds, Marquise stormed off. Jonaya, of course, followed him, and the look on Nusef's face when she did was priceless.

Jonaya returned about five minutes later without Marquise, scowling hard before sitting next to me and Waayil. Rori and Eko came over as well, looking like they had just gotten into a fight with some bears. Both Jonaya and I gave her a look, but she pretended not to see and began singing along to "Mask Off" by Future.

I leaned back into Waayil's chest, and danced a little as he kissed on my neck and locked his arm around my waist. After a while, everyone started to calm down and enjoy themselves, even Jonaya.

POP! POP!

"Aahh!" people screamed and scrambled around at the sound of two gunshots, and the chandelier falling down onto a couple people before breaking. Waayil had tossed me behind him so quickly, that I wasn't even sure how he'd done it. When I looked towards the door, I saw it was Marquise holding a gun, along with some other guy.

"Oh, you about to kill somebody?" Waayil chuckled as he started towards him. The music was now off, and everyone was still as hell.

"Waayil, come back," I whimpered, not knowing what the fuck Marquise was gonna do.

"Marquise!" Jonaya hissed, a little bit of fear in her voice.

"I came to warn yo' bitch ass brother," Marquise spat. "He needs to leave my girl alone."

"Warn me then, nigga," Nusef called out, walking towards Marquise like Waayil had done.

"Don't pull yo' shit out if you not gon' use it, bruh." Waayil laughed as if everyone else wasn't about to shit on themselves. "See this right here." I could tell Waayil lifted his shirt to expose his gun, even though his back was to me. "If I pull this from my waist, I'm sending one through yo' dome, muthafucka. So I'm gon' give you 'bout five seconds to get up out of here before I do that."

With his chest heaving up and down and nostrils flared, Marquise was looking like a raging bull right now. The whole party was doing the mannequin challenge as we waited for Marquise to decide his fate.

"Jonaya, come with me," was all he said before turning and leaving with the same guy he showed up with.

Jonaya grabbed her purse and stood, but I grabbed her wrist.

"Don't leave with him, Jo, what the fuck!"

"He ain't gon' do nothing, Kay."

"Jonaya, no." I glared at her, putting my big sister hat on. She stared at me, snatched her wrist, but then sat her ass back down on the couch.

"Fuck y'all standing around for? Ain't this a muthafuckin' party?" Waayil shouted with an adorable smile, showing off his deep dimples. The music came right back on, and everyone gradually resumed dancing, smoking, and drinking.

About twenty minutes later, Alba walked through the door with two girls and when her eyes landed on me in Waayil's lap, she looked like she was about to burst into flames.

To fuck with her, I began dancing extra freakily in his lap as she walked by us. Jonaya, Rori, Sax, Eko, and Nusef were laughing once they realized what I was doing, but Waayil was too busy enjoying the view of my ass to notice. "Hey, Waayil." Alba waved.

I gave him a look like 'he'd better not speak' and he didn't. He told me he didn't believe it was his baby that she was carrying, but it was a possibility. So in my eyes, until it was proven that she was his baby mama, he didn't need to make nice with this hoe.

"Oh, she got you trained now, Yil?" Alba turned her lip up. One of her friends looked scared and the other was trying to convince her to leave it alone.

Waayil nodded 'yes' with a smirk to her question, making us all laugh loudly as hell.

"Good pussy will do that to a nigga, ma," he added before placing a kiss on my neck.

Instead of continuing into the party, Alba turned on her heels to leave, and her friends followed. These little parties stayed with the drama...

29

———

DREE

It was 7 p.m. at night and I was sitting in the library with a headache out of this world. I'd only started law school a week ago, and I was stressing already. There were so many damn laws and law terms that it was ridiculous. I thought I would be ahead of the game by reading up on material prior to starting school, but that definitely wasn't the case. Half the shit I learned, I have forgotten now. I guess there wasn't enough space in my brain yet to contain so much damn information.

To make matters worse, I couldn't really complain because of all the shit I talked before the semester started. If I, Dree Goode, admitted that I was having a hard time after only a week in, I would never be able to live that shit down.

"Oh my gosh," I groaned at the table adjacent to me. It was surrounded with a group of students who clearly didn't know that you needed to be quiet in a library. They'd gone from laughing, to arguing, to just plain shouting in a matter of 15 minutes.

"Is this seat available?"

I looked up to see Sean grinning down at me. From the looks of it, you would never know we had pretty much all the same classes and coursework. He was well put together right now and I was clearly losing it. Don't get me wrong, I was still dressed to impress because that was just part of being me, but I felt like I was losing my mind.

"Yeah, go ahead. All seven of these seats are available."

"So how far have you gotten on the assignment?" He sat down next to me and slapped me in the face with his cologne. He'd laid it on thick, but it made me smile because I knew why.

"I'm still on the first question. I cannot remember the details of some of this shit for the life of me." I placed my pen down and sat back. "I don't think I'm ever gonna be a lawyer."

"Dree, come on now. It's hard right now, but after a while it's gonna be like second nature to you."

"What? How do you know? You've been a law school student for as long as I have, Sean." I chuckled with a frown because he spoke as if he'd been practicing law for decades.

"My dad is a judge, and my mother is an attorney," he replied proudly with a cute smile.

He was so cute. He and Canyon were worlds apart, not just in personality but in looks too. Canyon was a bit rougher around the edges with the facial hair and tattoos scattered over his tall built frame. Sean was a bit leaner, free of artwork from what I could see, and had not a single hair on his mug. Canyon's voice was even deeper, whereas Sean's was on the softer side. Both were my type, however: fine as hell.

"Wow, so I'm guessing they told you all about law school, huh?"

"Oh yeah, even when I didn't want to hear it."

The loud laughter from the table next to me interrupted our conversation and even my personal thoughts. I closed my eyes in irritation, and massaged the area between my eyes for a moment.

"I think we can get more studying done at one of our houses." Sean looked to me.

"Well my house is not an option because I have a big family."

"What's big?"

"Big is three younger sisters, four if you include my mother, and then my mother's boyfriend. My house is never quiet. My nephew, Lonan, and I are the most civilized ones, and he's newly one."

We both chuckled in unison at my light humor.

"My house is an option. I mean, I only have my parents and that's it. I always wanted a sibling though."

"You can have all three of mine if you'd like." I gulped some of my water down. "But I don't know if I should go to your house. I mean, I have a... situation."

I didn't know what Canyon and I were. After that night we went out and had sex, we'd spent a little more time together and had a lot more sex, but no conversation on what we were had ever taken place. I was just one of those people who needed to hear verbally that I was with someone. I wasn't just gonna assume anything. And I hadn't even met his son yet.

"That *situation* prevents you from studying with a classmate?" Sean raised a brow.

Suddenly, I felt stupid.

"You know what? No, it doesn't." I smiled and closed my thick ass book, shoved it into my bag, and then rose to my feet.

Sean and I left, and I trailed him in my car to his home. He lived in a really nice house out in Belle Meade, with a long driveway. I thought my stepfather's house was nice, but this one damn near took the cake. I mean his front yard alone could fit two other single-family homes right there. My jaw was literally sitting in my lap as I came to a stop behind his car. When I got out, he laughed at the look on my face.

"You like it?"

"I love it!" I met him and we started towards the front door. "So this is how you live when you marry another lawyer, huh?"

"Yeah. My father is a little older than my mother though, which is why he's a judge now and she's still an attorney."

We entered his home and my jaw was right back on the marble

floors. He showed me around the whole place, and then finally, we went to the study so we could crack open these books. Sean turned on the fireplace as if it was cold, and then we sat at the low-level table.

"So what do your parents do?" he asked after we'd been reading and exchanging for about fifteen minutes or so.

"Let's see... my real father is some man that I have never met. My stepdad, Jasper, who I call Dad, is a plastic surgeon. My mom is..." I tilted my head so I could think. "She's a restaurant owner."

"Wow, what restaurant?"

"Natasha's Waffle House."

"Oh." Sean nodded and laughed nervously. "An authentic place."

"You mean ghetto."

"Well, I've been there and while the crowd was a little too rowdy and loud for my taste, the food, service, and cleanliness was pristine." I just shook my head and we went back to reading for a moment. "So this *situation*... is it serious?"

"I don't know. I mean it could be. We haven't really talked about it."

"Are you in love?"

"I... I love him, yes, but I don't know... I don't know, why?"

For some reason, I didn't want Sean to know that I loved Canyon because I felt like he would back off and I kind of didn't want him to. I didn't want to lose Canyon either, but like I said, I wasn't tied down to anyone.

"Just wondering."

"Mr. Ike, is rosemary garlic chicken okay for dinner tonight?" Some woman dressed in maid's attire entered the room and smiled.

"Did you call my father?" Sean turned to her and she nodded. "Then yes, that's fine. I have a guest, so please include her as well."

"Of course, Mr. Ike." She then looked to me and nodded with a smile. I didn't know what to do, so I waved weirdly.

"What the hell!" I cheesed, making him chuckle sexily.

We kept at our work, and by the time we were exhausted, dinner was ready. His parents weren't home, so he and I just ate in the large dining room together.

I enjoyed our conversation, which was different from the kinds I'd had with Canyon. Sean and I mostly talked about our career goals and things of that nature whereas, Canyon and I kind of talked more about our personal life, likes and dislikes, and damn near everything *but* career stuff.

After that good ass dinner, Sean offered to put a movie in and since I didn't have class tomorrow, I agreed. I noticed that I'd left my phone in the study, and when I retrieved it, I had a couple texts and missed calls from Canyon. I decided I would just talk to him tomorrow when I woke up.

"You like scary shit?" Sean inquired once I entered the den.

"Don't like it, but I'm not some scary person, if that's what you mean."

"Good. Sit down."

I sat next to him, and soon after, the maid, housekeeper, whatever the fuck she was, brought us some popcorn and other snacks.

About halfway through the movie, Sean draped his arm around me and pulled me closer. I didn't do or say anything; I just kept my eyes on the movie. Suddenly, he turned me to face him using my chin, and then pressed his lips against mine. I tensed up because I was surprised, but then I relaxed as he pecked me again. Our slow kisses were interrupted by the sound of my ringing phone, and when I picked it up, Sean took it from me and placed it on the coffee table in front of us.

He pulled his lips from mine and got down off the large couch to reach under my skirt, pushing my panties to the side. I was in disbelief as he spread my thighs, and latched his mouth onto my clit.

This is so wrong, Dree!

I wanted to stop him because as many times as I'd told myself that what Canyon and I had wasn't serious, I knew deep down Canyon would go ape shit if he knew about this. Not to mention, if I even *thought* Canyon was getting head from some other bitch, I might cut his ass.

"Sean." I lightly pushed his head, but he didn't budge. He just kept attacking my pussy as if we didn't just have a three-course meal. "Oh shit," I panted as he spread my legs wider, pushing one thigh outward a little bit.

I tried, I really did, but Canyon wouldn't leave my mind, so I forcefully pushed Sean's face from between my legs.

"What's wrong?" He frowned, lips covered in my juices.

"I just remembered I have to be home in like five minutes." I quickly hopped up, turning my lip up at the gushy feeling between my legs.

"Dree."

"I will see you in class, Sean."

I rushed out of the house like a bat out of hell, making sure to grab my phone, and then my bags from the study. When I got in the car, I tried dialing Canyon but he didn't answer so I texted him 'goodnight'.

I loved Canyon but I hated to admit that I liked the possibility of growing old with the person that Sean would become.

30

―――――

NUSEF

I was getting my room ready because my first tattoo session of the day was in just ten minutes. I was booked solid today and I was thankful because my mind wouldn't be idle.

Every muthafuckin' second of the day it seemed, Jonaya crossed my mind. The way her ass kept this relationship with Marquise going had my fucking blood boiling. I wanted to roll up on their asses and fuck his ass up again, but I knew that wouldn't do shit but push Jonaya further away from me.

I didn't know what to do at this point, so I was just gon' take a step back and let her make the move. At least I was hoping I could take a step back. Shit, every time a nigga saw her I wanted to remind her that I loved her, hoping she would change her fucking attitude with her stupid ass.

"Hey, baby, your first appointment is here." Rebecca walked in my room and hugged me from behind.

Shit between us just wasn't the same no more now that I had spoken my feelings for Jonaya out loud. It's almost like me verbally expressing that I loved her, made it truer than when I was keeping the shit suppressed.

"Thank you." I gently peeled her arms from being wrapped around me.

"She brought you like a snack or something. Do I need to check her ass?" Rebecca raised an eyebrow and put her hand on her hip.

"Nah."

The client was Leighton, and I hadn't talked to her since I dipped out on that stupid ass double date. But her persistent ass called the shop and made an appointment with me. She didn't mind that I was booked two weeks out; she was willing to wait.

Rebecca left my room and went to fetch Leighton, bringing her to me. Leighton was in this dress that was barely holding on around her titties, and she was carrying a tray of some type of food. Rebecca stood in the doorway with a displeasing look for a little bit, until I nodded for her to get out.

"I hope you like cupcakes." Leighton smiled and looked for somewhere to set the tray before placing it on the counter in here.

"Damn, ma, why you make so damn many?"

"My cupcakes are really good, and since you're a pretty big guy, I wanted to make sure I had enough for you."

I nodded with a chuckle because she sounded stupid as fuck.

"Aight, so you said you wanted this on your lower back, right?" I held up the drawing I'd created based off what she'd emailed to me.

"Yes."

Before I could instruct her ass to do anything else, she lifted her dress past her thong, and laid on her stomach. She didn't have much ass at all, but her skin was nice and smooth.

I washed my hands, put on my gloves, and got my shit ready so I could get this tattoo done. I didn't want to fall a minute over, because I wanted to stay on track. The tattoo consisted of her grandma's name surrounded by a couple hearts, which was easy shit for a nigga like me. I was used to things way more complex, so it didn't take me long at all to perfect it.

About twenty-five minutes later, I was done, and she got up off the table to turn around and look at it through the mirror before I wiped it down and covered it up.

"You are so talented, Sef."

"Thanks."

She checked it out some more before making her way over to me. I protected then covered it, before she pulled her dress down slowly. I noticed she had a little bit of hips on her, making a few thoughts cross my mind that shouldn't have.

"So, is that girl who brought me back here your girlfriend now or something?" Leighton sat back down on the tattoo chair and furrowed her brows. "I know you said she wasn't when we were at the movies, but..."

"We're close as fuck, I'll say that."

"So close that you can't like talk to other people? Wednesday and Jonaya told me about her, but they made it seem like she was just something you were doing. She seems to think differently though."

"Fuck y'all discussing my business for?"

"No, nothing like that. I umm... I told them I liked you but I was worried about that girl because I'd seen you with her a few times."

"I get it. Well you good, ma, unless you have any more questions about how to take care of the tattoo, you're free to go."

"Why did you leave the movie like that? I know you weren't sick."

"I actually was. Movie popcorn always fucks with me and I shouldn't have had any of that bullshit. But, Leighton, baby, I have to—"

She got up and straddled my lap before I could even complete my damn sentence. For the first time since her ass had been here, I noticed she smelled good as hell. The urge to shove her hoe ass off me was slowly disappearing as her small soft hands dipped down into my jeans. Just as her fingertips brushed across my dick, she flew back off me and was being dragged across the floor.

"Rebecca!" I hollered, seeing her holding tightly onto Leighton's curls as she pummeled her face. "Quit this shit before y'all fuck some of my shit up!" I barked and yanked Rebecca backward.

"You stupid hoe! I knew to keep my fucking eye on you!" Rebecca shouted, panting heavily like a damn bear as Leighton slowly stood to her feet.

"Fuck you!" Leighton shouted and tried to run up but I blocked her, still holding Rebecca with my other arm.

Where in the entire fuck was everybody else?

"Sit down and don't move, Rebecca," I spoke in her ear with my teeth clenched.

"Nusef—"

"Sit down."

Rebecca sucked her teeth and plopped down in the chair in my tattoo room. I took Leighton's hand and then led her outside because she needed to go, but I wanted to make sure shorty was good. Rebecca was getting her ass. Granted she didn't really have the upper hand because she was on the floor getting her shit pulled, but fuck.

"You aight?" I asked Leighton once we got to what I assumed was her car.

"Yeah, but I'm gonna get her ass," she fussed and then touched her nose. It was a little bloody.

"You want me to get you something for that shit?"

"No, I'll be okay. I have something at home and I don't live far from here." She ran her hand through her curly mane and shook her head. "If she's not your girl, she surely acts like it."

"Rebecca is a little crazy."

"Well, her little crazy ass better be prepared the next time I see her because she's getting fucked up. Trying to sneak me. I don't like bitches like that."

I just chuckled because it was funny as fuck seeing her little ass so angry. But low-key, I was praying Rebecca and Leighton didn't cross paths again because I wasn't ready to break up another fucking fight. And if they did come in contact, I prayed I wasn't around. Shit, they could kill each other for all I cared at this point, just not in my presence or around my tattoo equipment.

"Relax yo' ass before you drive, ma."

"Fine, since you care so much." She smiled. "So can we chill together sometime? Not like a double date though, just me and you."

I stared down at her, seeing how pretty she actually was. Still didn't have no ass, but her nice round titties, hips, and legs made up for it. Her sexy vanilla complexion looked smooth, and shorty smelled good too, which was always a plus. I was definitely a little interested to see what that pussy was like.

"Yeah, we can. Put yo' shit in my phone." I handed her my iPhone, and checked over my shoulder as a patron entered my shop.

Leighton quickly typed in her phone number, along with her name, and when I saw she added her address too, I chuckled.

"You may need it. You never know."

"Aight, I'll check you later. Take care of that tattoo." I backed away, slapping hands with Moses as he entered the shop to work.

"I will."

"Bad as fuck. You messing with that?" Moses asked with his hand on the shop's door. He knew I had a little something with Rebecca and didn't want her to hear.

"I don't know yet."

We laughed in unison as we went inside, and I greeted the patron waiting as Chiara finally brought her ass in to work. She claimed she had a family emergency and was gonna be a little late. Her ass was a lot late though.

"I'm sorry, Sef! I promise it won't happen again!" Chiara said before racing to the back to put her shit up.

I headed towards my tattoo room to see Rebecca still inside, face full of anger. I closed my door and sat across from her, pulling her closer to me since the chair she was in had wheels.

"Why you do that shit, Rebecca?" She was looking off, so I tilted my head so we could make eye contact. "Huh? In my place of business?"

"Business? When I walked in here, it didn't look like business, Nusef! She was in your damn lap with her hand touching your crotch it looked like!"

"Lower your voice when talking to me, ma; you know better." I was calm, but she was gon' take me to another place by hollering at a nigga. "Talk to me like I'm talking to you."

She dropped her head and began to fidget. Suddenly, she was sniffling, and I exhaled heavily because I knew the waterworks were here.

"I can't do this anymore, Nusef," she sobbed.

"Do what? Ain't nobody ask you to fight that girl!"

"This! This not knowing what I am to you! It's making me crazy! I don't fight over niggas, and here I am dragging this bitch while I'm at work, over you!"

"So what's up then? You wanna kill this?"

"No, baby, no." She sniffled and placed her hands on the sides of my face. "I want us to be exclusive."

"Rebecca—"

"If you can't do it, Sef, then I can't be anything to you. So it's either you and me as one, or we can lead two separate lives."

The look in her eyes was serious. I didn't want Rebecca to be my girl, because like a bitch, I was still holding out, waiting for Jonaya to grow the fuck up. But on the other hand, I didn't wanna lose shorty, because I did love her. Right now wasn't the best time for me to witness both my bitches fucking with other niggas.

Damn, I was a selfish ass nigga sometimes.

"Look, ma, I love you, but I can't." I shook my head. The shit was killing me to let Rebecca go, but I knew if Jonaya snapped her pretty ass fingers, I'd be gone in a minute. Rebecca didn't deserve that shit.

"How do you know? You've never even tried."

"Shorty, I can't."

She gazed in my eyes for a few seconds, and then stood up slowly, tears streaming her caramel cheeks.

"Okay," was all she said as she left the room.

This was some bullshit.

31

———

RORI

I'd chosen to go to the library to do some of my homework, and since I didn't have any distractions, I'd finished pretty quickly with the rest of the night to spare.

It was going on 8 p.m., and I had never been free this early since I'd started school a couple weeks ago. I didn't want to go home because I didn't have to be anywhere early tomorrow, and I definitely wasn't in the mood to see Gavin. I loved him still, but the guilt of fucking with Eko made it hard to be around him. And lately, Gavin had been laying it on extra thick, making me feel even worse.

I'd gotten tired of using my mom's car, and my sisters' cars, so I somehow convinced my stepdad to let me use his while he was away in New York. He even had a gas credit card stashed in the glove compartment that he gave me free reign to use. By saying that, I didn't have to rush home in case someone needed their vehicle.

Gavin's named popped up on the screen of the car since I'd hooked my iPhone up, but I just let it ring because I knew he'd be trying to see me. Like a shady hoe, I instead made my way over to Eko's place. I saw his car was parked in the driveway, which was like hitting the jackpot because a guy in his profession was rarely ever home and extremely hard to catch. Plus, he managed a barbershop too, so his free time was scarce.

Getting out of the car, I made sure my hair was intact. The wind had made my curls extra frizzy, so I was looking like a ball of yarn. Tying it up into a big bun, I put on some more colored gloss, and then spritzed a little of the perfume I had in my purse as I crossed the street.

Approaching the door, I rang the doorbell, then inhaled and exhaled sharply as I waited. My heart dropped into my stomach when some White girl answered the door with a frown.

"Can I help you?" she asked. She didn't have an attitude, but I could tell she was wondering why I was here.

"I was look—"

"Jenni, what the fuck I tell you about answering my door?" Eko barged through, stepping around her.

This was Jenni? I had a totally different picture of her in my head; namely that she was Black. Now that I think about it, I'd seen her around Eko before, but they were never hugged up or anything so I didn't think she was *thee* Jenni. I always thought she was with one of the other guys that worked the trap, because she and Eko barely interacted, if at all.

She was very pretty, though, with greenish blue eyes, long dark hair, and full lips that appeared to be authentic. She even had a little shape on her from what I could see right now.

"I'm sorry, Eko, I didn't know you had company. I was coming to ask you about... to ask you about..."

"Nah, you good." Eko cut me off, smirking down at me from his doorway. "Jenni, I'll get up with you later." He looked over his shoulder at her. Her mouth went into a slight O shape as she stared up at him.

"Eko, who is she? Are you serious right now?" She pointed to me.

"I'm dead serious, ma," he said and then stepped out the way so she could walk out the door.

"Eko, it's fine. I didn't really want anything." I turned to leave, but suddenly this nigga picked me up from behind and carried me back into the house. I was just as shocked as Jenni right now.

"Jenni," Eko called her name sternly.

Jenni glared hard at me, and then grabbed her Gucci purse off the couch roughly. I didn't know why she was mad at me when he was the one kicking her ass out.

"Fuck you, Eko!" she barked and stormed out.

Eko placed me to my feet and went to close and lock the door behind her. When he turned to face me, I was scowling up at him with my arms folded.

"What you mad for?" His brows dipped.

"Did you seriously kick your girlfriend out for me? It's not that serious, Eko!" I shouted. "As a matter of fact, I shouldn't even be here with you! I have a boyfriend, and you have someone as well! What the hell am I doing?" I charged the door but he was blocking it. He lightly shoved me backwards and stared at me with an irritated expression.

"Stop acting stupid, Rori. You wanna be with Gavin's bitch ass as much as I wanna be with that bitch I just threw out."

"You don't know what I want, nigga."

"Yeah I do. Fucking your nigga's best friend ain't your style, Rori."

"Exactly why I need to take my ass home, instead of trying to be laid up in here with you. You need to move and let me by."

"No, that's exactly why you should be here. I have to be one special ass nigga for you to open your legs to me, shorty."

I didn't have a response right away because I sort of felt like he was right. I wasn't that girl who went behind her man's back and betrayed him, but it was something about Eko. And it wasn't like the way he treated me was something new; he'd always been there when Gavin was fucking me over in a sense.

Whenever Gavin would forget to pick me up, Eko would. Whenever Gavin would say some rude shit to hurt my feelings, Eko would always get in his ass. Eko had even brought me food when Gavin would have me sitting there, starving, while he handled 'business.' I guess I just never paid much attention to his gestures, because I just thought he was helping his best friend.

Suddenly, him calling Gavin a bitch brought my thoughts to a halt.

"When did Gavin become a bitch?"

"When he tried to fuck me over. Still is trying to fuck me over, but he's about to pay for that shit." He took a seat on his couch.

"Wow," I chuckled. "So you fucking me, is this a part of your plan? Something you can throw in his face? Or do you really like me how you say?"

"It's both, Rori. It was the latter first, though. I always had eyes for your pretty ass, but out of respect for that nigga, I kept it cordial. But now?" He frowned his sexy face. "Fuck that shit. I've always wanted you so I'm gon' have you."

He was so sure.

"Eko, I—" I paced in front of him and he pulled me down into his lap. I had a dress on, so I tried to adjust it but he stopped me.

Slipping his hand between my legs, he touched my pussy with his big hand, and she reacted almost immediately.

"I wanted this. I got it. And now I'm staking claim on it." He spoke seriously as he caressed my pussy through my panties. I wanted to scurry out of there, but I felt stuck.

"Eko—"

He shook his head so I stopped talking.

"I'm not playing with you, Rori," he almost gritted out.

I didn't know if I was afraid or turned on right now. Maybe it was a little bit of both.

Locking my arms around his neck, I crushed my lips against his. His hands moved up and down my back, before he squeezed my ass roughly. As we sucked one another's lips, we began to let out subtle moans, before he stood up and carried me towards his bedroom.

"Wait, did you just fuck her in here?" I pulled away from his mouth.

"Nah, I just got some head in the living room, but that was this morning. I don' showered and everything."

I smiled and so did he. He really thought what he'd just said was okay.

We fell back onto his bed, and he immediately began tugging my panties down. My dress had no straps, so before he even had my panties past my feet, he was yanking at the top of it.

"Mmm." I moaned softly once he began sucking my nipples hungrily, while toying with my clit.

Once he'd had his fix, he pushed my dress down past my hips and threw it to the side. I tossed my head back as he kissed down my body gently, while groping my thighs with so much aggression. He spread my legs abruptly, making me smile, and began to suck on my inner thighs as he made his way to my middle.

BAM! BAM!

"Eko! Open up!" Gavin's voice boomed through the house as he banged on the door.

I damn near jumped out of my skin as I crawled up the bed backwards with my eyes wide. Eko just chuckled nonchalantly as he rose to his feet. Even when he was annoying as hell like right now, he was sexy.

"What the fuck is funny, nigga?" I hissed, trying to scoop up my clothes.

"Stay like that," this nigga had the nerve to say.

"Are you fucking crazy? I have to get the hell out of here."

"Nah, it's about time he find out what's—"

"No, E! Please, do this for me. Keep this a secret for right now. I will tell him on my own."

Eko went to the front without saying a word, and before I could even get my panties on, I heard him letting Gavin in. How the hell would I explain my reasoning for being at his best friend's house and in his bedroom? Good thing Gavin didn't know my stepdad's car or I would be fucked!

The boys' voices sounded closer as I fumbled while pulling my thong up. The bedroom door was open, so the only thing I could think to do was get my ass under the bed, half-naked. The boys entered the bedroom having a discussion, and I could tell by the way Eko's voice trailed off that he was wondering where I'd gone.

"And you swear you ain't seen or talked to Neo?" Gavin asked frantically.

"No, nigga, I told yo' ass that. Why the fuck would I lie?" Eko hissed.

"Shit. I didn't... fuck!"

"What's the problem nigga?"

"I uh... nothing, I'll handle it." Gavin sighed. "What you about to do for the rest of the day though?"

"Chill with this shorty I been fucking." I could hear the smile in Eko's voice.

"Oh word? No more Jenni?"

"Not really. But look, she's waiting on me, and I been thinking about the pussy all day so I need to roll out and get up in that."

"Damn, she got you whipped already, mane?" Gavin chuckled, and I rolled my eyes. He needed to get the fuck on because I did not like laying my body on this floor and under this bed. What had my life come to?

"Nah, but she got a nigga, and we have to work around that. He's a little square ass muthafucka though, so it ain't gon' be a problem snatching her up when she's ready."

"His bad." Gavin laughed along with Eko. "Well aight then. Hit it extra hard for me."

"Shit, I will."

I snickered subtly at Eko's response because Gavin had no idea.

I heard them leave the room and then about thirty seconds later, Eko came back into the bedroom, calling my name. Slowly, I crept from under the bed and he burst into laughter. He had the cutest smile ever.

"Yo, you was up under there the whole fucking time?" He clutched his abs and bent over chortling like it was really that funny.

"Fuck you, I'm leaving." I stood up and snatched my dress up, but he yanked it from me.

"Lay yo' ass back down, Rori. You ain't going no damn where until I'm done with you." He pulled his shirt over his head to expose the top half of his chiseled six-foot-three frame.

The seriousness in his voice made me sit down on the bed as if I were a robot, waiting to make moves by his commands.

My ass had almost gotten caught, yet, here I was just as ready and willing to get the dick as before.

32

WAAYIL

My last tattoo of the day was done, and my client had taken their ass home. I was tired as fuck, and in need of a big ass blunt to calm my fucking nerves. I decided to roll one while I sat in my car in the parking lot, because I didn't like smoking around Yikayla's son, Lonan. Plus, I didn't want her ass trying to hit either.

As soon as I lit it, I took a couple puffs and let my window down a tiny bit. Just as I relaxed some, bobbing my head to "TELLME" by Adrian Marcel, there was a knock on my window. Irritated as fuck, I looked to my left to see who the hell it was. I couldn't do shit but chuckle angrily when I spotted bitch ass Roscoe standing there mean mugging like he was about to really do some shit. I took another hit, and then lowered the volume on my music, but not too much because this right here was my shit.

"What?" I spat.

"Can you step out the car for a moment?" He stepped back, hands still in his pockets.

"For what? Tell me why the fuck you out here and I'll decide if that shit is worth me stepping out of my shit."

"You know what it's about, my nigga; Yikayla."

"Oh, well then we ain't got shit to talk about, bruh."

"Yeah, we do, because regardless of what you think, you—"

"Hold up, hold up." I turned my car off and got out, blunt still in hand. Once I closed my door, I leaned up against it and said, "Now what was you about to say?"

I was sitting on muthafuckin' ready right now, so if he said anything I didn't like, I was going upside this nigga's head. And lucky for me, no one was around to block or keep me from doing that shit.

"I-I was saying that regardless of what y'all are doing, she's still my baby mama."

"What's your point?" I inhaled on the blunt. "Because right now, all you're doing is running yo' fucking mouth but not really saying shit. You interrupted me chilling for a minute, so you better have some good shit to say, bruh."

"I want you to back up off of her and let her make her own decisions." I couldn't help but to laugh as the smoke flowed from my mouth. "And... and, I don't want you around my kid."

"Too late for that shit. I been playing daddy for a while now."

"Nigga, what?" He moved towards me some.

"You heard what the fuck I said, nigga. And back yo' stupid ass up before I crack yo' shit," I hissed, leaning up off my car, ready to put hands on this nigga.

"Man, I ain't come here for all that fighting shit."

"Well I fight, muthafucka, so if you ain't prepared for that shit, watch how you move, nigga. Coming in all close and shit like you ready to handle something."

"Look—"

"Nah, bitch, you look; Yikayla is my girl and whatever comes with her is mine too. You ain't no fucking daddy, nigga, you a damn sperm donor. Quit acting like you care so damn much about either of them." I dropped the blunt and stepped on it. "This the last time I'm gon' let yo' ass slide, bruh. Stay up out my damn face, because on God, the next time I see yo' ass it's gon' be a mutha-fuckin' wrap. I don't do the talking shit, I lay niggas out, so take this pass and skip yo' broke ass on home. I don't play about Yikayla Goode and her son either, so heed to this warning, bitch. I'm begging you for yo' own good, bruh." I got real close to him as I spoke.

I had him a little bit on height, so he kind of looked up at me with his mouth twisted like he was itching to say something. My fists were balled, and I raised my brow, letting him know if he was feeling bold then to act on it. Instead, like a smart person, he sucked his teeth and turned around to walk off. He tried to fake it, but I knew I had that nigga all shook up like Elvis.

Once I saw him get into the passenger seat of some car, I got back into mine. Cranking my whip up and blasting my music, I let my windows all the way down, used some mouthwash and popped some gum, then sped out of the parking lot to get home.

I'd finally found an apartment, and I was gon' be looking at that shit tomorrow. My parole officer got on my ass about me staying in hotels and shit, so I had to stay with my parents like I'd put on my paperwork.

I hated being a grown ass man under their roof, but the upside was that I got to keep an eye on Wednesday, and spend some time with my little brother, Emil, which was rare, because he stayed out for some reason. We didn't hang with the same crowds at all, so it wasn't like I could see him in the streets.

When I walked in the house, I saw Yikayla, Lonan, my parents, and Wednesday in the den watching TV. I loved how close Yikayla was with my parents, especially my mother, who was a tough critic when it came to women. She hated Alba, and when I told her about the potential baby, she shook her head at me for what felt like an hour straight. I had to beg her ass to say something.

"Hey, honey, are you hungry? Kay made some really good baked potatoes." My mom smiled as she looked over her shoulder.

I nodded for Yikayla to come with me before saying, "Yeah, she's about to make me a plate right now."

"I am?" Yikayla raised her brow as if she wasn't about to do what I'd said.

"Yeah, come on." I watched Wednesday take Lonan from Yikayla and kiss his cheeks, then my eyes watched Yikayla's body as she stood up. "Where is Emil?" I inquired once I realized he was the only one missing.

"He went out," my dad responded, sipping his mug of beer.

I wanted to say something, but I had to remember Emil was grown and a man. Something just didn't feel right though. He was never here. I'd seen him maybe three times since I'd been out, and whenever I tried to hang with him, he acted too busy.

Emil and I used to be tight, along with Nusef, so his behavior was a bit strange to me. I thought he was angry with me for getting caught up on a murder charge, but Nusef told me he'd started acting distant like that towards him too.

"You want one or two?" Yikayla asked as she uncovered the tray of baked potatoes. They were covered in cheese, grilled sautéed shrimp, and spinach.

"Damn, shorty. Fuck you doing cooking for these niggas like that?"

"Waayil, this was nothing." She giggled when I hugged her body from behind and kissed her on her neck.

"This fucking body, man," I spoke lowly to myself as I pressed my dick against her plump ass and squeezed her breasts from behind. I bit my lip thinking about how I was gon' beat that pussy tonight.

"Waayil, I don't want your parents to walk in. Sit down."

"I ain't hiding my obsession with you from no fucking body, ma," I spat. Yikayla looked over her shoulder at me and half smiled before I pecked her lips. "I want two though."

I sat down at the table as Yikayla put my plate together and then got me something to drink. Her sexy cocoa skin had a glow to it, and the way her hair swept against her sexy back was turning me on like a muthafucka. Her dress was short and tight, but it was casual, not some shit you'd see in the club. My bitch was fine as fuck, and the sight made me shake my head.

"I've been looking at apartments and I think I've found one," she said as she set my food and drink down at the table and joined me.

"I already got one. You know that." I prayed and then stuck my fork into the potato.

"Yeah, *you* have one, but I don't."

"Fuck you need your own for, Yikayla? We together, right?"

"Of course, Waayil, but I've never been out on my own really, and now that I have this new job and stuff, I want to move to my own spot."

"Without me."

"Not like that. I don't mind living with you, but I want my own responsibility."

"Then you can pay half of the bills, but I don't see a point in us living apart. I been away from you for long enough already, Yikayla, and I'm not agreeing to us living in two separate fucking places, just to move in together months later."

"Okay, fine, you brat."

I chuckled at her dig and shoved some more food into my mouth.

"I saw Roscoe, had to let his ass know to back up off you."

"You did? When?"

"Tonight, just before I came home. Telling me he didn't want me around Lonan and all this other bullshit. So I told him next time I saw him, I was fucking his ass up."

"Waayil, he's Lonan's father, you have to be okay with him seeing his son."

"He don't wanna see his son, he wants yo' ass. And being Lonan's father gives him a reason to be around you, Kay. I hope you see that shit, because if not, we gon' have some problems, ma. If that bitch wants to be a dad, he'll act like it. He approached me because his concern is you, not y'all kid. If it was, he would have talked to you, right?"

"Yeah, I guess so."

"No need to guess, I just told you what it was."

"Shut up, nigga," she laughed.

I had no problem with Roscoe trying to be a father to his kid, but I could see right through that nigga. He didn't give a fuck about me being around Lonan. Shit, I could change Lonan's last name on his birth certificate for all that muthafucka cared, as long as he had Yikayla. And if I felt like he was about to try to put the moves on my bitch, I was prepared to push that nigga's wig back with the quickness.

33

———

JONAYA

It was still hot as hell in Memphis, so Leighton, Wednesday, and I decided to relax by the pool in my backyard. We'd just gone swimming in the super cold water, and now we were just laying out, enjoying the sun for a moment. I knew soon enough my ass would be right back in the water because the heat in Memphis was like being put in a steamer. It was that heat that made you frown for no reason at all.

"So, guess who I've been texting a little bit?" Leighton smirked as she looked from Wednesday to me.

"Who knows, you're a hoe," Wednesday half joked and the three of us laughed.

"If I'm a hoe then what are you, boo?" Leighton raised a brow and smiled.

To have such overprotective brothers, Wednesday did get more action than most girls with that type of situation, but definitely not as much as she could. I think it was because Waayil was locked up for a minute, and Nusef was too busy dabbling in his own personal affairs to watch her too closely *at times*. He paid enough attention to keep her from having a boyfriend though. As for Emil, he just wasn't that type of brother to clock Wednesday's moves. However, now that Waayil was out of prison, Wednesday had definitely slowed up. And ever since Waayil threatened and pulled a gun on her latest junt, Ty, she was really on her best behavior because Ty was ghost now.

"Tell us, I don't like guessing." I laid my head back against the lawn chair, twisting my face at the burning sensation of the sun.

"Nusef."

I almost broke my neck when I sat up to look her way in astonishment.

"My brother, Nusef?" Wednesday inquired to be sure. "I thought after the double date that was done?" I was hoping she said no, but in all the years I'd been living in Tennessee, there had only been one Nusef.

"Hell yeah, your brother. After he tattooed me, and his stupid ass fuck buddy put her hands on me, we exchanged numbers. I didn't say anything because I thought he was still gonna be bullshitting, but nope!" she giggled excitedly. "He actually texts back and we made plans to chill tomorrow."

"So what, you're planning to get some dick and move on?" I raised a brow.

"I mean, usually that's my move, but I actually like Nusef. Plus, any woman that doesn't lock Nusef down, if given the chance, is a fool. That man is Earth's gift from God, and I'm gonna accept that shit and unwrap it as soon as I can."

"So you and Rebecca can be sister wives?" I chuckled.

I admit, I was hating and I didn't know why. I mean I did... but why? And the fact that Nusef and I barely talked anymore made hearing this even worse. We would text occasionally, but he was never really into the conversation. And when I would call, he'd always be in the middle of something and would have to go. He made me so fucking angry.

"He told me he's done with Rebecca. I asked about it."

I was kind of speechless at this point. I wanted to be a hating ass bitch and tell Leighton that Nusef had an STD, but that wasn't like me. None of this bullshit was like me. I didn't get jealous, and I didn't have feelings.

Take my relationship with Marquise, he called himself being angry with me and giving me the cold shoulder, but I couldn't have cared less. I guess he realized it though, because now he was texting me and I was barely replying.

"Ladies, I think I've had enough sun and pool for today. I need a shower and some of that air conditioning inside of my house." I got up and grabbed my towel to wrap around my body.

"Jo, I'm making lunch for you guys, but here is some lemonade." My mom sauntered out in some tiny shorts and a crop top.

"Thanks, Mama. Just set it on the table for them."

She nodded and gave me a kiss on the cheek, before I passed her and went into the house. I heard some giggling and laughing as I bypassed the den, so I peeked in to see Canyon and Dree on the couch, cuddled up and looking hella gay. For a minute, I just watched them interact, and seeing the wide ass grins on both of their faces. They'd been in love for years, but I guess they were just now realizing it.

Seeing that made me feel some type of way, so I started towards the stairs so I could shower in my bathroom. Once I was cleaned up and cooled down, I joined my friends for the lunch my mom prepared and just relaxed with them in the back until the sun went down.

Rori, Dree, Yikayla, my nephew, Lonan, and Canyon had joined us, and once it got to be around 9 p.m., I retired upstairs.

I hadn't been watching TV in the dark for ten minutes before there was a knock on my bedroom door. Before I could say come in, the door opened and in walked Nusef. Seeing him caught me so off guard that I didn't say anything as he shut the door behind him. He looked good; really good. He was wearing a hoodie, basketball shorts, socks, and slides. The hood was pulled up over his head, but I could still see his beautiful face, adorned with his freshly lined facial hair.

"Why you not in the backyard with everybody else?" He moved further into my bedroom as I sat up in my bed.

"I was tired."

"Where yo' bitch at?"

"My bi—" I made a face and rolled my eyes when I saw that sexy grin appear on his face. "Marquise is not a bitch, Sef."

"Walks like a bitch, talks like a bitch, and got his ass whooped like a bitch, so to me, that's a bitch." He sat on my bed, and the light from the TV flickered against his handsome mug. "I bet he fucks like a bitch too."

"Sef."

"What?" He shrugged.

"Don't be mean. You guys used to be friends."

"Yeah, but that's over with. It was over with when I fell in love with you and when he decided to press me outside of my place of business."

"Well I'm sure he's sorry."

I watched him remove his shoes just before he kicked his feet up onto my bed. He then got back off to remove his hoodie, and I got a glimpse of the V that led to something I'd never wanted to see until now. His cologne wafted past me as he got under the covers with me.

"Nusef, you have on your street clothes."

"Shut up sounding like somebody's muthafuckin' mama," he spat, making me chuckle. I was serious, but I had missed him so, that I decided to drop it.

We watched TV for a couple hours, talking and laughing like old times. I hadn't felt this happy in weeks, and it was starting to seem like I had my best friend back. It got late before we knew it, so I turned the TV off and slinked down under the covers. Nusef followed suit and hugged my body from behind. That was normal, but then he decided to talk.

"Jonaya."

"Nusef."

"I love you."

My heart seemed to stop upon hearing him say that shit yet again. I chose to pretend I didn't hear, and just kept my eyes closed. Nusef clearly wasn't giving up though, because he hugged my back tighter into his strong chest, and moved my long hair out of the way, using his chin so that he could kiss the nape of my neck. My clit tingled at the feeling of his lips against my skin, and suddenly, I was hornier than a teenage boy. We'd never been intimate in anyway, yet, he knew just where to place his lips on my neck.

Turning me onto my back so that I could see him, he whispered, "I love you."

"Oh my gosh," I mumbled, covering my face with my hands.

He moved my hands from my face and pinned them to the bed. I attempted to free myself, but he was so fucking strong. It was like someone had bolted my wrists to my pillow. He maneuvered himself on top of me and in between my legs, and since I just had on some thin silk shorts on my bottom half, I felt his brick hard dick pressing against my pussy. My clit was throbbing like a heart right now. I couldn't believe I was craving Nusef Christian like this.

He kissed me, and chills traveled down my body every time our lips came in contact. After sucking my lips for a few moments, he kissed down my face to my neck, onto my collarbone, and down my stomach. He finally released my wrists, and gripped the waistband of my silk bottoms before tugging them down.

"Sef."

"Tell me you love me and I'll stop."

"Nuseeefff," I whined as he tossed my shorts off the bed. I didn't wear panties to sleep, so there he was, face to face with my pussy.

He wasted absolutely no time placing my thighs on his shoulders and lifting my bottom with his hands. He buried his face between my legs, and an uncontrollable moan burst through my lips when he began to suck on my clit. I tried to pull away, even though I didn't want to, but his grip on my ass gave him leverage over me. He pushed my vagina more into his mouth, and flicked his tongue over my clit a little before sucking it again.

"Fuck," he mumbled against it, driving me crazy.

I'd never cum this quick, and I felt it on the horizon.

"Wait, Sef." I was trying to get him to stop, but he was like a lion to its prey right now as he devoured me with so much passion.

My nails scraped against his fresh fade as he pressed my right thigh into my stomach for more access. I trembled and came hard, but Nusef ignored it.

"Oh my gosh," I damn near screeched, praying no one heard me.

I pressed my palm against his forehead to get him away, but it was like the nigga did neck workouts because it didn't help one bit.

"Give up," he said, before slurping and sucking me into oblivion.

I was tired from the way he was eating me, so I did just that. I relaxed, and spread my left thigh out more since he still had my right one pressed against my mid-section.

My body suddenly became paralyzed almost as an overwhelming feeling of pleasure shot through me. I released so explosively, that my voice trembled as I whimpered softly. Nusef kissed my pussy nastily for a few; sexy lips doing the most as my clit pulsated.

When he was done, he got from between my legs and I hugged my knees into my chest. I was so thrown off and still in shock from cumming like that. As I did my best to recoup, I heard him getting out of the bed and rustling with something. I looked over my shoulder to see him pulling his hoodie back on.

"Where are you going?" I panted.

"Home."

"But it's late and—"

"It aight."

"So what, you just came here to do this?" I frowned, slightly upset.

"To eat ya pussy and tell you I love you? Yeah."

Before I could think of anything to say, he was closing my bedroom door behind himself.

That nigga knew what he did. I'd be fantasizing about tonight for years to come.

34

CANYON

The smell of pancakes permeated through the air in my bedroom as I pulled my polo over my head. I smirked at the fact that I had Dree's ass in there making me breakfast. If you knew Dree, you knew she wasn't the type to do a damn thing for a nigga, so the fact that she was cooking for me spoke volumes. Not to mention, she woke me up with some head that had my toes curling.

I grabbed my phone off the dresser once I had my Nikes on, and it started ringing in my hand almost immediately. Continuing on my route to the kitchen, I looked down to see it was my sister, Jupiter, so I answered as I took a seat at my kitchen table.

"What's good, baby sister?" I cheesed as Dree set a plate covered in pancakes, breakfast potatoes, grits, eggs, and bacon in front of me. I gave her fine ass a thumbs up, and she smiled.

"Stop calling me that, Canyon. I'm just letting you know that Portia said she saw Luna at the club last night."

The word 'so' almost slipped out of my mouth until I remembered my son was supposed to be with her. Luna was my baby mama and when we first started fucking around, it was just on some bed buddy shit and nothing else. But when I realized Dree wasn't fucking with me, I put in a little more effort over that way and got Luna pregnant. And it was like once she had my baby in her, she turned into somebody else. All she did was go out, complain, and beg for shit she didn't need. It was almost like her stupid ass thought she could do whatever the fuck she wanted now that she had me for eighteen years. It only got worse when I decided I couldn't be with her ass no more.

"The club? That's impossible, Jupiter."

"She sent me pictures, bro. Luna was at the club and stayed until the shit closed damn near. I'm pretty sure Cade is with her sister."

"This some bullshit. Aight, thanks." I hung up the phone and stared down at my plate. My appetite was no longer as thoughts of strangling Luna's ass up a wall invaded my mind.

"What's wrong?" Dree questioned.

"I gotta make a run real quick. You wanna roll with me?" I stood up and pocketed my phone. "My baby mama, Luna, you know her. She's fucking up, and I have to go get her together and then take my son to her."

"Maybe I shouldn't go, Canyon. I mean, I'm sure she won't wanna see me."

"I don't give a fuck what that bitch wants! Fuck I look like worrying about what makes her stupid ass uncomfortable?"

Dree nodded and then got up from the table. After she covered the plates in foil and put them in my fridge, we were out the door.

I could tell her ass didn't wanna come, but she didn't have a choice right now. It was no point in me going out, and then coming all the way back here to get her. If she was gon' fuck with me, then she was gon' have to see Luna's ass a time or two.

"I hope you ain't gon' act like that all day, Dree." I came to a red light.

"Act like what?"

"All somber and shit. If you gon' be with me, seeing and dealing with Luna is gon' be a part of that shit."

"I know, Canyon."

"Good."

On the way to Luna's house, I dialed her sister and she told me that she indeed had my shorty.

I finally made it Luna's house, and parked in her driveway. Dree wanted to stay in the car, and because I just wanted to get this shit over with, I let her. Walking up to Luna's door, I banged on the screen until I heard her loud ass voice asking who it was.

"Open this shit up!" I barked.

It got quiet all of a sudden, so I knew her ass was afraid. She had no damn business dropping our son off with her sister when it was her damn time with him. It'd be different if she only did the shit occasionally, but every muthafuckin' time she got my son, she was tossing him onto her sister and running the fucking streets.

"Open this fucking door, Luna, before I bust open this window!"

Finally, I heard her unlocking the door, but she stayed behind the screen as she tied her robe close.

"Canyon, Cade is asleep so come back later with--"

"Rain already put you on front street, ma, so kill them fucking lies."

"Why can't I ever have some time to myself! You act like because I'm a mom, I can't ever go to the damn club! Where you think I met your cheating ass!"

This bitch was crazy, and when I say crazy, I mean bat shit. I'd never cheated on her stupid ass, but she loved to say it for some reason. People all over told me that she was saying we'd broken up because I was unfaithful and she couldn't do it anymore, when really, I left her mentally challenged ass.

"Luna, open this screen door."

Sucking her teeth, she unlocked it and pushed it out. I checked over my shoulder to see Dree deep in her phone, texting away.

"Is that a bitch in your car, Canyon? You have the nerve to show up here with some hoe?" Luna hissed as she stared up at me.

"Watch ya mouth." I closed the screen door behind me. "Look, clean this shit up and clean yourself up. I'm going to get Cade and then I'm gon' drop him off here. If I find out you gave him back to Rain, Luna, I swear on my mother's grave I'm gon' fuck you up."

Only reason I was even doing this shit instead of taking my son home, was because he needed his mother. I'd rather force her ass to do right, than deprive my son of his mama.

"Okay, okay, damn!" She watched me with them puppy dog eyes before asking, "Who is that woman?"

It was like everything I'd said went right over that disheveled ass weave.

"Stay out my business and get to fixing shit up. I'll be back in about thirty minutes."

Luna followed me to the door. I made it to my whip, and when I got in, I saw Luna standing in the doorway squinting her eyes and trying to see who it was in my passenger seat. She knew who Dree was and if she found out we were fucking around, Luna would probably lose what little mind she had left.

"Can you take me home?" Dree sighed as soon as I'd backed out of Luna's driveway.

"For what?" I sensed she was on some bullshit.

"Because I don't wanna do this."

"Do what, Dree?"

"This with you. I'm not for the baby mama drama, so like I said, take me home please."

"Baby, I'm sorry our plans got pushed back because of this, but you're doing too much right now. The shit is about to piss me off, and I don't wanna get pissed off."

"I don't care what you get, nigga. I said I wanna go home, and I don't wanna fuck with you no more. Get as pissed as you want, but you'd better drop me off."

Canyon, don't unlock her door and kick her out onto the road.

"So that's it then, huh?" I chuckled, mad as a muthafucka. "You're stupid as fuck, Dree, but it's cool, ma. I'll take yo' ass home."

"Good. And you're stupid too, nigga."

I tucked my lips in and nodded my head because I was just milliseconds away from breaking her neck.

"Keep talking shit, Dree. On God, we gon' have a problem. Don't let these degrees and good job fool you, ma."

She smacked her lips but she shut the fuck up. She stayed quiet all the way to her house, and quickly opened the door to get out.

"Bye, baby."

"Fuck you." She slammed my door and switched up her parents' driveway.

I'd let her think we were done for today, and shit, maybe even tomorrow morning. But by tomorrow afternoon, I'd be in them guts, making her ass apologize.

35

————————

YIKAYLA

Tonight, Waayil and Nusef were throwing a party at Monarch Tattoo, just to celebrate their success and having been open for three years now. It was so exciting to see how far the shop had come, because I remember when Nusef was going through all those changes trying to get it built and all this other stuff.

A couple times he wanted to give up, but Waayil had convinced him to pull through. That twin shit was real, because it seemed like his whole mood would change after speaking with Waayil. I sighed at the thought, because those were the days that I couldn't even stomach the name Waayil Christian, and here I was, on his arm, staring up at him like he was the greatest thing since sliced bread.

The place was packed with tattoo artists that worked here, their significant others, all of my sisters, Waayil's sister, Wednesday, and plenty of other people that I guess had gotten tattoos here. I did notice the chick with blue hair named Alyssa was in the building, and every time I looked her way, she was saying something to her friend while eyeing Waayil.

I wasn't really the jealous type, but Waayil brought it out of me. I, at times, tried to keep it at bay because I didn't wanna be like Alba, but I was starting to see where homegirl came from. Speaking of that bitch, you know she wasn't missing the chance to be in Waayil's presence.

"My brother and I just wanna say thank you to everybody here, because I'm sure some way and somehow you've contributed to the success of the shop." Nusef smiled, holding up his cup of Hennessy. "Now y'all know my brother doesn't talk much, he'd much rather whoop a nigga's ass, so I'm the only one making a speech tonight."

Everyone laughed in unison at Nusef about Waayil, because most of us here knew how true that was.

Once Nusef was done, the hired deejay turned on "Slippery" by Migos. Everyone went back to sipping their drinks, swaying to music, and having conversation.

"I just stopped by to say congratulations to my baby daddy." Alba came up to Waayil and me.

"Alleged." I fake smiled.

"*Anyway*, I'm proud of you, Waayil."

"Thanks." Waayil nodded and then led me away. "Calm down." He spoke against my lips and pecked me.

Waayil leaned up against the wall with a bottle of Hennessy that he was drinking out of, and he pulled me in front of him. He let me have a sip out of the bottle, and then he kissed me softly as hell. My hand slipped behind his head and we began tonguing it up like we were about to fuck right there. And as hot as he had me, I just might have. I turned my back to him and began to dance against his dick to Migos.

"Kay, you about to get that shit tonight," he chuckled, dimples showing out.

I chuckled at him and when I glanced to my right, I saw that receptionist bitch looking. Her expression was somewhat blank, but I saw a hint of something else. I didn't know if it was jealousy or even worse, hurt, but it looked like maybe a mixture of the two.

"Hi!" I called out over the music.

"Girl, bye!" She waved me off.

"Yikayla!" Waayil called my name and reached for my arm as I started to walk over to her. "Aye, come here." He picked me up from behind and carried me towards the back until we were in the office. Sitting me down and then his bottle of liquor, he said, "Why you be acting like you don't know who this dick belong to?"

The lustful look in his eyes was so sexy as he walked towards me slowly. Before I could respond, he made me face the wall and began to lift my skirt. Gripping the waistband of my thongs, he started to pull them down while he kissed and sucked on my exposed shoulders. I was already leaking as I listened to him unbutton his jeans, while now sucking my spot on my neck.

"Mmm," I mumbled, loving the way his mouth felt.

I gasped lowly at the feeling of him at my opening, and just as he barged his way inside of me from behind, he yanked down my tube top to expose my breasts. Grabbing them roughly, he began to slowly move in and out of me, getting my pussy adjusted to his length and girth.

"This pussy was molded for my dick," he whispered, sliding his hand between my legs to toy with my clit.

Once he was all the way inside of me, and sliding in and out with ease, he began pounding me nice and hard. Our skin smacked together loudly as he beat it up, making me gush all over his pole. I released rather quickly, but he kept pummeling me, causing my mouth to open widely in pleasure.

"Waayil," I managed to whimper.

He swiftly bent me over the desk, and went ham, fucking me so hard I had to grip the sides of the desk so I wouldn't cry out too loudly in pleasure. He slipped his hand in my hair, and yanked my neck back by it, not slowing up at all with his strokes. The curve in his dick pounded my spot repeatedly, making me explode so hard that I felt it between my thighs.

"You gon' quit acting up?" he quizzed me, still beating it up.

"Mhm," was all I could get out, just as he gripped both my ass cheeks to spread them while he pounded me.

"Say 'yes daddy,'" he demanded, and almost made me reach my peak off that alone. "Say it, Kay!" He smacked my ass.

"Yes, da-daddy," I cried out, feeling this dick-down in my damn knees!

"Ahh fuck," he moaned softly in his deep voice, which was such a turn on.

You could literally hear him plunging into me because of how soaking wet I was. It was even louder in combination with our skin clashing together constantly. We began moaning together, as he brought me to another orgasm, just before letting loose himself.

After catching his breath, he pulled out of me, then kissed my pussy as I lay over the desk. I finally stood up, and after he tucked himself away, he helped me straighten my clothes. We then went to the bathroom to clean ourselves up and wash our hands.

"My panties!" I whispered harshly before going back into the office.

He chuckled as I picked them up from the floor. I looked at them trying to decide what to do because I didn't want them back on. Waayil took them, and stuffed them in his shirt pocket like a damn fool.

"Waayil, you are not about to go out there with my panties sticking out of your pocket like a handkerchief!"

He scooped me up and I locked my legs around his waist.

As he carried me back towards the front where the party was, he said, "What I tell you about that mouth?"

"I'm sorry, daddy." I pouted playfully, and he bit his lip while squinting his sexy honey colored eyes, like what I'd said turned him on. He squeezed my ass so hard, my lower lips spread a little.

"Mmm, you ain't got no panties on no more. A nigga wanna eat ya pussy now." He licked his thick lips. "Kiss."

I pecked him sensually and repeatedly until we made it to the front, and as soon as we did, receptionist hoe had her eyes on us.

Don't worry, bitch. I got my eyes on you too.

36

———

EKO

I was finally home from a long ass day, and before taking my shower, I just sat down on the damn couch for a second. I'd been moving and shaking all fucking day, and just needed a moment. I thought about calling Rori, but I was just gon' pull up on her ass in the morning, take her to breakfast or some shit. Little ass stayed hungry, so I knew I wouldn't hear any of that flip ass mouth if food was on the table.

Just as I let my head rest against the back of the couch, my phone rang. I exhaled heavily and then picked my head up to look at my screen. I saw it was Jenni, so I hit ignore on her ass and dropped my phone on the cushion next to me. I was sure her ass didn't need shit, and even if she did, right now I didn't give a fuck. Not but two seconds later, my shit was ringing again, so I sat up abruptly and answered the phone.

"Jenni, you better be in a muthafuckin' burning building, bitch, bec—"

"Eko!" Rori cried, catching me off guard.

"Baby, what's wrong?" I shot up from the couch, already on ten because I didn't know what the fuck had her so upset.

"It's Gavin. He's gonna kill me," she sniffled.

"What? He ain't gon' kill you. Where the fuck you at, ma?" I was panicking like a muthafucka. I didn't know where she was, and even though she wasn't mine yet, I didn't like her being at some random location and afraid.

"He- he..." she stammered.

"Baby, calm down and talk to me." I had gotten my gun and made sure it was loaded, before pocketing my keys and leaving the crib.

I could faintly hear sounds in her background, like someone was yelling and banging on a door.

"I-I found earrings in hi-his bedroom and when I told him I was done with him and leaving, he went crazy," she sobbed. "I'm in his bathroom with the door locked, but he said he's about to shoot it down."

By this time, I was in my car, driving with the gas pedal to the fucking floor. If Gavin laid a finger on Rori, I was blowing his fucking head off, and that was on everything I loved. Thankfully that nigga lived fairly close, and since it was nighttime, the traffic was light to nonexistent. I made it to Gavin's crib on the Southside, and blocked his driveway instead of looking for a park.

"Aye, open up!" I banged on his rickety wooden door as hard as possible. He came and yanked it open, scowling hard as hell. "Man, what the fuck you in here doing?" I barged in and he shut the door behind me.

"This bitch got me fucked up!" He darted towards the back. "Bring yo' ass out, Rori, before I shoot yo' ass!"

"Nigga, step the fuck back! You ain't about to shoot no damn body!" I hissed, yanking him from the bathroom door. "Rori, it's Eko, open the door for me please?"

"Eko?" she repeated.

"Yeah, ma." I glanced over my shoulder at Gavin who was panting like a bull, clutching his 9mm. "Give me that shit, man, fuck wrong with you?" I snatched his gun and he punched the wall just as Rori cracked the bathroom door.

"You ain't going no fucking where!" Gavin pointed at her. When she stepped out the bathroom, he charged towards her and she got behind me. "Move, E."

"Nah, nigga, back yo' ass up. I'm not about to let you put yo' hands on her, bruh. If she don't want yo' ass, accept it."

"This ain't got nothing to do with you! That's my bitch!"

"Not no more!" I roared and he backed down a little bit, looking me in the eyes like he didn't know me. "Now get the fuck out my way."

I escorted Rori towards the door, and told her to go to my car while I removed the bullets from his gun. I then tossed it on the sofa, as he stared at me in disgust.

"Why you in another nigga's business?" he asked, tone much calmer.

"Because I care for her and I'm not about to let you beat on her or worse, kill her just because you got caught fucking around."

"Care for her? Why? That's mine."

"Because I do."

We stared at one another for a few seconds in silence.

"Oh what, you got a crush or something, Eko?" He laughed wryly. "You think if you save her, she gon' let you fuck? Well that ain't gon' happen, homie, because that's mine. Everything about Rori is mine."

Out of respect for Rori, I didn't want to come out of my mouth and tell him how I'd been fucking on his bitch for some time now. Plus, there was no need for me to try to get one up on this nigga. He was clearly worried and I wasn't at all.

"She's out there in *my* car though. She called *me* to come get her."

His jaw twitched and his nostrils flared, as I stayed calm.

"Don't touch my girl, Eko."

I simply smiled and left out his spot, closing the door behind me.

I walked to my car and opened the passenger door to see Rori sitting there but much calmer. Placing one hand on the hood of my car, I leaned down into her face and just looked at her.

"I got you, shorty, so relax, aight?" I assured her.

Resting her hand on one side of my face, she caressed it and then kissed my lips.

37

———

DREE

I hit ignore on Canyon's fourth phone call tonight as Sean's driver helped me out of the back seat of this all-black Escalade. I smiled upon seeing his beautiful house again, as I fixed my short black dress. Tonight would be our first real date, and he decided to have it in the backyard, which was large and beautiful.

As I started towards the front door, I placed my phone on vibrate so that if Canyon called me again, it wouldn't interrupt. Ever since the day I told him I was done, he'd been trying to text, call, and chill with me, but I wasn't having it. I'd been secretly spending time with Sean, and upon witnessing Canyon's baby mama drama, I quickly realized that he was *not* the man for me. I wanted someone like Sean, a drama-free nigga who was on his way to being successful.

"Right this way, Miss Goode."

The housekeeper answered the door and escorted me through the large house and out to the back. When I stepped out, I saw Sean looking so handsome in a Gucci suit. I knew my fashions well, especially expensive brands. His hair was freshly cut, and his sexy mocha skin was gleaming under the beautiful lights that decorated the area we were to dine in. It was a large white gazebo, with three steps to walk up into it.

"You look beautiful," Sean commented, as he took my hand to take me to the table. On it was a bucket of ice with some champagne sitting inside it.

"Thank you. You look nice as well."

Sean pulled my chair out, and once I was seated, he rounded the table to sit across from me. Some man dressed like a butler removed the Dom Pérignon from the bucket of ice, popped it open, and then filled our champagne flutes with some. The taste was so crisp and smooth going down that I had to close my eyes to enjoy it.

"On the menu tonight is spicy shrimp tossed in a creamy fiery pesto sauce as an appetizer, filet mignon cooked in a special blend of spices, accompanied by mashed potatoes and asparagus, and then cheesecake drizzled with a homemade strawberry sauce for dessert," the man explained to us. "Can I get you anything to drink that's nonalcoholic before I bring the appetizer?"

"Just water, Marshall, thank you," Sean answered. He grinned when I gave him a look. This date was definitely more my style than the one with Canyon. "I was a little surprised you decided to come on this date."

"Why? We've been spending a lot of time together." I sipped my champagne.

"Yeah, but you're always a teeny bit standoffish, and I guess that was because of your *situation*."

"Well, I am happy to let you know that I no longer have a situation."

"For real? May I ask what happened?" His perfect white smile lit up the area even more.

"He's just not what I'm looking for. I think I was just caught up on what he and I used to be, and I had to realize that I'm not the same Dree I was back then. I don't want the drama he brings."

"You're too beautiful to have to deal with drama."

"You sure know what to say," I giggled. "So you don't have any baby mamas or girlfriends I need to worry about, right?"

"Absolutely not. Do you think if I did, I would be able to have you at my home?" He cleared his throat. "I don't play games, Dree. When I see something I want, I go all in, and I don't keep anything on the side."

"You see something you want?"

"Definitely."

Marshall returned with our appetizer, and refilled our glasses with more champagne. The shrimp was so good that I wished I didn't have to share with Sean. As the night progressed, I realized that I'd made the right decision in choosing Sean over Canyon. Sean was just the type of man I'd been yearning for all this time. He was very handsome, smart, tall, and most importantly, he didn't have any attachments.

"So can you stay the night?" Sean asked as we entered his home from the backyard. Everyone was still in the backyard cleaning up our mess.

"Aren't your parents here?"

"Nope, out of town."

I'd only met his parents once, and they seemed to be very involved in their work. They were like a law power couple, and it made me smile thinking Sean and I would become that one day.

"Umm, I would love to, Sean, but I think if I stay, I may do some things I'm not ready to."

"I'm not expecting anything, Dree. I just don't want this shit to end yet."

"No, I know, but I'm worried about myself. I may be the aggressor."

We laughed in unison as he nodded, sliding his hands into his Gucci slacks. He was so debonair from his head to his toes. No tattoos, no hood talk, and no facial hair. I usually liked a nice mustache or beard, but I think Sean looked better without it.

Sean walked me out to the Escalade where his driver got out and pulled the door open for me.

"See you tomorrow then?" he asked, and I shook my head 'yes,' before he snaked his arms around my waist and kissed me.

On the ride home, I couldn't stop smiling. My life was close to perfect. I was in law school, I had my health, my family, and now a wonderful guy.

As the truck came to a stop in front of my home, I waited for the driver to let me out. Once my stiletto heel hit the ground, I noticed a figure sitting on the porch like they were waiting.

"Have a good night, Miss Goode."

"Thank you," I replied lowly to the driver as I made my way up the driveway.

Getting closer, I realized it was Canyon, dressed in gray sweats and a white t-shirt. He was looking like a straight up gangster, and even though I didn't like that, he looked sexy as hell.

"So that's why all of sudden I'm too much drama, huh?" He laughed as I walked up the porch steps.

"What are you talking about?" I frowned and shook my head once I made it to the top. He stood up, towering over me, and shoved his hands into his sweatpants. His cologne was subtle but apparent; smelled nice.

"So who is this nigga that got drivers and shit for you."

"Nobody, Canyon."

"So you coming back with a driver and wearing this little ass dress for what then? Tell me what the fuck I wanna know, Dree. Did you toss me for another nigga or nah?"

I looked away briefly and then back up into his eyes.

"I didn't do it on purpose. He and I just kind of happened." Canyon nodded as I spoke. "Canyon, come on. What we were doing was just finishing up something that never got closed out. You don't wanna be with me and you know it."

"Speak for yaself, shorty, don't speak for me. I wanted you back then and I *did* want you now, but after tonight." He shook his head as he looked me up and down. "I don't want shit to do with you. You ain't nothing like I thought you were."

"Excuse me?"

"You ain't deaf, Dree. From here on out, I don't fuck with you as friends or anything else. You'd rather chase after a nigga because of the material shit he can give you, versus being with the man who actually loves yo' ass. And that's not the type of bitch I wanna fuck with."

"Canyon!" I reached for his arm as he walked off, but he moved from my touch.

"Nah, fuck you, Dree."

I watched him walk away, sexy as fuck, with his educated thug ass. As much as his words messed with me, I was sticking with Sean.

38

———

WAAYIL

This nigga, Neo, had been blowing me up about that stupid ass situation I'd gotten myself into while locked up. I was close to changing my damn number, but I knew that shit wouldn't help. I would have to deal with that bullshit head on.

I entered my parents' crib because my mom had texted me, letting me know she heard Emil come in. I wanted to talk to his ass and shit; catch up, I guess. The nigga had been like a damn ghost since I'd been out. We barely talked when I was locked up, because my phone calls would have to be split up between everybody in the house. That shit reminded me to try and visit Midori's ass in college.

I went upstairs and down the hall, and when I reached Emil's door, I knocked lightly on it. I heard rustling like he was hiding some shit, so I knocked again.

"Emil, it's Waayil."

"Umm, yeah, what you need, bruh?"

I twisted the doorknob but it was locked.

"Man, open this door, I wanna talk to you."

"Oh, Waayil, I'm not feeling too good right now, but umm, I'll text you later or something, aight?"

"Emil, don't make me kick this shit down. I don't know what the fuck you got going on, but let me in this muthafucka."

He groaned and then it got quiet for a few seconds. I then heard him unlocking the door, and then silence again. Twisting the knob, I pushed the door open and walked in, checking the scenery out, hoping to spot whatever he was trying to hide. When I turned to look at him, I saw someone had clearly whooped his ass like he stole government cheese.

"What the fuck happened to yo' face, Emil?" I frowned, ready to set some shit off about my younger brother.

"Waayil, man, it's aight." He grinned like a maniac.

"It's aight? Nigga, somebody stomped a mud puddle in yo' ass and you're talking about its aight?" I almost couldn't believe my muthafuckin' ears or eyes. "Who did this shit to you?"

"Nobody—"

"Tell me who the fuck did it, Emil! I'm not fucking around right now. I'm hot as fuck, and you'd better speak the fuck up right now, bruh!"

He shook his head like he was saying I wouldn't get it.

"Waayil, I'm begging you to leave this alone."

"Well I'm not." I shrugged. "Get to talking," I stated sternly.

"These dudes, Grant and Eddie. They be outside the store on Grand and Park." He plopped down on the bed and dropped his face into his hands.

"Fuck they beat you up for?"

He was shaking his head as he kept it down in his hands. He finally lifted up, and tears were pooled in his eyes.

"Emil, what the fuck is going—"

"Because I'm gay, Waayil!" he hollered.

For the first time in this whole conversation, I was stuck like fuck. I ain't know what to say or how to fuckin' respond. My eyes were wide; I could feel them, as I scanned my brother like I didn't know him.

"Them niggas found out and they jumped me! Now you fucking

know!" he sobbed. "Now I'm asking that you give me some privacy. Please," he begged, hands in prayer mode.

I nodded and left the room, closing the door behind me.

Gay or not, that was still my little brother, so I went straight to my car and drove to the liquor store on Grand and Park Avenue. I parked a little down the street, and got out to walk back down. I saw two niggas standing outside smoking cigarettes, and looking way too young to be doing so.

"Aye, I'm looking for Eddie and Grant," I said.

"Who you?" the light-skinned one asked, tossing his cigarette to the ground.

"Waayil. Who the fuck are you?"

Chuckling as he sized me up, he got up off the wall he was leaning on and moved towards me with his homie trailing. I was way bigger than this nigga, height and muscle wise, but clearly, he had confidence.

"I'm Grant, and this is Eddie." The light-skinned one pointed to himself and then over his shoulder at his chubby brown-skinned homeboy. "What can I do for you, *Waayil?*"

WHAM!

I socked that nigga so hard he stumbled back about one hundred yards before falling to the ground. His chubby homeboy watched it go down, and as soon as we made eye contact, I gave his ass a two-piece, sending him to the gravel as well.

"Y'all got a problem with gay people?" I inquired just before kicking the shit out of the light-skinned nigga.

"Ah!" He clutched his stomach, showing off his bloody ass teeth as he clenched them.

"Huh?"

WHAM!

I went across the chubby one's face again, and he yowled before covering it.

I continued on, punching and stomping each one of them as I saw fit, while they hollered out and cried. I saw red as I fucked these two little bitch ass muthafuckas up. They'd learn not to fuck with anybody even remotely related to my ass.

"Ahh, oh! Oh shit!" they both whimpered and cried, as I squatted down and grasped them both by the hair. Both of their dusty asses needed a haircut, but it worked in my favor in this moment.

"Next time you see my brother, Emil, you'd better look the other muthafuckin' way. If he tells me y'all little weak crusty ass bitches even made a peep in his direction, I'm gon' have some heat for y'all asses." As I spoke, I glanced back and forth between the two, as they groaned in pain from me gripping what little hair they had, in combination with the ass whooping they'd just endured. "A nigga like me don't give a fuck about going to jail. So play around and make me catch a case if you want to. We clear?"

"Yeah, yeah, man," they both answered simultaneously, sniffling and shivering like two hoes on the street corner in the winter.

"Good."

I threw their heads to the ground, and rose to my feet. Like nothing happened, I walked back to my car and drove home to get some pussy.

39

———————

JONAYA

"**D**amn, bitch, your step dad got every damn thing." Leighton stared at my stepdad's liquor wall in awe.

She, Wednesday, and I were down in his bar, looking for something good to go with this pineapple juice we'd gotten.

"Just get that Grey Goose," I said.

Wednesday took it off the shelf, and then we sat down on one of the butter leather couches with some glasses. After I filled a silver bucket with some ice from my stepdad's ice machine, we started filling our cups with vodka and juice. We'd just had some big ass cheeseburgers, so we were prepared to drink as much as we wanted to.

"So Nusef's flip flopping ass is acting distant again." Leighton rolled her eyes.

"Nusef is a player, girl. He's only gon' be nice to you when he wants to fuck you. That's how my brother is," Wednesday responded, as she gulped her drink down.

"Y'all slept together?" I damn near shrieked.

Nusef and I hadn't talked much since he ate me out and left me to stare at the wall for an hour. He would text me here and there that he loved me, and I just wouldn't respond because I couldn't. And no matter what I texted him, he would respond with 'I love you,' so I stopped hitting him up. Then on top of that, Marquise hadn't given up, so I decided to start letting him come around again to keep my mind off of Nusef. I didn't know what I was doing with my life, which is why I needed these drinks.

"I sucked his dick and that's it," Leighton replied, making me choke on my drink.

"How the hell did that happen? I wish I would suck a nigga up and he send me home." Wednesday sucked her teeth. I nodded in agreement. Leighton's ass was dumb.

"I was over his house and we were watching a movie, in the dark. So he was just like 'show me something,' out of the blue, and was taking it out. I didn't know what to do, so I just started sucking it," Leighton explained as she rolled one up.

Wednesday and I doubled over in laughter at this bitch. I didn't like hearing about Nusef and other girls at the moment, but that shit was funny.

"Wow, he got yo' ass, and easily too." I shook my head.

The three of us continued drinking, and then smoked as well. An hour and a half later, we were drunk, high, and running in and out of my stepfather's bar bathroom to pee.

"What's the worst thing you've ever done?" Leighton slurred.

"Who?" I inquired.

"Both of you, but since you asked, you go first."

"Worst as in like sex, orrrr?" I furrowed my brows. I was too twisted for this.

"Okay, I will go first so y'all can get an idea." Leighton sat up, eyes low as hell from the weed and drink. "I fucked my sister's boyfriend after I convinced him that she'd cheated on him."

"Leighton!" Wednesday screeched.

"Damn, bitch, you're a fucking hoe." I laughed.

"Just a little." Leighton chuckled. "Okay, Jonaya."

"Shit, umm... I was talking to this guy once, and when I went to his house, I saw his brother looked better so when he fell asleep, I fucked his brother."

"What the fuccckkkk!" they both shouted in unison, making me laugh way too hard because I was under the influence.

"I think yours is the worst, Jo," Leighton said.

"I've never done anything shady like that." Wednesday shrugged. Her eyes were damn near closed because she was gone.

"It doesn't have to be sexual," Leighton exhaled.

"Okay, okay," Wednesday slurred and smiled. "You guys can't say shit though."

"Bitch, go! As fucked up as Jonaya's and mine were, we will not tell your little secret," Leighton assured her and I nodded to agree.

"Okay." She sighed. "I lied to Waayil about Uncle Harry."

BECOME A VIP READER!

*To join my mailing list text **SHVONNE** to **66866** and stay up to date! Also, join **Shvonne Latrice Reading Group** on Facebook!*

www.ingramcontent.com/pod-product-compliance
Lightning Source LLC
Chambersburg PA
CBHW061344310726
48974CB00001B/186